# A Promise
## of Safekeeping

**Lesson One:** You already know how to do this. You've been doing it all your life. As an infant, you studied your parents' faces even as they studied yours. You learned the meaning of a smile, a frown. And then you learned the meaning of a bashful smile, a disappointed frown. All people are open books, and you're hardwired to read them. Your instincts will guide you. Just listen.

# A Promise
# of Safekeeping

# A PROMISE
# OF SAFEKEEPING

# LISA DALE

**B**

BERKLEY BOOKS, NEW YORK

**THE BERKLEY PUBLISHING GROUP**
**Published by the Penguin Group**
**Penguin Group (USA) Inc.**
**375 Hudson Street, New York, New York 10014, USA**
Penguin Group (Canada), 90 Eglinton Avenue East, Suite 700, Toronto, Ontario M4P 2Y3, Canada
(a division of Pearson Penguin Canada Inc.)
Penguin Books Ltd., 80 Strand, London WC2R 0RL, England
Penguin Group Ireland, 25 St. Stephen's Green, Dublin 2, Ireland (a division of Penguin Books Ltd.)
Penguin Group (Australia), 250 Camberwell Road, Camberwell, Victoria 3124, Australia
(a division of Pearson Australia Group Pty. Ltd.)
Penguin Books India Pvt. Ltd., 11 Community Centre, Panchsheel Park, New Delhi—110 017, India
Penguin Group (NZ), 67 Apollo Drive, Rosedale, Auckland 0632, New Zealand
(a division of Pearson New Zealand Ltd.)
Penguin Books (South Africa) (Pty.) Ltd., 24 Sturdee Avenue, Rosebank, Johannesburg 2196,
South Africa

Penguin Books Ltd., Registered Offices: 80 Strand, London WC2R 0RL, England

This book is an original publication of The Berkley Publishing Group.

This is a work of fiction. Names, characters, places, and incidents either are the product of the author's imagination or are used fictitiously, and any resemblance to actual persons, living or dead, business establishments, events, or locales is entirely coincidental. The publisher does not have any control over and does not assume responsibility for author or third-party websites or their content.

PRINTING HISTORY
Berkley trade paperback edition / January 2012

Library of Congress Cataloging-in-Publication Data

Dale, Lisa.
  A promise of safekeeping / Lisa Dale.—Berkley trade pbk. ed.
    p.  cm.
  ISBN 978-0-425-24514-9
  1. Women lawyers—Fiction.   2. Ex-convicts—Fiction.   3. Judicial error—Fiction.
4. Richmond (Va.)—Fiction.   5. Forgiveness—Fiction.   I. Title.
  PS3604.A3538P76 2012
  813'.6—dc22

                                                               2011019254

PRINTED IN THE UNITED STATES OF AMERICA

10  9  8  7  6  5  4  3  2  1

*To Cathy*

# CHAPTER 1

The day news broke that Arlen Fieldstone had been released from prison was the day the first flutterings of Lauren's heart began. The muscle that for all her life had pumped so courteously and discreetly within her chest suddenly clamored for attention. As she stood on the sidewalk at a busy newsstand, adding low-cal sweetener to her morning coffee and trying to ignore Arlen Fieldstone's sad eyes on the front page of the newspaper, she felt an odd thump behind her ribs, as if a small firework had gone *pop*—just once—before it disappeared.

She paused, and after the twinge subsided, she went about the rest of her day as gently as she could, trying not to pay too much attention to her heart for fear that she would invent a problem where none existed.

At her office not far from the Albany, New York, courthouse, she waved over her assistant, Rizzi, to ask how her son was doing with his broken wrist. She ordered an extra cannoli with her lunch as she sometimes did when she was feeling indulgent, and she adjusted her schedule to allow for an extra half hour at the gym. She reviewed the files on the potential jurors she would meet that afternoon for a case against a pharmaceutical company, and she popped a few antacids. The morning's odd tremor of her heart was nothing more than a muscle spasm—no different than if she'd gotten a cramp in her foot.

But when she arrived at the courthouse, the courthouse where she'd worked a thousand times, and where she and the opposing counsel were now readying to interview potential jurors, the heart stutters returned.

She felt just one little spasm at first, as if her heart had been jerked on a string. And though the beat faltered, she did not. She stayed focused with a tenacity that she'd practiced for so many years she no longer thought of it as tenacity at all.

Candidate after candidate came into the room, and she proceeded with her line of questioning to determine who would be the most sympathetic to her billion-dollar client: *Do you consider yourself a religious person? Do you believe there's a limit to the amount of money a company should be penalized for pain and suffering? Do you or does anyone in your family have a condition that requires regular medication?*

Thirty minutes later, what had been a hiccup in her chest was now an earthquake. She felt as if the fat, round ball of her heart was attached to a wooden paddle and a rubber band. She hadn't realized she'd stopped talking.

"Ms. Matthews?"

Burt Sternfeld, who usually called her *Lauren* unless they were in public, sat at her side. He swiveled his chair toward her as she put her hand on her heart; underneath the fabric of her suit jacket and the silk of her shirt, the ventricles that normally moved so fluidly were gulping and sputtering. She tried to tell him she was fine, but somehow, there weren't any words—only her breath, going in and out of her lungs with alarming quickness. Only her heart, sending up smoke signals that something was wrong. Darkness burned holes in her peripheral vision.

Someone asked, "Is she okay?"

And it was only when she opened her eyes again that she realized they'd been closed. She must have fallen off her chair because she was on the wood floor, her pencil skirt riding alarmingly high on her thighs. She tried to sit up, to cover up and pull herself together. Burt cautioned her to relax.

"What happened?" she asked.

"You passed out," he said, bending over her but not touching.

"For how long?"

"Just a few seconds," he whispered to her. "Lauren—are you pregnant?"

"What? No."

He sat back on his knees with some awkwardness, given his bulk. Though his voice was gentle, he probably didn't realize his mouth had pulled for the quickest flash of a second into a frown. But Lauren saw everything, every micro expression that could cross a person's face in a moment—it was what she got paid to do. And she knew that in some subconscious place deep below his very sincere compassion, he was somewhat repulsed by her breach of decorum. Fainting during voir dire proceedings was not professional at all.

"I'm fine," she said, propping herself up on her elbows and testing for dizziness. She pulled down her skirt a few more inches, bent her knees so she could sit up straighter, and put a hand to her forehead. Though she'd sat at the defense counsel's desk many times, she'd never seen the underside of it before. "I'm fine."

Burt shook his head. "I've already called the ambulance. They're on the way."

Lauren didn't protest. She pressed her hand to her chest again. Her heart was still knocking her ribs like a fish trying to bust the surface of an icy lake. Burt and the others were staring at her with a mix of repulsion and surprise and concern, and she could hear people ducking into the room to see her—curious as onlookers who slow to see wrecked and mangled cars. She closed her eyes.

*Please,* she told her restless heart. *Please just stop.*


Will Farris didn't consider himself the most observant man in Richmond, but he knew enough to know that the sleek black sedan parked for the last three days across from his antiques shop probably didn't belong to one of the many college students who lived in the neighborhood. And so instead of buying himself one cup of coffee at the shop in the morning, he bought two.

The kid in the black sedan jumped clear out of the driver's seat when Will knocked on the glass.

"Hey, man," Will said. The guy rolled down the window, composure returning to his sleep-rumpled face. He wore a Redskins hat and a good twelve hours' worth of blond stubble. The kid pulled himself up straighter in his seat—Will could see the fight instinct of a good cop kick in, the flashing awareness of being boxed into the driver's seat. Will smiled and held up the second cup of coffee. "Thought you could use this."

For a moment, the kid hesitated—looking at Will, then the cup, then back at Will, obviously trying to work out whether taking the coffee would mean acknowledging that his cover had been blown. In the end, the caffeine was the bigger draw, and the kid reached out the window for the paper cup and said thanks.

Will leaned his elbow against the roof of the car as the kid peeled the lid off his drink. "I guess you drew the short straw."

"Something like that."

"How long they gonna keep you sitting out here?"

"Hard to say. Depends."

"On what?"

"On how long you keep him living in that apartment above your shop."

A delivery truck drove past them, rattling hard on its shocks. Will glanced toward his building, which he'd bought at a foreclosure sale with his own pennies when he was just twenty-two, back before the street became trendy and the art galleries and vegan restaurants moved in. Like other shops in Carytown, Will's building was a mid-century house, fit for any middle-class family, that had been reincarnated for retail. At street level, wide bay windows—protected now by a metal grate—were crowned by a gilt sign that said only ANTIQUES. On the second floor, an air conditioner hummed and one light was on.

Will drummed his fingers on the roof of the car. "They realize he's *not* guilty, right?"

"We don't want no trouble in the neighborhood. That's all."

"I suppose you're gonna tell me the twenty-four/seven surveillance is for his protection?"

"And yours," the boy said with perfect earnestness. "Some folks ain't too happy about your putting him up like this."

Will laughed. "I'm not in danger and you know it. Y'all just want to keep an eye on Arlen, far as I can tell."

The boy shrugged. "Just following orders."

"Well, don't trouble yourself. Arlen's not gonna cause any disturbance unless people start causing it with him."

"You never know. Prison'll change a man. Believe me. I seen it with my own eyes."

Will patted the roof of the car twice. Already, the hot August sun was blazing, and the black car was little more than an oversized oven.

"Seriously, man," the boy went on. "Be careful."

"Arlen's as good as anybody," Will said. And yet, the brick wall of his confidence was weakened in places, because Will really didn't know Arlen anymore. Nine years ago, Will would have sworn on the family Bible that Arlen was incapable of murder. But now? Will's faith in Arlen stood on one wobbly leg: a friendship that had been severed when they were just boys.

"Enjoy the coffee," Will said.

"Hey, pal," the kid called out as Will crossed the street. "Next time, can you make the coffee *iced*?"

"Don't push your luck."


At four thirty in the morning of her first day in Richmond, the time of day when Lauren always felt she made the most sense to herself, she woke and didn't know where she was. Her alarm hadn't gone off, and yet her eyes had come open as if they—and not her digital clock—were plugged into an outlet and set for a certain time. She sat up, rubbed her face in the darkness. She listened to her body: in her chest, her heart was opening and closing like a fist, quiet and even, for now.

Maisie's spare bedroom was half storeroom, half B and B. A stack of neatly labeled Tupperware bins was lined up against the wall. A hand-stitched quilt hung over the back of a rocking chair in the corner, lit softly by streetlight. A round braided rug floated atop a wooden floor that had been layered up by decades of paint—the latest being cornflower blue. Lauren dropped her bare feet off the side of the high bed, her toes skimming the floor.

Four thirty in the morning. If she were at home in her Albany condo, she would stand and get herself ready for her morning workout, taking the elevator to the gym downstairs to hit the treadmill and get her blood moving. Then a four-minute shower, a high-protein shake, and it was off to the office, where the only person she would meet on her way to the sixty-first floor would be

Ted the security guard, whom she chatted with for a few bright moments each day. Ted would worry about her when she didn't show for work today. She wished she could have warned him.

She stood, feeling lost and meaningless without her usual routines. Out of habit, she plucked the fraying threads of the bracelet on her wrist—a gift from her niece. It clashed with everything she owned, and it always looked out of place with her severe suits and that no-nonsense toughness she'd learned to cultivate at work. But she loved it—just like she loved her niece, just like she loved her whole family . . . her family who did not yet know she was gone.

She eased open the slats of the blinds to see through them: the whole of Monument Avenue was deserted, a lonely streetlamp shining like a spotlight on an empty stage. Richmond was a stranger to her—vaguely menacing in the shadows. When she moved, the boards of the old house creaked.

She turned on her laptop, the light filling the room like the sunrise, and she logged into Maisie's Internet connection. There were eight e-mails waiting for her about Dautel Pharmaceuticals. She was glad to see them. She climbed back into bed and began to type, eager for the night to be over, eager to get a head start—as if she might beat the day to whatever it had in store and reclaim from fate her lost upper hand.


Richmond was no stranger to ghost stories. Its white-columned verandas and wide streets had been haunted since the first Europeans arrived on Virginia's tobacco-friendly soil. Churches and whorehouses alike burned to the ground during the Civil War, and from their steaming ashes the stories of hauntings arose: shadows of hanged slaves appearing on brick walls, little girls floating above wooden floorboards, mischievous old beer drinkers loitering for centuries in dark taverns . . .

Over the years, Richmond had come to embrace its ghostly past. In certain parts of the city, evening brought tour guides in Confederate gray leading groups of camera-toting tourists down alleyways and side streets, people hoping for the thrill of glimpsing ghosts—or perhaps just their own powerful imaginations.

Despite his reluctance to materialize outside Will's apartment building, Arlen Fieldstone knew that the residents of Carytown whispered about his presence with the same horrified captivation that compelled them to tell ghost stories. The "Infamous Innocent," the papers were calling him. From his perch on the second story of Will's shop, Arlen watched the frenzied bustle of Carytown— surveying the daylight mayhem for an opening to rejoin the stream of the world.

When he was in prison, he'd made promises to himself. Many promises. He promised that when he got out, the first thing he would do was go straight to a bar and say, "A round for everyone, on me." He promised that, as soon as they cut him loose, he would lie down in the grass—any old patch would do—because he missed grass terribly, the smell of it freshly cut, the tickle of it on his skin.

And yet—here he was. No bar. No grass. More ghost than man. He hardly slept. He twitched like the deer that had grazed so nervously in his mother's yard. His bedroom felt unsafe and overly big—so big that he might as well have been sleeping on a park bench under the sky.

Outside, Carytown partied and shopped till it dropped. Arlen watched. Listened. Once, when the shop was closed and Will had gone home, Arlen walked himself up to the front door and even gripped the hard brass handle. He stood that way for a long time, Richmond calling to him like a siren, beckoning with promises of every kind. His palm sweated. His heart raced. But still, he had not been able to bring himself to turn the handle. He was Richmond's newest ghost story—trapped by specters of iron bars.

* * *

Will didn't get up immediately when the front door to his shop squealed open. The type who visited in the middle of a workday were either semiprofessionals looking for a steal—in which case they could show themselves around—or down-on-their-luck men who wanted to see how much they could get for their mother's jewelry or an old watch. Either way, there was no sense in standing on formality.

"In here!" he called from his office, which was little more than a room that happened to have a computer in it, along with mountains of copious and sundry collectibles. He whistled a little as he skimmed through an antiques magazine, keeping an eye out for familiar items with the same sense of ease and interest that some other person might feel when stumbling across the face of an old friend in a high school yearbook.

"Hello?"

He stopped reading. The woman's voice was unfamiliar—a nice, neat, tidy little *hello*. A *hello* appropriate for a massage parlor or bridal boutique. "Yeah. Be with you in one sec."

He closed the magazine and made his way to the front of the shop, picking a path among haphazard piles of treasure. Over the years his mother and sister had tried a handful of times to come in and "spruce up the place." Annabelle complained that the shop always smelled like dust and grandmothers, and his mom's aversion to clutter went back to her housekeeping days. But Will did his best to keep them from meddling too much. True—the place looked dreadful: ripped cardboard boxes, shelves heaped with teacups, steamer trunks full of ancient antimacassars. But to his mind, an antiques shop without a good coating of dust would be like the Statue of Liberty without her fine green patina.

In the rubble and chaos of his collection, the woman standing in the front of his store was completely out of place—though he could not perfectly put his finger on why.

"Can I help you?"

"I hope so. Are you the owner?"

"Yes, ma'am," he said, lifting himself onto the countertop and sitting.

The woman was small and boyish, with a neat bob the exact color of the Brazilian cherry chifforobe he'd bought at an estate sale last week. She wore a tan cotton dress that was a little too stiff to be called a sundress—not a frill, bow, or ribbon to be seen among fitted seams. "What can I do you for?"

"The apartment above your store," she said. Her gaze was calm and level, and her voice smooth. "I can't figure out how to get to it. Where's the call box? Or the door?"

He laced his fingers together. There was something familiar about the woman. Had she been in the shop before? Her wide-set eyes and heart-shaped face struck him as throwbacks to the days of speakeasies and ragtime. In some intuitive and murky part of his brain, alarm bells rang.

"Who you looking for, darlin'?"

"It's *Lauren*. Not even my father calls me *darling*."

"You're a Yankee."

She nodded.

"Well, nobody's perfect," he said. He pushed himself hips first off the counter and dusted his hands on his old cargo shorts. "Who you looking for, *Lauren*?"

"I'm trying to find Arlen Fieldstone," she said.

"You a reporter?"

"No."

To cover his reaction he walked around to the back of the little counter. Lauren . . . not a reporter . . . looking for Arlen . . . Lauren *Matthews*. Her name was a lead weight. She was older than when he'd last seen her on television. Her hair was short now, falling no lower than her earlobes, and her bangs were a hard, thick line above her eyebrows. Her skin rode close to the muscles and tendons beneath her dress straps. Her heels looked demonic. He did the math—he and Arlen were twenty when the trial had happened, and she'd been twenty-five. She was thirty-four now.

It was coming back. The television cameras had loved her—a pretty and improbable young redhead in a suit that always seemed too big for her even though the cut was right. Every time Will saw her on the news, reporters surrounding her like she was a rock star, his blood boiled with outrage—outrage that his good friend had been accused of a crime he could never in a thousand years commit. Outrage at the farce of justice. And as if that weren't enough—Arlen's fate had resided not in the hands of sagacious and hoary old judges, but with a beautiful and impertinent twenty-something prosecutor who controlled the jury the way a conductor would lead a choir.

Echoes of old hatred welled up. Lauren was obviously no longer a wonder kid, but she'd become a wonder woman. After Arlen's verdict, Will had followed her career for a little while, furious and fascinated to watch her move on to bigger and better things while Arlen faded into obscurity in his jail cell and Will scraped to get by.

Occasionally, she would pop up as an expert on a nightly news program—looking prim and polished in colors that were too dark for her skin. And a couple years ago she wrote a book about interpreting body language (Will had bought it, read it in one night of fervent focus, then brought it back to the bookstore for a refund). Eventually, he'd lost sight of her—or he'd deliberately looked away—and he realized that maybe he'd been a little more angry at her than she deserved, and a little too obsessed with her in some twisted part of his mind. He supposed it was only natural that the next place she would turn up would be in his store.

Will leaned as casually as he could on the counter and smiled at her. He didn't want to give away the fact that he'd recognized her despite the long years that had passed since Arlen's trial. And yet, with his gesture, something about *her* changed—as if she'd heard what he was thinking and knew the moment he'd put two and two together and realized who she was.

"Arlen ain't here," he said, and he rubbed his nose with the back of a finger.

She laughed, so quietly he might not have heard it if the traffic hadn't eased for a moment outside the store. "I happen to know he is here."

"How's that?"

"You just told me."

He crossed his arms. "What makes you say that?"

"You scratched your face."

"I had an itch," he said.

She lifted an eyebrow. "Some people's bodies release adrenaline when they're stressed or when they lie. Adrenaline causes the capillaries to expand—hence, your itchy nose."

He knew he was staring at her, that his jaw was probably on the ground. "Fine. Here's the truth. I know who you are, *Lauren Matthews*, and there's no way in hell I'm letting you upstairs."

The imperious look on her face settled into its previous blankness.

"But I guess you knew that too, didn't you?" he said.

She nodded.

"Because I have a 'tell'?"

"Everyone does," she said, almost a little shyly now. "And anyway, it's a good thing."

"How's that?"

"Lots of people touch their faces when they lie. It means they're uncomfortable doing it—and that they don't lie often. For you . . ." She opened up a microscopically tiny black purse and pulled out a beautiful silver pen. "For you, it means you're willing to fib a little to protect a friend. But that you're probably not going to make a regular habit of lying because you don't think it's right."

He couldn't help it; he stepped back a little as she bent to write her name on the back of a postcard that one of the local bands had dropped off. He wished he could say that meeting her in the flesh had dispelled all the myths about her from the television and newspaper reports. But if anything, her appearance had only confirmed the typecasting.

"Listen," she said. When she looked up at him, her gaze was neither pleasant nor challenging. In person, her eyes were a strange color: a coppery pond lit with sunlight and flecks of mossy green. Peering into them felt as oddly compelling and intimate as looking deep into the center of a tiger lily. He decided he liked her better on TV.

She went on. "I don't want to cause any trouble for him. I really don't. I just . . . I need to speak with him. And I hope he'll want to speak with me too. As soon as possible because I have to get back to Albany. So please? If you wouldn't mind?"

She folded the postcard in half and held it out for him in small fingers.

He didn't take it right away. "I can't promise he'll see you."

"I'm not asking you to."

He looked at her—her jet-black mascara, her white gold necklace and diamond solitaire, her glossy, cherry cola hair—and he believed her.

"Fine," he said. He took the card and shoved it into his shorts pocket.

"Thank you," she said. There was something uncomfortably

still and placid about her, as if she breathed less air than he did or needed to exert less energy to hold herself upright. "I don't think I got your name."

"I didn't give it to you."

"But I'm asking."

He smiled. "Well, in that case. It's Will Farris."

"Are you Arlen's friend?"

"Since we were thirteen."

She nodded. And before she turned and left, he was surprised to see that something about the information had made her glad.

For a moment after she was gone, he leaned against the counter, his blood buzzing with the same loathing and fixation he'd felt toward her during Arlen's trial, now magnified to monolithic proportions without the filters of miles, pixels, and commercial breaks. He had the urge to kick something. But if anyone had a right to be angry, it was Arlen. Not him. He picked up the phone and dialed.

"Yeah?"

"Donnie?" he said. "Will Farris. You still got that old toy cannon collecting rust out back?"

Donnie laughed. "I told you before and I'll tell you again. I ain't coming down on the price."

"That's okay," Will said, a little breathless. "I'll take it."

He hung up, and waited for the relief to set in.

**Lesson Two:** Learning to read people closely, to understand and even predict their behavior, is not without its dangers. At any given moment, our brains simply cannot take in and process all the data flooding our circuits. By necessity, we've got to cherry-pick what information we notice and what we ignore. Many of us are predisposed to focus on either the best or worst in those we meet. When you begin to scrape away your own natural prejudices and inclinations, the results can be enlightening in any number of ways.

# CHAPTER 2

Jonah: The thing you'd like most in Richmond: the Egyptian Building on the front of this postcard. So strange and unsettling among stately old brick. It might support your theory about an ancient alien race. Least: the heat. You could fry an egg on my BMW. No, I'm not going to try. Hug and kiss Dakota for me. Lauren

P.S. Enclosed please find an imaginary ham biscuit, a Virginia specialty. Don't wait too long to eat it. It might go bad.

In the late afternoon, rain fell on all of Richmond with no exceptions. It washed into the gutters and sluiced into drains, and in Carytown young people with bright umbrellas ducked beneath awnings and into cars. Will, who had not been caught in the summer storm, stood and watched the downpour from the window of his rental apartment, where he'd once lived and where Arlen now stood at his side. The wind blew hard and flung drops of water against the glass.

"Hoo-*wee*," Will said. "Bad out there."

"It's . . . incredible," Arlen said.

They stood for a moment, watching. When the storm began to let up, they went together into the bathroom, Arlen standing in the doorway and Will bending over the toilet bowl. He lifted the lid of the old beige tank, turned brownish by years of buildup, and he plunged his hand inside.

"I got a joke for you," he said as he worked. "How can you tell when a lawyer is really, really cold?"

"I give up."

"He's got his hands in his *own* pockets."

Arlen made a noise, a cross between a groan and a chuckle, and Will felt a bit happier. He adjusted the flap in the back of the toilet so it created a tighter seal, and the hiss of running water was silenced a moment later. Will stood, put the heavy porcelain lid back on the tank, and wiped his hands on a towel. "All fixed. If it starts running again, let me know and we'll get a new flap. But you oughta be okay."

Arlen stood leaning against the doorjamb of the closet-sized bathroom, and yet his face was as blank as if he were daydreaming from some scenic vista. He was a big man—he'd always been big—but the soft fat he'd grown up with was gone now, replaced by cords of hard muscle. His eyes were very round and pronounced, flecked with gold. A few freckles peppered his dark skin.

"Arlen?"

He shook his head slightly, his eyes clearing. "Thanks. I wouldn't have known how to fix it."

"Naw. Don't sweat it," Will said, struck by Arlen's situation— his perfect lack of adult experience. He didn't even know how to adjust the flap in a toilet tank. In some ways, taking in Arlen was like taking in a teenager instead of a grown man.

They walked into the small living area. There was no furniture apart from an old pink couch fit for a nursing home and a small television propped up on a cardboard box. The apartment was simple and practical enough—even a little cheery when the blinds were open and the sun came in—and Will was glad he could offer it to his friend. He dropped himself into the cushions, took off his baseball hat, and blotted the sweat from his forehead with the front of his shirt. When he spoke, he did his best to sound casual. "You had a visitor today."

"Eula?"

Will's heart sank. "No. Lauren Matthews. Remember her?" Arlen was quiet. Thunder rumbled, weakening in the distance. "All these years, and still wound tighter than a Gibson guitar."

"What she want?"

"She didn't say," Will said, and he tried not to show that the question bothered him. What *did* Lauren Matthews want with Arlen? He thought of her—her sheath of a dress, her sharp little face. He had the sense, even when he stood in the same room with her, that she was looking at him from behind a two-way mirror, so that he couldn't quite get a read on her but she saw everything about him.

He'd never perfectly grasped what it was about her that some-how both attracted him and repelled him. Lauren was the perfect opposite of his ideal woman in every way. He liked women who weren't afraid to be a little bit broken down, rusty around the edges—women who were confident and knew how to get their hands dirty and have fun. What he did not like was pretty, better-than-thou redheads who started snooping around at his best friend's apartment, causing trouble for a man who'd had more trouble in his life than most people could stand.

"She say anything?" Arlen asked.

"Not really." Will pulled his hat back on. He dug into his pocket for her contact information. Her handwriting was neat and blocky—she could have been an architect if she hadn't gone into law. "She left this address and phone for you."

Arlen held out his hand. He looked at the postcard for a long moment as if it might tell him something—a secret message, a code to unpack letter by letter. Will saw the transformation: Arlen's face, usually as placid as a mountain lake, turning stormy.

"This woman—" Arlen shook his head, choking off words.

"What?"

"Nothin'."

"She's a little bit of a freak, isn't she?" Will said—anything to keep Arlen talking. "Like she's part psychic."

"Naw, she ain't psychic." Arlen's fingers twitched at his side. "Man, if I could tell you how many times I dreamed . . ." He met Will's eye full on—a stare tough as oak. "All I'm saying is that I couldn't've committed the act of murder *before* they locked me up."

Will hesitated. The boy cop's words echoed in his ears: *Prison will change a man.* "And now?"

"I'm just saying—that girl best not be coming around if she knows what's good for her." He crumpled her note in one fist and tossed it back to Will. "Throw it away."

Will shoved it in his pocket, out of sight. He didn't think his friend was capable of murder. Exaggeration, maybe. But not murder. Arlen was angry—and he had every right to be.

Will looked hard at his new tenant—his shoulders that were more muscled now, his eyes that had lost some of their light. The outlook for men released for false imprisonment wasn't exactly good. Prison life was a life of violence, where the potential of threat—physical and otherwise—lurked everywhere, ubiquitous and unavoidable as the institutional fluorescent lighting. What kind of man did Arlen have to become to withstand years behind bars? Lambs among wolves did not survive.

Will got to his feet.

"You heading down?" Arlen asked.

"Yeah. Sometimes I actually have work to do. Care to come with?"

Arlen may have considered it a moment, but he shook his head.

Will walked across the tiny living room to the door. "I got another one for ya," he said. "If a lawyer, a judge, and a jury consultant were trapped on a desert island and you could only save one of them, would you go to a movie or out to a bar?"

"I ain't going back to jail," Arlen said. "I'd save them all."

By evening, Lauren's secretary, Rizzi, had called three times. The whole office had gone mad as hatters in Lauren's absence—mercury in the watercooler. Burt was a complete bear, calling on the interns for tangential research that he obviously didn't need but absolutely had to have right away. Lauren's colleague Bryce Pinker was furious because Lauren's biggest case had been temporarily dumped on him, and he was trying to get Rizzi to take his kids to band practice. And, to top it off, the copier had died.

"It's nuts here without you," Rizzi said. "Like an eclipse, when all the birds go crazy because it's night in the middle of the day."

Lauren chewed an antacid quietly so Rizzi couldn't hear. "I promise. I'll be back soon. This shouldn't take too long."

"The quicker, the better."

"Have you heard anything about when they might be having the vote?" Lauren asked.

"Nothing unexpected. But don't worry, hon. I'm your eyes and ears."

"Good," Lauren said. "You know how much I want to have my name on the door."

"Well, maybe being away for a day or two will make them see that you should have been a partner two years ago instead of that deadbeat Rich Weller. But what do I know? I'm just the secretary."

Lauren laughed. "I owe you. We'll go out for tequila when I get back."

"Are you the DD?"

"Yep."

"I hope to God they do make you a partner. Somebody's got to get me a new copy machine."

Lauren's father was less sympathetic than Rizzi when she called to tell him the news that she'd left Albany. Lauren walked down the street as she spoke to him, searching for a gym. She would need a good hour on the treadmill after she got off the phone with her dad.

"Is there a man?" he wanted to know. "Is that what this is? Some moonstruck-lovers kind of thing?"

"Yeah, right," Lauren said. "It's business. In a way."

"How is apologizing to Arlen Fieldstone business?"

"I have to be able to hold my head up in a courtroom, don't I?"

"Not if you lose your job."

Lauren stopped on the sidewalk and looked behind her, wondering if she'd walked past the gym. She'd decided that the best way to break the news to her parents that she was going to take a tiny little hiatus from work was to tell them over the phone, *after* she'd already done it. She would have preferred to drive over to their big stone house overlooking the Hudson River and then settle into their outdoor living room for a heart-to-heart. She wished she could tell them—could talk with them—about Arlen, about how his conviction had undermined everything she'd believed in.

But her parents, who were always supportive, weren't always

understanding. Her father had pushed her to graduate high school early—for her own good. He'd pushed her to earn her JD in an accelerated program. He'd coached her, and cheered her, and used his political connections to help make her what she was. But when it came to matters of the heart, "Go tell it to Oprah," was what he liked to say.

"So where are you staying?" he asked. "A hotel?"

"No. You remember Maisie—my roommate from college. I'm staying with her for a while."

"What do you mean by 'a while'?"

"I don't know. Not long."

"Well . . . what about Jonah?"

A pang of longing for her brother swept over her as she crossed the street. The picture of him that she carried in her mind was a snapshot of the way he'd looked a few years ago—when his hair had been buzzed to protect against lice, and the severe cut had made his eyes look bluer, bigger, even more vulnerable. He would be horrified to know she still thought of him that way: her brother who used to make charcoal sketches of the night nurses and who'd worn his name on a bracelet at his wrist.

"I said good-bye to Jonah," she said.

"Well, then, what about Dakota?"

Lauren laughed. "She's *four*. And I'm only going to be here a day or two. She won't even notice I'm gone."

"Well, your boss certainly notices."

"It doesn't matter. Dad—"

"It most certainly does matter," he said. His voice was scratchy on her eardrum. "You've dedicated your whole life to that firm. You can't just go blow it all because you're confused about how you feel right now."

"I'm not confused. Don't you understand? I need this. Maybe . . . maybe Arlen needs it too."

"What could you possibly say to Arlen Fieldstone that would make up for nine years in prison?" her father asked.

Lauren was glad her father couldn't see her, because she winced.

"And besides, it's not your fault. All the evidence was there to convict him."

"That's not what the appellate court thought."

Her father gave a frustrated *huff.* "If that woman's cocaine dealer—what was his name?"

"Chris Witte."

"Right. If he hadn't gone and started bragging, Arlen would still be in prison to this day. There's nothing you could have done differently. *Nothing.*"

Lauren found the gym and leaned against the wall outside the door. She knew her father wanted what was best for her. To him, she was blameless. He simply couldn't understand why she felt such personal responsibility about Arlen's conviction, and because he couldn't understand, he was annoyed. He was a man who loved with grit, gumption, and authority. He was pitiless—yes—but it was love that made him that way. He'd never held Lauren to standards that he didn't hold for himself.

Lauren tried to look natural leaning against the brick of the old building, her cell phone at her ear. Her chest felt tight and pressure was building between her temples. She forced herself to relax. She wished she could tell her parents about her heart, her trip to the doctor's, his warning that she find a way to make the palpitations stop. But how could her father understand what she was going through if he didn't believe she was going through anything at all?

Better to keep him out of it.

"Well, is it *safe*?" her father asked. "I don't want you agreeing to meet this guy in the middle of the night in some deserted parking lot."

"You're watching too much *CSI*," Lauren said. "And anyway, that's exactly the point. Arlen is *not* a murderer."

"But he's a stranger that you helped incarcerate. Don't think Burt doesn't tell me about the threats."

Lauren sighed. She'd been over this a hundred times with her father, who'd been her boss's golfing buddy since before she was born. Working on high-profile cases meant she *did* get the occasional threat. She'd received a new letter just last week, before she'd decided to leave town. They were always the same—passionless Times New Roman font, misspellings that would make a five-year-old cringe, and usually some kind of vague and dramatic overture like "watch your back."

More than once, she'd left her office to discover that her tires had been slashed (she'd had them insured after the first incident, since the parking lot security was worthless). And last year, someone had keyed her passenger-side door—but she'd decided to be amused by it rather than angry, because the vandal had spelled the word *whore* wrong.

In the beginning, when her work had first attracted public attention, the threats had scared her—deeply. She'd gone to the police department, but there was little they could do. She took self-defense classes and got a home security system. She refused to walk to the parking lot alone if the sun was down.

Years passed. The threats trickled in now and again . . . and yet, apart from mildly annoying acts of vandalism, nothing ever happened. Logic replaced fear as Lauren began to understand the type of people who hated her.

The threats were about some anonymous and angry person blowing off steam, not about actual violence. In her heart, she began to feel a sort of tenderness toward people who had resorted to such cowardly acts. They weren't the kind of people who had learned to express themselves through art, or dance, or writing, or even professional therapy. They had no outlet—except for a few symbolic yet largely harmless acts of rage.

"Just promise you'll be careful," her father said. "And promise you'll come home soon. You've spent your whole life working to get where you are today. I'd hate to see you blow it on an unnecessary apology to a man who doesn't even know your name."

"Thanks, Dad."

"I'm always looking out for you. You may be the first woman partner in the country's most prestigious jury consultancy—"

"I'm not a partner yet."

"Either way, you're still my little girl."

"Thanks, Dad," she said. Then, with a blast of air-conditioning hitting her in the face, she pulled open the door and went into the gym.


In prison, Arlen had learned to sit for hours, not moving, with nothing in his head except the thoughts that floated here and there as gently as feathery seedpods on a summer wind. His mother used to have a cat that lazed in the window and blinked at the sun. He'd felt bad for the animal, for how bored it must have been to do nothing but sit and stare at the blowing cornstalks across the road. Now he understood just how much there was to see, when a person really could see what there was.

Richmond—Carytown—was fascinating; he felt greedy with the need to take it all in from his place at the window. Sometime in the last decade, men had started dressing like women in tight shirts and skinny jeans, and the women had started dressing like hobos—or, at least, the young ones did—walking out the door in whatever slouchy and mismatched things they happened to grab. He couldn't look away. People were always doing two things at once, talking to a friend and playing with their phones, hurrying and listening to Walkmans the size of postage stamps, or walking without looking where they were going and working a flattened-out computer with their thumbs. Arlen—who could barely do one thing at a time and feel he was doing it well—was rapt.

A teenage boy rode past on a bicycle, and Arlen's own muscles twitched as if he could feel the pedals under his feet. White cords from the boy's headphones dangled down his chest and disappeared into a pocket. As the bike moved through the frame of the window, Arlen turned his body to the side, put his head against the glass, to watch the boy push into the periphery.

And when a car in an intersection stopped fast, and the boy flew headfirst over his handlebars, Arlen saw that too.

The adrenaline came quick—a shot of energy and strength. His armpits prickled with sweat and his heart sped. Nine years in prison, and his body responded to danger in the time it took a bolt of lightning to jump from clouds to ground. He didn't think about what he was doing—he just ran downstairs, through the antiques shop (where Will was polishing a banged-up trumpet), and to the door.

But when his foot hit the concrete step that led to the sidewalk, he stopped as if he'd been turned to stone.

Outside.

The outside world in full swing—Richmond on a Monday evening. His heart pounded hard in his chest, blood heating his muscles.

"What's wrong?" Will stood behind him, but Arlen didn't turn. He once saw a guy get jumped in the prison yard with a shank made out of a toothbrush. The man's throat was slit from earlobe to earlobe, and he bled out on the pavement before the guards and medics could do a damn thing. Arlen had stood by then too, paralyzed. It was the first time he'd seen a dead body, but it wasn't the last.

Now, when he spoke, he felt as if he'd needed to pry the words out of his brain one by one. "The boy . . . on a bike . . . an accident . . ."

Will shouldered past him. "I'll be right back!" Then he was gone.

Arlen slunk backward into the shop.

Fifteen minutes later, Will returned; his cheeks—which were always a little reddish—had become a deep mauve in the heat. His red-blond hair was messy, curls nearly translucent as a baby's, matted by heat and sweat.

"The boy's fine," he told Arlen, breathing hard. "Just a bump on the head. He was up and talking, no problem. They called the ambulance just in case."

"Crazy kid," Arlen said. "That's what they get for trying to walk and chew gum." He had no reason to hang around in the antiques shop, feeling so much like an antique himself, so he started back toward the stairway that would lead to his bedroom on the floor above.

"You were gonna help that boy," Will said.

"I didn't."

"You can't leave?"

"Course I can," Arlen said. "Just didn't care to."

Then, because he didn't want to have to explain what he didn't quite understand, he walked foot over foot back upstairs, back through the living room, back to the window, where he saw the ambulance going down the street, the lights and sirens muted, and the people on the sidewalk having no sense that anything was or had ever been wrong.

Lauren kicked off her sandals and propped her bare feet on the railing of Maisie's balcony. She leaned her head back against her chair and breathed in. The air, so saturated with humidity, was not entirely unpleasant, and she thought that at any moment it might slide down her skin like water droplets on a cool glass. Above, a striped green awning blocked out the sun's last rays, which were pinkened with haze and heat. The streetlights were starting to flicker.

Lauren had spent a full day in Richmond, and she hadn't seen Arlen. One day down.

She jumped when Maisie punched her in the arm. "Hey. Enough of that."

"What?"

"I can hear you thinking from a mile away."

Lauren laughed. Maisie was lazing at her side, one hand hanging limply off her armrest, the other clutching a highball of sweet tea. Ice tinkled when she moved. "I thought *I* was supposed to be the people-reader."

"We lived together in a dorm room the size of a shoe box for two years. I can't read people, but I can read *you*."

"Oh, really?"

"Like a book."

"What am I thinking now?"

"That your friend Maisie is the best hostess in the whole world?"

Lauren touched her forehead. "My God. That's amazing! We'll have to train you in speed-reading next. So you can size up a person even before they say hello."

"No, thanks. That would take the adventure out of dating."

"Don't I wish!" Lauren said. And out of a bad habit, she glanced at her cell phone on the table beside her. But there were no calls.

"So spill." Maisie propped her legs up on a small stool. After her shift at the hospital, she'd changed out of her scrubs and put on an emerald sundress so slouchy and elastic it might have been pajamas. "How did it go with Arlen?"

"I didn't see him. His landlord recognized me. He wouldn't let me upstairs."

"So what will you do?"

"I don't know." Lauren thought of work—of the things she'd left undone. Leaving had been a spur-of-the-moment decision. She'd left a half-sipped glass of wine on the kitchen counter; the vacuum in the living room was plugged in. When she got back, it would all look the same as when she left it. "If I don't hear anything by tomorrow afternoon, I'll go back over there."

"You're really in a hurry to go home."

Lauren glanced at her friend. Where Lauren was small and athletic, Maisie was broad and curved. Her blue eyes spoke of beaches and palm trees, even in the winter. Her brown hair bounced with natural curl, caught in a ponytail. On Lauren's rigidity scale—a system she'd invented to help her estimate a potential juror's nature—Maisie was a marshmallow.

"I'll try to get back down here to see you again over Christmas," Lauren said. "When we can spend more time together. But I'm hoping to make the trek up north again by tomorrow night."

"Are you telling me that for all that luggage you dragged in here, you're only staying for two days?"

"You know me. What I pack for two days is someone else's weeklong cruise," she said, mocking herself a little. "It's all about being prepared."

"Impossible. You can *never* be prepared."

"Well, I still like to try."

Maisie was quiet for a moment. Lauren could tell she had reservations about speaking again: her tight lips and slightly narrowed eyes gave it away. "What are you going to do if Arlen won't see you?"

"I'm optimistic that he will."

"You've got so much riding on whether or not he forgives you. What if he doesn't? What then?"

Lauren's heart jumped in her chest, and she waited a moment before she spoke, commanding it to settle down. "He has to."

"But why?" Maisie asked, pleading now. "Is it because of Jonah? Because if it is . . ."

"It's not about my brother," Lauren said.

"What happened to Arlen—and Jonah—wasn't your fault."

"It wasn't *entirely* my fault. But it was some."

Lauren stood and made her way to the railing of the balcony. The breeze that blew against her hot skin was barely a breeze at all. "You would want to make this right too. If you were me."

"Probably. I'm not trying to second-guess you. I'm just trying to help."

Lauren glanced over her shoulder and offered her warmest smile. "You help me more than you know."

She looked back to the street, where a man was walking a huge white dog down the sidewalk. The doctor had warned her. After she'd picked herself up off the floor of the courthouse and they'd brought her to the ambulance, she'd been subjected to a series of tests. The doctors scrutinized not only her heart, but her life. They wanted to know: *Did she take illegal drugs? Legal drugs? Did she drink coffee? Alcohol? Did her family suffer from heart disease? And what about her stress levels; how would she describe them?*

Forty-eight hours and one Holter monitor later, a specialist sat her down in his office. He'd told her the impulses in her heart were firing out of rhythm, so that the well-timed pulses of electricity were less like clockwork and more like lightning in a storm. He'd thrown words at her—*palpitations, sinus tachycardia, atrial fibrillation.* The doctor had told her that if the misfiring didn't stop, she could face more serious long-term consequences. Lauren had demanded the bottom line. *Look,* he'd said. *I probably shouldn't put it this way. But I think it's an old-fashioned nervous breakdown.*

Lauren had been shocked. She'd always thought of nervous breakdowns as ailments that were more made up than real—mythical "female diseases" from some other time when women wore corsets and hid their pregnancies.

How could *she* have a nervous breakdown? Her schedule was grueling, high-pressured, and dangerous—and for years she'd weathered it. No—she'd conquered it. Struggle had made her strong. There was no way she could go back to her office and attempt to explain that there was nothing wrong with her other than what was in her head, that she'd simply had a—she hated to even *think* it— nervous breakdown.

She *had* to get Arlen's forgiveness. Closure was not merely an amenity that would allow her to look herself in the mirror again; it was necessary. Before Arlen's retrial, she'd felt untouchable. A monarch ruling her own life—to the awe and amazement of everyone who saw how young she was and how much she'd accomplished.

But now she'd lost her confidence—and she couldn't work cases without it. She didn't want to have a stroke before she turned thirty-five. Arlen's forgiveness would go a long way toward undoing what had been done. What *she* had done.

The last of the pink smears of sunset faded behind the big houses across the street. "Well," Maisie said, "it's nice to have you down here visiting. You need a break from all that court stuff. A few days in Richmond will do you good."

"I wish I could stay longer," Lauren said.

"You're welcome as long as you like. Stay the year. Stay two. Lauren . . ." Lauren turned, and Maisie reached across the small balcony for her friend's hand. "If it were up to me, you wouldn't go back to Albany at all."

The narrow brick alleyway alongside the antiques shop smelled of yeast—and when Will dragged the garbage to the sidewalk for tomorrow's morning pickup, he knew why. Two days ago, he'd bought Arlen a thirty-pack of beer. Nothing fancy—just the same kind of pilsner served at picnics and dive bars. Now the whole pack was gone.

Will headed back into the shop, then up the stairs that led to the apartment where Arlen was staying. He knocked and entered. Arlen looked up from his perch at the window. The TV was muted but on.

"I'm heading out. You need anything?" Will asked.

"Naw. I'm fine."

"You should make a grocery list. Otherwise I have to guess."

"Just don't get anything I have to assemble myself. Those little cups of macaroni were good. Fast."

Will nodded, again struck by how much Arlen was like a teenager—except that he was different from the one Will had known. The last time Will had seen the Arlen he knew, the person he recognized on some fundamental level, Arlen had been a newlywed. He'd saved up a little money, and he'd been able to plan a short trip to Albany to visit a sick cousin. Almost a decade later, Arlen was finally back in Virginia, but Will had the sense that he didn't consider himself to be *home*.

When they were kids, living in the backcountry, they'd liked to head down to the old flat brook, fishing rods balanced on their shoulders like muskets, coolers of pilfered beer in their free hands. The cicadas would wheeze in the treetops, the creek would come alive with water bugs, and they would sit feeling alone and safe until the sun went down.

Their home lives weren't bad, exactly, but in a town with more people than jobs, more bars than churches, they didn't have what outsiders called "advantages." Arlen's mom had been a widow; his dad had died from emphysema after fifty years of working the mines in the summer and the fields in the fall. His mother managed to pay the mortgage, but not much else, by holding an illegal day care in her living room.

Will's situation had its challenges too. His dad was gone as well; he was a trucker whose only reason for coming home seemed to be to get Will's mom pregnant. She'd just had her sixth baby when his father took to the road and didn't come home again. Will's mom did her best. The government helped. It was almost enough to get by.

Will found refuge in his friendship with Arlen. In the halls of their high school, they were joined at the hip. Neither had nice clothes. Neither was popular with girls. But together, they talked about everything, sitting on the boulders beside the creek. Both of them had wanted something better, and mostly what they wanted was money. They swatted at mosquitoes and dreamed that they would start some business together and get out of town.

But these days, even when Will was beside him, Arlen seemed to consider himself alone.

"All right," Will said. "Long as you don't need anything. You got a key."

Arlen turned back to the window. "So long."

Will walked down the stairs to the first floor, the old boards creaking heavily under his weight. Twice today Arlen had scared him: First when the strength and force of his anger at Lauren Matthews had made Will's skin crawl. And second when Will realized that Arlen couldn't go outside.

Will wanted to *know* his old friend again. But how could he when Arlen wouldn't let him? For one week Arlen had been out of prison. Will had searched for signs of his old friend in this new guy's face, but Arlen remained a stranger.

He shoved his hand into the pocket of his cargo shorts, where Lauren Matthews's note had been folded into a square. And he thought about her, much more than he meant to, as he let the Virginia roads take him out of Richmond proper, take him home.

**Lesson Three:** Learning to pay attention to personal appearance is a vital first step to truly seeing people. How we dress or don't dress, how we style our hair or don't style it, the ways that we alter our bodies (weight loss, plastic surgery, tattoos, piercings)—each element of our personal style is a choice—an elective trait—and each choice is a proclamation to the world that says, *This is who I am.*

But don't think that because a woman wears no jewelry, she's poor (she may be allergic to certain metals, or not like the feel of it on her skin). And don't think that because a man is well dressed, he must be rich (men who wear the best suits may go home to rooms full of old furniture and curtainless windows). The image a person projects is only the beginning of your search for clues.

# CHAPTER 3

On the evening of Arlen Fieldstone's conviction, Lauren and her colleagues treated themselves to a night of celebrating. Lauren had taken on the Fieldstone trial after a freak accident—when both the district attorney and his assistant had been injured together in the same car crash as they went out together for their lunch break. Lauren—with all the exuberant courage of a young woman who meant to get a foot in the door come hell or high water—was called to stand in until one or both of her bosses recovered. She hadn't needed to hear the gossip to know what the legal community was whispering about her. There was talk of finding a replacement. But she rallied, worked under her bosses' supervision, and then, in front of national television syndicates and politicians everywhere, she made the case her own. When she won, she wasn't lauded like some winning hometown quarterback; she was hailed as the whole team.

*We, the jury . . .*

On the night of the verdict her colleagues joked about carrying her through the streets on their shoulders. And though they didn't lift her, the suggestion was enough to make her high. She pictured it: streamers and confetti fluttering earthward as they paraded through the concrete caverns of downtown Albany—the scene no less real because it was imagined. They rolled into the bar, the usual bar, as if they owned every napkin, coaster, and glass. At some point Lauren lost track of the number of drinks thrust into her hand.

Burt Sternfeld, who was a partner in a private firm of lawyers and jury consultants, gripped her arm. *A prodigy*, he'd called her. She was a *prodigy*. She'd heard the word before—when she'd graduated early from her private high school, when she got an accelerated BS, when she had her JD at twenty-two. But it wasn't until Burt said *prodigy* to her that she thought, *Maybe*. He'd put an arm around her shoulders as if she—and not her father—had been golfing with him for a decade, and he said he'd heard a rumor about her interest in jury consulting. He asked her to make an appointment with his secretary. She nodded politely. Her toes in her shoes curled so hard they hurt.

All of Albany had turned its eyes on her. The bartender gave her his number—an odd but delightful occurrence given that she'd seen the man at least a dozen times before and he'd never flirted with her until that night. And Juliette Peterson, the secretary who always gave her such a hard time when Lauren asked for copies, swallowed her usual irritability and said congratulations. *Everyone* knew Lauren was not just another wannabe. She was the real thing.

*. . . find the defendant . . .*

Lauren's victory was one for the history books, a victory that almost hadn't happened. She'd stood trial in her own way, and she'd won. After the verdict had been announced, Senator Raimez had found her in a quiet corner of the courthouse. His eyes were full of tears and he held her hand somberly—not quite a handshake but an embracing.

"Nothing changes the fact that my wife is dead," he'd said to her, right in front of the cameras. "But justice lives on."

*... guilty as charged ...*

That night in her bed, her head swimming with alcohol and compliments, her legs exhausted because she was not yet used to working a full day in high heels, she saw flashes of the future before her. Her proud parents (she would buy a house to rival theirs). The wardrobe she would have when she got her new job at Burt's firm (which was just about in the bag). The respect she would command when she walked the marble corridors across the country. She fell asleep half dreaming that a great road was becoming clear before her—a path that she herself had cleared even though it stretched far out in front of her, into places she hadn't yet been.

If she thought of Arlen Fieldstone again—as a *person* rather than an *event*—it was only in passing. The Fieldstone conviction was washed away on a tide of vodka, congratulations, and then the rush of wildly successful years.

From his little apartment—which he'd come to think of as a prison tower—Arlen had studied the mechanics of the antiques trade. It seemed simple enough. Will lugged armfuls of junk into the shop; strangers lugged them right back out. Rusty tricycles, advertisements for gasoline, plastic superheroes still in their boxes ... The place was an ant farm for pack rats. Yesterday, Will had wheeled in a cigarette vending machine that, far as Arlen could tell, had no hope of being useful again except for target practice. But Will had whooped and smiled like it was Christmas day over the thing, even as flakes of rust were falling from it like snow.

Now, Arlen stood in the shop. Will had put him in charge—walking out the door even while Arlen argued. "Back in twenty," he'd said.

That had been an hour ago. But luckily, nobody had come in. Arlen was alone with empty fish tanks and costume jewelry and pull-string dolls. Over the counter, Will had hung a sign: WORK IS FOR PEOPLE WHO DON'T COLLECT ANTIQUES.

Arlen wondered: What did Will see in all this junk—this stuff that smelled so bad, coated in dirt and rust? He'd thought Will had meant to get all rich and upstanding when he grew up. Instead, he collected old crap.

He noticed, for the first time, a shelf within eyesight of the office and a sign that had curled in at the edges:

NOT FOR SALE.
AND NO, YOU CAN'T TALK ME DOWN.

Arlen peered closer. A cast-iron dog. Tickets to a Redskins game. Keys and a replica Ford truck. Will's old Ford. And a whistle that Arlen himself had whittled one day with his very own hands.

He stepped back.

These were Will's things. His personal things. Arlen reached out, thinking of what it would be like to hold that old whistle—he could remember sitting on his mother's porch when he'd made it, stopping now and again to watch the sky change and the robins peck at the dirt. But then something dark twisted around in his belly and stopped him from picking it up.

"Hellooo?"

He jumped clear out of his skin. He hadn't heard the front door open.

*A customer.*

He pulled his shoulders back and walked slowly, slowly to the front of the store, all his senses alert and his brain screaming and telling him to just slink away before anyone knew he was there. He emerged from behind a tall bookcase, and there in the middle of the entryway, standing and looking befuddled, was a middle-aged white woman. Her shin-length skirt was printed with tiny green and white flowers, and her blouse was buttoned down over giant breasts. She wore an old visor over her tufts of coppery hair.

"Oh, there you are," she said.

Arlen managed to nod. He couldn't get enough air.

The woman tipped her head and smiled. "Hot enough for you?"

He tried to speak, but the words got stuck, so he made a sound to show he agreed.

"Well, then," the woman said, clasping a shiny red purse before her in two hands. "It's my husband's birthday next week and he collects bottles. The little blue ones. I'm wondering if you have any."

Arlen didn't have to think long about the answer. He'd seen a few blue bottles on a shelf in the middle of the heap that was Will's store. He gestured for the woman to follow him. And to his surprise, she did. No hesitating because he was leading her back into the maze of junk, away from the door. No saying, *I'll come back another time*. She just followed him. Totally unafraid. He realized she had no idea who he was.

At Will's glass display—which was a few shelves of dusty vases and bowls—she stood for a moment, looking at the jewel-blue apothecary bottles. She held them up one at a time. They caught the light and shimmered like tropical fish. On the shelf, they'd been lifeless; they came alive in her hand.

He clasped his fingers together in front of him. He missed women—boy, did he ever miss them. This woman smelled like an imitation of the lilac bushes that bloomed beside his mother's clothesline. In the spring, his shirts and coveralls used to pick up a bit of the scent. The smell of the outside world was one of the things he'd missed most in prison; he'd spent ages breathing filtered, temperature-controlled air. But Richmond, it was a feast for the nostrils. He couldn't help himself; he leaned toward the woman, her faint cloud of lilac so thick she almost seemed to be in a haze of purple, and he breathed in.

"I'll take this one. And—Oh!"

She turned her head. Arlen straightened up, caught. The woman's eyes grew wide under her white visor, and her mouth was open so far that he saw she had lipstick on her teeth. He knew enough not to apologize, because if he said he was sorry he would have to explain himself. He wasn't certain she knew *why* he was leaning toward her; she knew only that he was.

She turned bright berry pink and held up a few more bottles for Arlen's inspection. "I'll, um, I'll take these as well."

Arlen nodded. She hurried to the front of the store a little more quickly than she'd walked into it, and Arlen followed. Behind the register the cashbox was locked up, but Will had shown Arlen where he hid the key. Arlen made change for the woman, then carefully rolled each blue bottle in brown paper and secured it with a bit of tape. And it felt good—so good—to be packing them up and handing them off. He liked the idea that the woman thought he did this all the time.

"Thank you," she said. "You have a nice day now."

"Same to you," he said.

And he realized they were the first words he'd spoken to anyone but Will since he'd been freed.

Lauren and Maisie had breakfast in the sun-filled kitchen—hazelnut coffee, toast, and sliced melon. Maisie's sleep-rumpled hair and foggy eyes reminded Lauren of mornings spent on the beds of their dorm room, chasing mild hangovers with cups of orange juice and analysis of the night before. Before Maisie left for work, Lauren thanked her and gave her a long hug in the doorway. If Lauren connected with Arlen today, she would leave right away.

With the house empty, Lauren dialed her brother, tucked her cell phone against her shoulder, and washed the dishes. Jonah's phone rang and rang. She was just about to disconnect when her niece picked up.

"Hello, this is Dakota speaking."

"Kota! It's Aunt Lauren."

"Hi!"

"How are you?" Lauren asked.

"Fine."

"Yeah?"

"Uh-huh."

"Doing anything fun?" Lauren asked.

"Yes."

"What?"

"Playing."

Lauren put a mug into the drying rack. She'd fallen head over heels for her newborn niece when Dakota had burped on her shoulder and ruined her favorite shirt. Lauren wanted to keep her talking, just a little more.

"What are you playing?" Lauren asked.

Dakota made a good effort at conversation. She was trying— Lauren could tell. But the fact remained that human beings weren't designed to talk to each other via screens and fiber optics. Adults learned to work around the relative "blindness" of cell phone calls and text messages. But Dakota had yet to develop the proper brain muscles and attention span for artificial communication. She just wanted to get off the phone.

Eventually, Lauren let her go and her brother got on the line.

"Hey, Laure! Checking up on me?"

"Just calling to get the latest from my favorite stay-at-home dad."

"Dakota's driving me crazy," he said. "She just learned about tap dancing. Now she wants to be a Rockette."

"I thought she wanted to be president."

"That was last week," he said.

Lauren smiled and adjusted the phone on her shoulder, careful not to get suds on her cell. Jonah and his wife—who had been his nurse when he'd been incarcerated—had managed to work out a good life for themselves despite Jonah's early setbacks. He didn't have a good track record when it came to holding down a job, but he was an amazing father. Some people said he was immature; Lauren liked to think that he'd simply never lost his innocence.

"So did you see Arlen?"

"I'm working on it." She turned off the faucet and put down the dish sponge. "I have to be honest. It didn't occur to me until I got down here that Arlen might not want to talk to me."

"I could have told you that."

"I figured he would *want* to see me. You know, for closure."

"Did you at least get a look at him?"

"No."

"Let me know when you do. We'll take him apart—figure out a plan. We'll win him over yet!"

Lauren opened a cabinet and grabbed a clean dishcloth to dry the wet plates. "What would *you* do if the person who put you in jail showed up at your house and asked you to forgive her?"

"It's different with me."

"But what would you do? If you were Arlen?"

"Let's review. What do we know about him?"

"What I remember most is how quiet he was," Lauren said. "Soft-spoken. People would have called him a man of few words. But I don't think the quietness was because he lacked things to say."

"Right. He's quiet not because he doesn't have opinions, but he feels like he doesn't need to express them. His opinions belong to him and him alone. So keeping quiet becomes a kind of power, in a way."

"Maybe his only power, given the situation."

"He had a crappy defense attorney," Jonah said. "That woman thought he was guilty."

"Maybe," Lauren said. Since they were children, Jonah had always been the better people-reader of the two of them. Lauren's teachers and parents had assumed she was a natural—that she had an inherent talent for seeing beneath the surface of things. But while she did have *some* talent, she was no match for her brother. He saw everything. Every secret was a broadcast. Every minor emotion that crossed someone's face was magnified tenfold. People thought that her gift had made her a prodigy. *His* gift had once driven him insane.

He said, "Arlen might not want you to know whether or not he forgives you."

She stopped drying dishes. The towel sagged in her hand. "It would be nice if I knew. But even if I never know, fine—maybe I don't deserve to. I still have to tell him that I'm sorry for my part in what happened. It's the right thing to do."

Jonah sighed. "I wish I could have watched the trial. I probably could have told you he wasn't guilty right off the bat."

"Probably," she admitted. Her mind flashed to an image of herself as a young woman scrutinizing the jury, looking for reactions—the flash of a frown, the twitch of an eyebrow—so she could better lead them, guide them, *force* them to reach the conclusion she had already reached: that Arlen was guilty. Unfortunately, she'd never thought to look at Arlen.

She heard Dakota singing in the background. "I should let you go."

"Laure?"

"Still here."

"Don't you dare come home early because you're worried about me. You stay down there till it's done."

She smiled. She thought she'd called her brother because he needed her to. Now she knew that was wrong. "I don't think I'll be too long."

"*Be* too long," Jonah said. "Be very long. What's up here for you except a bunch of old, egoistic curmudgeons who get off on arguing with each other?"

"Those egoistic curmudgeons are considering me for a promotion."

"Great," he said flatly. "So you'll be head curmudgeon."

"I'll call you later."

"I'm here if you need me."

She dried her damp hands, then shut her cell phone. It rang, almost instantly, again.

The granite along the shore of Belle Isle was knotty and muscular, stone stretched like taffy, then left in the hot sun to bake. The air smelled of sweet green leaves and the coppery tang of river. Lauren stood among sunbathers, splashing infants, children hopping boulders and squealing. A family had made a picnic on a large flat rock surrounded by white water. Lauren couldn't help herself: she pried off her sandals and slipped her toes in the cool, swift river. When her legs tired, she sat on the heated stone so her feet could dangle in the current. Will Farris was late; she didn't care why. She'd lost track of time.

Finally, a cool shadow came over her—not a cloud or a bird— and when she craned her neck to look, he was there. He wore a ragged white shirt and wrinkled shorts the color of dried clay. Even sitting down she could see that he hadn't shaved since yesterday. His stubble was fuller and blondish red.

Her mind went to work. Did he always look so disheveled? And if so, where did it come from? Laziness? Poverty? Or did he simply not realize how people might see him? He hadn't seemed quite so slovenly yesterday. He'd seemed comfortably and practically dressed, but not slovenly, not like this . . .

She told herself, *Knock it off.*

"So what do you think?" he asked. He gestured to the swift river, the Robert E. Lee suspension bridge, the sweeping vista of the city, and Hollywood Cemetery on the distant ridge.

She climbed to her feet, not bothering to put her shoes back on. "It's fascinating."

"Not the word most people would use."

She shrugged. She liked the juxtaposition of motion and still-ness, of the wild water rushing over the rocks and the blocky shapes of buildings and highways. But she could see a trace of mockery in Will's eyes, and she wasn't about to explain. She crossed her arms and gave him all her attention. "What did you want to talk to me about?"

He smiled a little. "You do cut right to the heart of things."

"When I have to."

"But small talk's like foreplay. It sets the mood."

She laughed. "Yes. But *you're* using it as a tactic for stalling as opposed to seducing."

He looked over her shoulder—just a glance—and she could tell he was uncomfortable. "You want to know why I wanted to meet you—"

"I doubt it was to practice your sexual innuendos."

He considered her. Then he began to walk away. "Come on. Let's go."

"Where?"

"To find some shade." He faced her, squinting in the sun. "Unless you want to get burned."

She slipped into her sandals as gracefully as she could; then she followed him.

He was a good person, she supposed. He'd taken Arlen in. He'd even protected him—albeit from her. Under different circumstances, she might have liked him. But it was clear enough that he didn't want her to.

She followed him to the stark line where the rocky beach ended and a tangled wood—trees and shrubs she couldn't name—closed in. In the shade the air was ten degrees cooler. A slight breeze fanned the sweat on the back of her neck.

"Is this okay?" he asked.

They'd walked only an eighth of a mile, but Will had brought them to a large boulder, half-submerged in earth like an iceberg in water. There was no trail nearby, but little slices of the river glinted through the openings between the trees.

"This is fine," she said, and she sat down on the large rock. Will settled himself as far away from her as the stone would permit—and facing the exact opposite direction. If he slid a few feet nearer, they would be sitting back-to-back.

She had to twist her body, hard, to see him. His hair was a messy, reddish blond—not like hers, which was sometimes red, sometimes black, depending on how the light hit it. His hair was the reddish blond that fell somewhere between beech and clay. His face was bronzed across the cheeks, nose, and forehead— weathered, she might say—though he was probably a few years younger than she was. She guessed he'd spent a lot of time outside, and from the hints of lean muscle in his arms and legs, he'd spent it working.

"Stop doing that," he said.

"Stop what?"

"Keep your eyes on your own paper." He pointed toward the patch of trees in front of her. "Got it?"

And then she realized—while she'd been completely engrossed by reading him, he was positioning himself not to be read.

"Sorry," she said, and she looked straight forward. Through the trees and bushes, she could see the ruins of some old building.

"That's better," Will said. "Don't move."

She bent her knees and drew her legs up before her. Her skin prickled. She felt blindfolded. She was conscious of herself in a new, excruciating way: of the fact that she hadn't worn a bra under her brown halter top, of the high hitch of her shorts, of the way her hair was sticking to her skin. She could feel him looking at her, scrutinizing, and she resisted the urge to fidget or talk—though she desperately wanted to.

For as long as she could remember, people who didn't know her very well often remarked that she was a good listener. But those who were close to her knew she was more than that. What she heard when she listened wasn't the words that were spoken, but the spaces between. And as she got older, she began to have the sense that at any given moment there were really two different worlds operating: the world of the surface, where a person could say, "I'm so sorry to hear that," and seem to mean, "I feel bad for you"; and the world underneath the surface, where a person could say the same thing, but mean, "I don't want to know."

She loved people—loved them hard and with her whole heart. And she loved children especially because they didn't fib or evade in quite the way that adults did. But she knew that if she wanted to love people fully and completely, she would have to love them with exceptional strength—to accept everything good that people wanted her to see in them and everything bad that they couldn't hide.

As Will stared at her, she wished there was some way to explain herself to him. But he wanted to see for himself.

"So what do you want with Arlen?" he asked.

"I want to talk with him."

"About what?"

"About what happened," she said.

"That's it?"

"No. No, that's not it."

"Tell me," he said, his voice softening.

Her cheek was warm under his stare. She lifted her chin. "Can you imagine," she asked, "what it was like when they told me Arlen wasn't guilty after all? That he'd lost nine years of his life because of a trial I'd helped orchestrate?"

He said nothing.

"I was in the hospital a week ago." She laughed a little at herself and shook her head. "As of this moment, the only other person on earth who knows that besides my doctor is you."

"You haven't told anyone."

"No."

"Why?"

"There was no reason to worry anybody." She leaned one palm back on the rock; pebbles and grit stuck to her skin. It bothered her that after keeping her emergency room visit a secret for so long, here she was spilling her guts to a stranger—a stranger she couldn't see even though he was only a few feet away.

"Is it your heart?" he asked.

She hadn't realized she was touching her ribs, rubbing the spot where her heart lay quiet. Embarrassed, she drew her hand away. "I guess it was trying to tell me something."

"What?"

For the first time, she was glad she couldn't see him. "I owe Arlen an apology. And more."

Will sighed, a long, masculine sound of consideration and decision making all in one. "Why didn't you tell your parents? Your boyfriend?"

"There's no boyfriend," she said.

"Girlfriend?"

She laughed. "Go fish."

"So you didn't tell them, but you're telling me."

"It's easier to tell things to strangers." She twisted her hands together and wished she could see him. "Plus, the first thing they teach you in behavioral psychology is how important it is to reveal things about yourself if you want to establish trust."

"You want me to trust you."

"I do."

"Why?"

"Because despite what you may think, I'm not a bad person."

"What else?" he asked.

"No one but you has the power to convince Arlen to speak with me."

"Otherwise you wouldn't have told me?"

"I'm not sure," she said. "But I did tell you. And . . . I'm glad."

He got to his feet and made a slow circle around the giant stone—something in his languorous gait put her in mind of the big cats that paced in their cages at the zoo—until he came to stand in front of her. His arms were marked here and there with mosquito bites and scars. He ran a hand through his hair, his face shadowed with frustration. "It seems like you and Arlen both need to talk to each other."

"Arlen wants to talk to me?"

"Hell, no. But . . . I think it might be good for him. He needs *something*. And I'm not sure that talking to you is the answer, but I'm working with what I got."

Lauren nodded. "So you'll help me."

"For a price."

She laughed a little. The pieces were coming together. Will *was* poor after all. "Money won't be an issue. Just tell me what you need."

"I don't need your money," he said. And she didn't need to be looking to feel the shift in him, a tensing and drawing away. "I need your help. An eye for an eye."

"What?"

"My sister Annabelle just had a baby."

Lauren flushed. "I don't know if I'm that good with kids . . ."

"I don't need you to babysit. I need you to go with me out into the field. I've got some great leads lined up for the next couple days, and people are much more open to letting me rummage around in their spare rooms and attics if I've got a woman with me."

"So you're a picker," she said.

He smiled—something sharp in the pull of his lips. "Best in Virginia."

"You don't have a friend who can do it?"

"I don't have a friend who *wants* to do it. It's not exactly a glamorous job."

Lauren mulled it over. She didn't love the idea of traipsing around strangers' personal junkyards and looking for antiques, but she did want Will's help. She also wanted to show him that she was serious—that she wanted Arlen's forgiveness and would do anything to get it. She would do her penance in outbuildings, and attics, and private junkyards.

"Look," Will said. "You're only here for a few days, right?"

"Hopefully less than that."

"Well, if you help me get through these next couple leads, it'll give me enough time to take out an ad and try to find somebody else. In return, maybe I'll work on Arlen. *Maybe*."

She got to her feet. Because the rock was gently sloped away, she hadn't realized how close Will had been standing, his feet only inches from hers. Now she was close to him, closer than polite conversation allowed. She stayed as still as she could, hands at her sides, her head tipped back to hold eye contact. The polite thing would have been for him to step away. He didn't.

"You want to keep an eye on me, don't you?" she asked.

"You got me," he said. "Are you healthy enough to tag along? I mean—with your . . ."

"It's nothing. It's just . . ."

"It's just that you need to square with Arlen."

"Yes." Her sense of smell had been trained to pick up details about a person, and men like Will usually smelled musty—like dust, grease, polish, or simply the smell of clothes left too long sitting on some floor. But Will smelled . . . fantastic. A combination of deodorant or detergent and his own natural scent. The smell didn't fit with his wrinkled clothes and stubble; somewhere, there was a missing link. She couldn't say if she was more bothered or intrigued.

"It's a deal," she said.

He shook her hand hard, palms brutishly clasping. "I'll pick you up tomorrow at five."

"That late?"

"Five *a.m.* Try that *early.*"

"That's not early for me," she said. And then she kicked herself. Why did she feel the need to prove she was *tough* to this man?

"You know your way back?" he asked.

She nodded. "I'm going to hang out by the river. It's not often I get to be outside in the middle of the day."

He looked at her once more, and she didn't shy away; she looked back. Will's face couldn't be called handsome. He didn't have a leading man's jaw or a news anchor's waxed hair. But his high forehead sloped down to a slightly rounded nose—not a small nose, but nice—and his mouth was a good mouth, with a curvy upper lip that a woman might not notice unless she was looking. The reddish stubble on his cheeks intrigued her; she liked men who were clean-shaven. Men who took care of themselves. Edward— and all her boyfriends, ever—had been clean-shaven. And yet, some small part of her wondered what it might feel like to drag her cheek across such rough terrain.

He stepped aside and she walked a few feet toward the river. She held up her hand in a halfhearted good-bye.

"Lauren?"

She turned.

"If you need to call someone about that heart, you call me. I'll take you over to the hospital, or I'll just go over and sit with you. And I won't tell a soul."

"Thanks," Lauren said. She read him for ulterior motives—his squinted-up eyes, his relaxed mouth—but found none. And the heart in question jumped once again in her chest, but for entirely unexpected reasons.

**Lesson Four:** You can't read a person without reading the context that the person is in. A man wearing a tie on his way home from work is one thing. A man wearing a tie at a bowling alley is something else. A woman who laughs loudly at a bar while talking on a cell phone might indicate that the conversation has her full attention. A woman who does the same thing in a library is attention-hungry, insensitive, or obtuse. To really get to know someone, get them out of their comfort zones—out of their usual context. Then watch and learn.

# CHAPTER 4

Dear Jonah: I picked this postcard up for you at a history
museum. It's the old capitol building—white columns
and pediments . . . not especially imaginative, you'd say.
Tomorrow, I'm going picking—which I'm given to understand is like stealing antiques for money—with a man I
met who is Arlen's friend. No, it's not like that (and yes, I
am reading your mind). The only thing I'll be picking up
on this excursion is probably fleas. LOVE!

Early Wednesday morning, Will had thought about honking the
horn in front of the house where Lauren was staying, but she beat
him to the punch. She was out the door in a moment—her sneakers
blurring with speed as she came down the stairs, legs trim and
tough beneath what he guessed were her workout clothes. Old
resentment flared, and he thought, *Maybe this wasn't such a good*

*idea.* Already, the morning was steamy—residual heat from yesterday. The sky was a powdery white blue and the moon was translucent as a feather hanging in the sky.

Lauren opened the car door; it creaked on the hinges.

He hated how pretty she was—her pink lips, heavy bangs, and disarmingly sweet face. Her hair was pulled up in tortoiseshell barrettes on each side, and it struck him how young she looked when she wasn't dressed up. If she were a stranger on the street, she would have been the kind of person he'd want to be nice to.

"You ready?" he asked.

She peered uncertainly into the interior of his car, with its ripped seats and sun-faded dashboard. He'd started restoring the old Studebaker pickup last year. Normally, he would have brought his van, but he knew they wouldn't be looking at any big items today. Plus he wanted to see how the truck held up: it was only last week that the engine finally coughed to life.

"We can take my car, if you want," she said.

"Which is your car?"

"That one." She pointed across the street. Her black BMW gleamed like candy in the sunlight—prettier now because of the junker idling beside it. Something in Will's gut went sour. But he forced himself to grin.

"Aw, come on," he said. "Look at this thing. It's a rocket ship. It's a piece of history."

She climbed in. "It smells like wet dog."

"So it does. You might wanna roll down your window there, *darling Lauren.* We're going au naturel today. No AC."

She had to use two hands to crank the window open. It stuck halfway. The car gave a soft clunk when he put it in drive. He took them out of Richmond, past the red stone masonry of the old train station, and west until the buildings loosened their grip on the soil and were replaced by trees. He'd started to say, "So, how do you like Richmond?" when her phone rang.

"Excuse me," she said, though there was no apology in her voice. She flipped open the phone and turned her face toward the window. While he drove, she talked about work: bits of a conversation he couldn't understand except to glean that she was up for some kind of promotion. After a moment, he knew she'd forgotten about him entirely, so that she was completely absorbed by the person on the other end of her phone. A little fissure of jealousy opened inside him; he muscled it closed.

When he'd watched her on his parents' beat-up television all those years ago, nobody in the whole courtroom had ever made him feel worse than she did. His clothes had been literally threadbare; his teeth had been crooked as country tombstones in his mouth. He hadn't gotten braces until he was twenty-two. While she spent her twenties making television appearances, he was scrambling to collect junk—anything to make a buck. Some part of him wanted to rub it in her face—how opposite they were. How hard he had it and how easy she did.

When he was downright honest with himself, he had to admit that he hadn't really needed her today, but he'd been obsessed by the idea of bringing her along. He couldn't explain that to her—he hoped he wouldn't have to.

She had him all knotted up. Maybe it was because of how reserved and cucumber-cool she always seemed to be. Maybe it was because she'd thrown his best friend in jail. Or maybe it was because he thought it the most hideously unfair and cruel thing in the world that a woman as smart, rich, and sexy as she was could be so morally deformed under all that blinding beauty. She'd claimed she'd come to apologize; he wasn't so sure.

As the highways thinned to a mere trickle of country roads, and

Lauren went from talking on the phone to dashing off e-mails with it, Will watched her secretly out of the corner of his eye.

In Beaufont, not far from the Cloverleaf Shopping Center, nobody needed to tell Eula Oates that her ex-husband had been let out of prison, and certainly nobody needed to tell her for the tenth time. And yet, here she stood, doing something as innocent as buying a book of stamps at the post office, and Mrs. Lawry was standing in line in front of her wearing her big blue net hat and sticking her nose where it didn't belong.

"Do you think he'll look you up—you know—even though you divorced him so fast?"

"Well," Eula said. "If he does show up at my house, I'm sure somebody in this town will ring you up and let you know even before I can answer my front door."

She left without waiting for her stamps, and she hurried out to her car. When she opened the driver's-side door, heat blasted her like she was climbing into the jaws of hell. She leaned her forehead against the steering wheel, just for a moment, before she put the car in reverse.

Nobody faulted her for doing what she did after Arlen got convicted; if anything, they felt bad for her. *Poor Eula. Marrying a murderer. Who could have known?*

But now that it turned out Arlen wasn't guilty after all . . . she might as well have been Lady Godiva riding naked in the street, for the way people's tongues wagged. Eula could read between the lines: *If only she'd been a more faithful wife. If only she'd trusted him more. If only she wasn't so selfish as to let him go.*

*If only, if only, if only.*

Arlen wasn't guilty—that was fact. And in the papers, they lauded him as a man who was nearly a saint—all sweet and gentle as a newborn calf. But Arlen was as capable of violence as anybody, if not more capable. And only Eula knew.

On the day she heard that they were letting him free, she finally got around to changing the locks of the house that she'd bought with him all those years ago, the house where they were gonna rock their babies, and nag each other about the dishes, and grow old, sleeping in each other's arms.


The sun had done nothing to make the morning less steamy. Moisture rose up from the fields and hung heavily in the air. The clouds seemed to boil in the sky. Half an hour ago, Will had sent Lauren to pick among the falling-down outbuildings and oxidized piles of car parts that dotted the ground in the shade. He'd assigned himself to the old cow pasture, where the sun scorched the grasses to brown. *Anything unusual,* he'd told her. *That's what I'm looking for. Something that catches your eye.* So far his traipsing and trudging and climbing had led only to a few old oilcans and a bee sting.

He listened for the sound of her. He hoped she hadn't gotten too far away. Properties like this could be endless—miles and miles of junk strewn like leaves on a forest floor. Will understood why people kept their old baby cribs and worn-out dressers in buildings that let in rain and snow and mice. Maybe the antiques left to bleach in the sun were ignored, but that didn't mean they weren't *wanted.*

He caught the sound of Lauren's voice on a gentle wind—*Who was she talking to?*—and he traced it back until he found her. From behind an old shed he watched her a moment. She was crouched down, poking at something in the dirt. Beside her was a little boy who might have been five or six. He crouched too, and whatever he was looking at had him fascinated and a little afraid.

"It's okay," Lauren said in a soft voice. "Look. It won't bite. It's nice."

The boy's face, a smaller version of the face Will had seen when the property owner had greeted them, was freckled and tanned. He wore a ragged red T-shirt with a frayed hem, shorts that were two sizes too big, and a pair of small work boots. Lauren dropped the stick and moved to pick up whatever they were looking at. Probably she wanted a better look. But the boy was staring at her.

Will came out of his hiding spot. "What you got there?"

The boy leapt up and jumped behind Lauren, and Lauren, too, turned to him with a startled gasp.

"Oh. Sorry," Will said.

"It's okay. We found something. Look."

Lauren stood and Will walked toward her to peer into her hands. Inside was a fire-orange newt. He wouldn't have pegged Lauren as the type who would pick it up.

"Oh, that's great!" he said with too much enthusiasm. The boy eyed him suspiciously. A moment ago, the kid had been talking a mile a minute. Now he just glared. "How 'bout it? Did we catch ourselves some dinner?"

The boy looked for one more long moment at Lauren, then abruptly turned and went running and hopping through the woods like a startled deer. Lauren put the newt on a decaying log. "I think he likes you," she said.

He watched the newt hurry into a deep greenish fissure in the center of the tree trunk. "And you must miss your lawyer friends."

"Why do you say that?"

"Hanging out with slimy, cold-blooded bottom-dwellers—"

"I get it," Lauren said, and she laughed a little. She wiped her hands on her shorts, leaving a loamy smear. "Believe me. There's not a lawyer joke I haven't heard."

"Oh no?" He crossed his arms and thought for a moment.

"Okay. How about . . . Why does the law prohibit sex between lawyers and clients?"

She smiled. "Double billing for the same service. You're going to have to do better than that."

Will tried to ignore the way the morning's anger was beginning to soften. Dealing with Lauren was easier when she was a heartless egoist bent on world domination—as opposed to a woman who played in the dirt with lizards and kids. "So did you find any actual antiques for me? Or just reptiles?"

"Actually I did find something," she said, gesturing for him to look toward the ground. "It's a telephone. Cool, right?"

He looked at the old phone, an oak wall mount with a hand crank, by Lauren's feet. He saw that it was coated with moist, fresh dirt, and that Lauren's bleach-white sneakers had suffered a similar fate. She must have had to pry the phone out of the ground. When he looked up at her face again, she was beaming with pride. He knew that feeling well: the joy of discovery. Some part of her pleasure echoed in him.

He said, "Not bad for a beginner."

"How old is it?"

"I'm not sure. Old. Maybe around 1906?"

"How much can you get for a phone like that?"

"'Bout as much as a person is willing to pay for it," he said. "Maybe five, six hundred. But if somebody wanted it bad enough, there's no telling."

"So it's really just about how bad a person wants a thing . . ."

"Everything in the world's about that."

They stood a moment in silence that wasn't as awkward as Will might have expected, staring down at the phone Lauren had found.

"Will?" Lauren was looking at him. The light caught her eyes, lit them like a sunbeam through a glass of iced tea. "Are you the one who paid for Arlen's lawyer? At the retrial?"

"Do I even have to reply if you're just going to know the answer anyway?"

She smiled. "I knew it was you. I'm glad you did it."

"Someone had to," he said.

"I know," she said, her face stricken with what could only be guilt. "I should have been paying more attention. I just . . . I need to apologize."

Will held her gaze. He knew what she was getting at. She wanted to know if he'd talked to Arlen—if he was going to make something happen for her. He hadn't, yet. "But apologizing . . . that's about *you*, isn't it? Not him?"

"I'd like to think it's for both of us." She took a step closer. He wondered if she was thinking of touching him—like she might reach for his shoulder or take his hand. But her arms stayed at her sides. "You'll help me, won't you? You'll talk to him for me?"

Will needed some space. He couldn't think. How could a person have such guileless eyes and yet be so disconcertingly *knowing*? He took a few steps away for no reason except that she was standing too close. "I don't know if I can help. He's carrying around all this anger like nobody I've ever seen. It's unlike him. And I'm worried . . ."

"You're worried that the old Arlen is gone."

He tried to conceal his reaction. He hadn't expected her understanding. He didn't want her to know how much it mattered. "Everybody keeps telling me to watch my back. I don't think Arlen's bad. But he could *go* bad if he doesn't change course. I won't let that happen."

"That's why you came looking for me."

He nodded. "You show up in town, hoping that Arlen's gonna be nice to you. Hoping he'll forgive you and you can start feeling better again. But here's the thing: Everything Arlen hates about the world, everything he's angry at, *all* of it is condensed down into one single point."

"*Me*," she said. It wasn't a question. She took in a deep breath and when her phone buzzed in her back pocket, she did something to silence it. "And you feel the same way about me, don't you? I'm a symbol of everything you don't like in the world. Everything that went wrong."

Will held her stare. In some small way, she brought out the boy he was when he was fifteen—rejected, poor, and pissed off at the world. He was annoyed that she knew what she did to him. "This isn't about me. There's only one reason I'm doing this. If *Arlen* can forgive you, he just might have a chance."

"That makes two of us," she said.

A light wind made the leaves above them whisper, and the anger that Will had managed to hold on to throughout the course of the morning left him, suddenly and completely, like a rope slipping between his fingers. Lauren looked up at him. Her eyes hid nothing. He wondered what kind of woman she was, to work all the time, to bear the burden of insight into people's secrets, to drive herself all the way to Virginia to see a man who hated her guts. She had demons. Just like anyone. Just like him.

"Don't worry," he said. "I'll try to get you out of here soon."


There was no blasting of trumpets or sounding of alarms when Arlen stepped out of the antiques shop in the middle of the day. No one on the street paused to gawk. Time did not stand still. No cameras flashed. The street just went about its business as usual—never mind Arlen's fraught rebirth into an afternoon that smelled of yeast, asphalt, exhaust, and something newly fried.

Arlen had decided that the way to break out of the antiques

shop was *not* to talk himself out of it, but rather to simply not talk himself into it in the first place. He'd been clinging to the idea that going outside would take great courage, and determination, and precise timing. But as it turned out, all it had taken was the realization that he'd run out of beer. He needed another beer more than he needed another episode of *The Price Is Right*. He wished he'd known earlier that escape was just an easy shift of mind.

He turned right heading out of the shop. The streetscape gave him a strange feeling of being out-of-body. Stoplights changed from red to green, morning glories in window boxes swayed slightly in a nearly imperceptible breeze, the traffic roared, and pedestrians passed by with such indifference that Arlen wouldn't have been entirely surprised if it had turned out they could go right through him. It made no sense, how mindlessly everyone went about their business, as if his walking down the street was entirely normal, when in fact it was anything but. Didn't they realize Arlen Fieldstone was walking among them? Convicted murderer who hadn't murdered? He didn't know what he'd been hoping would happen when he left the shop. But it wasn't this. It wasn't *nothing*.

When they let him out of prison, a guard had driven him to the public parking lot in a dingy gray van that smelled like cigarette ash. The door to the van slid open—a roar in his ears—and then a wall of a thousand television cameras pointed at him like some kind of firing squad. He climbed down from his seat and paused a moment before he put his foot on the pavement—there were no fences, no bolted doors, no shatterproof plastic panes, no bars.

*What now?* the reporters had asked. *Are you going to sue somebody? Are you going to find your ex-wife? What was it like to be in prison when you didn't do anything wrong?*

Arlen had just smiled a little and waved, and it took him a while to realize that one of the faces in the crowd was familiar—was Will. The closest thing to kin he had left. Will's expression was grave; he stepped forward out of the tangle of wires and lenses and micro-phones and pulled Arlen into a long, tight hug. Flashes snapped.

At that moment, Arlen understood what it was to belong fully to himself and only himself. Freedom was the taste of the sky on his tongue. Anything had been possible. Anything. He was free. What more did he need?

Now he walked past the shops on the block—the nail salons with painted windows, the take-out restaurants with their menus posted on their doors, the boutiques of old clothes made trendy again. He forgot about the beer. He walked and walked, and soon he didn't know where he was. All the streets were unfamiliar. All the streets looked the same. And yet, there was no begrudging guard to tell him what to do or where to go next. No cameraman asking for an interview. No senators or congressmen promising to help him make a new life.

Arlen had to jump to avoid a car when a stoplight turned green. Sweat made constellations on the front of his gray T-shirt. No one cared. And he didn't either. He didn't think about the antiques shop, his promise to Will that he would watch it, the fact that he'd left the door unlocked.

He had no idea where he was or where he was going or why no one gave a crap. And there was something safe in the feeling of total indifference, so that nothing and no one mattered. He thought, *Maybe* not caring *is what it means to be a free man.*


Lauren had never wanted a shower more in her life than when Will pulled his old beast of a car up to the curb in front of the antiques shop. Her shorts were sticking to the backs of her legs. Her hair was damp with sweat. She had the same hot and sticky feeling she'd had as a kid after a long day of playing in the ocean surf. She'd almost fallen asleep on the ride home.

"Looks like you got some color," he said.

She touched her face; her skin felt hot. "Maybe."

"What do you think of picking? Ready to quit your day job?"

"Not exactly. But it was fine. Interesting."

"Interesting?"

"I learned things," she said. She glanced at him across the cab of the car. His face was brightened by a streetlight. "You're like a walking Wikipedia."

"Walking Wiki—*what*?"

"Please tell me you're joking."

He looked at her, straight-faced and with dire gravity. She started laughing, and he did too. She leaned back against her seat, caught off guard by Will's teasing. She liked him—when he wasn't busy hating her.

When her laughter faded, he pulled the key from the ignition. His voice was low and smooth. "Why don't you come inside with me?"

A fiber of heat snaked through her, a longing that was entirely unexpected and entirely sexual. Her muscles tightened; her skin flushed.

Will went on. "Arlen's inside."

*Arlen.* "Oh. Of course." The heat that had been coursing through her hardened into ice, and her heart did a slow roll that made her touch her chest. She took in a deep breath.

"You okay?"

"Fine. I'm fine."

"You're nervous. You're really nervous."

"Of course I am," she said, more curtly than she'd meant to. He scooted closer to her across the long bench seat and put his arm on the backrest. He wasn't crowding her, but he was closer. He smelled like a long afternoon in the sun. And to her complete shock, she—who liked men who regularly used hair product and cologne—wanted to press her face against him and breathe in.

"Arlen's a good man," Will said. "I've known him since we were just boys."

"Did you grow up around here?" she asked, to distract herself.

"No." He laughed. "You ever been out to cow country?"

She smiled slightly.

"That's a big city compared to where I lived."

"So Albany must be—"

"The Kingdom of Oz," he said.

She was surprised when he took her hand—not to hold it, but to press the tips of his middle and ring fingers to the inside of her wrist. Such a light touch—and startlingly intimate. She wasn't surprised that Will was easy about touching her; after watching him all day, she could tell he was comfortable in his own skin. She briefly considered drawing her arm away, setting boundaries, but she found she didn't want to. The ribbon of attraction that had formed within her now curled on itself like a twist of smoke hanging in the air. Curiosity compelled her to sit still, apart from him except for the press of his fingertips on her wrist.

"Your heartbeat," he said. "What did the doctors say was wrong?"

She stared with intense focus at his hands, the circles of dirt under his nails, the whitish-gray scars set here and there on tanned skin. She rarely liked to acknowledge weakness, but there was something about Will that made her feel safe. "I've had episodes of irregular heartbeat. Palpitations. It's . . . it's a little scary when it happens. Like your heart is an alarm clock going off—like time's running out."

"They don't have drugs to help?"

"They have lots of drugs," she said, thinking of Jonah and the endless medications he was on, the medications for his medications; she did not want to start down that road. The pressure of Will's fingers on her skin shifted, and heat rose within her. When she spoke, she made sure her voice was even. "This is just a . . . a stress thing. I can get it under control on my own."

"What if you can't?"

"I can," she said.

Will brushed the slightly raised cord of a tendon with his thumb. "It's getting faster."

When she looked up at his face, there was no way to describe what she felt except the word *collision*. The impact of one thing and another. In the streetlight, Will's eyes were an indefinable shade of green gray that she wanted so much to name but that eluded her even as she looked directly at him. Her face flushed. She knew with certainty that he was attracted to her. She drew her hand away.

"Let's go in," she said.

From the back of the pickup Will retrieved a box of their picks, and then she followed him into the antiques shop. She had a good view of his body as he walked. He was fit and trim, dressed in work clothes but not quite as rumpled as he'd been on Belle Isle. At one point during the afternoon, he'd lifted the bottom hem of his shirt to blot his face with the fabric, and she'd seen the strong, coarse muscles of his stomach and chest, the slight shading of dark hair. She'd had to look away.

Of course, she knew enough about herself to recognize what this was. *Rebounding.* Things had fallen apart with Edward only a month ago, and she'd done her best not to spend that month wallowing. Now here was Will—attractive and enthralling in the way that an overgrown garden could be enthralling: a tangle of thorny roses, a weedy flower bed, stems putting down roots on rock. Everything Will was, was the opposite of Edward. Lauren needed to watch herself and take care.

"Ladies first," Will said, pushing open the shop door with one hand. Inside, he went to the counter and set down the box of things that he'd come away with today—a glass vase, a jump rope, a cast-iron horse. The old phone was still in the truck.

"Arlen?" Will called.

Lauren held her breath, coaching herself. This was what she'd come to do. To see Arlen. To throw herself at the mercy of his forgiveness. To confess to and face fully what she had done—and, maybe, be absolved.

There was no answer.

"Did you tell him I'd be here?" she asked.

"He knew you were coming with me today."

Lauren frowned. She caught Will's eye—the slight apology there—and she knew he was thinking the same thing she was.

"I'll just check upstairs," Will said.

Lauren held her breath as Will ducked into a room that must have been an office; then she heard the sound of his feet climbing stairs. She looked around at Will's collected treasures. Some things stuck out from the heap: an original box of Crayola crayons. A folksy painting of a cow. A birdcage. A bell. Above her head, she heard Will's boots thump the floor.

When he came back, he didn't need to speak for her to know that Arlen wasn't here. What worried her was Will's reaction. He was trying to appear calm but the set of his shoulders had shifted incrementally. He leaned forward, just a little, when he walked. He didn't so much as glance at her. He walked to the counter, reached underneath, and pulled out a gray tin box with a flimsy lock on the front. Will popped the box open. It was empty.

"What happened?" she asked.

"I don't know," Will said. "He's gone."

**Lesson Five:** If you're reading a person visually, you should be listening too. Tone, rhythm, diction, volume, even the micro-pauses we unconsciously take to breathe—all of these character-istics give insight into a speaker's true feelings or character. Someone who speaks more loudly than a situation calls for may be insecure about being heard. Someone who speaks too softly might be shy, or she might be demanding your attention by ask-ing you to focus, to lean in, to listen hard. The words we actu-ally speak are only one tiny part of the way we communicate; words, after all, are first and foremost sounds.

# CHAPTER 5

Arlen hadn't wanted to meet the woman who would one day be his wife—not at first—though he'd heard all about her. *A sweet girl,* his mother had told him as she stirred big pots of peanut soup on the stove in her house. *And you need to get yourself a girl, Arlen. I won't always be around to keep you in line.*

Arlen found that the best way to get his mother off the subject of this Eula person was to not respond, to let his mother just burn herself out. With each new description, Eula became more beautiful, more intelligent, more generous, more everything. She was a good cook, and Arlen's mother wanted a girl who would cook for him since he'd never so much as lifted a finger to butter bread. Eula had ambition too—she was a senior in high school and she made top marks, especially in her computer classes. Plus, she towed the line when it came to religion; she was the daughter of a deacon at his mother's church. Arlen, who had to listen to his mother's monologues about the endless talents of Eula Oates while he was scarfing down dinner, sometimes asked polite questions, sometimes changed the subject, and sometimes told his mother, flat out, *No.*

Eventually, when his mother grew tired of waiting for Arlen to show interest, she arranged for Eula to come over to the house to help her with canning the peaches that grew in the far corner of the property. Eula, who wasn't exactly dutiful but who didn't mind helping either, had walked into the house while Arlen was drinking straight from the milk carton with the refrigerator door open and his oldest pair of work jeans on. When he turned to her, he felt as if he'd been hit in the chest with a basketball, the breath knocked out of his lungs. He asked her out that day, sure that she'd come to the house in secret pursuit of his affection, because she and his mother were obviously in on the scheme together. But Arlen's mother hadn't known Eula as well as she'd thought: Eula hadn't fallen on her knees in gratitude that Arlen had asked her out—not by a long shot. She'd finished stocking the jars of fresh preserves in the pantry, and then she'd said, *Maybe. But I don't know.*

The summer storms came and went, and for two months, Arlen did his best to win Eula's attention. He started going to church again; he ironed his own suit because his mother wasn't getting the pleats exactly right. He dropped by the drive-in movie theater where Eula collected ticket stubs; he saw the same three movies half a dozen times. When he could stand it no longer, he found out from Will that Eula was quite possibly seeing another guy.

First he was angry. Then beaten. He avoided the drive-in. He began to mope. His mother dropped his plate of eggs and bacon down on the table with an accusing thud. "Didn't I raise you to be better than this?" she asked him, jabbing her pointer finger. "You want something, you gotta fight for it. You can't give up."

Another week passed before he dragged himself back to the drive-in, where he was probably the only person in the field under the giant screen who watched the film alone. He was adjusting his radio when he heard a knock on his window, and when he turned his head, a man he didn't know was there scowling at him, bending down.

"You Arlen?"

Arlen rolled down the window. "Who's asking?"

Eula was running up from behind the man a moment later, breathing hard, her eyes wide with panic. She wore an orange shirt and little shorts that showed off her curves. She took the guy by the arm. "Don't. Leon, don't. Please?"

Leon shook her off him, so violently and condescendingly that it made Arlen fume. "No, no, no," Leon said. He tugged the door of Arlen's car open. All around them, people had started rolling down their windows, paying attention to the drama that was unfolding under the big screen. "You said this is the guy who's been coming around bothering you?"

"I didn't say he was *bothering* me," Eula said.

"Well, he's bothering me," Leon said. He wasn't a big man— nor did he seem to be any older than Arlen—but his eyes had an out-of-control luster that Arlen would later come to recognize as the precursor to violence. Designs of lightning bolts had been razored into the man's hair above his ears. His hands were oversized for his smallish frame, but he held himself like an athlete. He leaned on Arlen's car, overly cool. "Why don't you get on out here and talk to me?"

Arlen didn't hesitate. He heard Eula making excuses, saying, *This is ridiculous*, and, *Leon, you leave him alone*. But the words barely registered. The movie went on. There was some amount of posturing and posing. Arlen could still remember the unflinching hardness of Leon's eyes. People shouted for them to shut up or fight already. The eyewitness accounts were conflicting: Some said Arlen threw the first punch. Others said not. However it began, the outcome was clear: Leon was a broken, sniveling, and bloody mess on the ground.

By the time the police came, Arlen was sweating and so pumped full of adrenaline that he couldn't feel his knuckles beginning to swell. But he had regained enough of his composure to know he should be embarrassed. With Eula shaking her head and looking on, a cop put handcuffs on Arlen's wrists and pushed him against his own car. He'd broken Leon's nose, and an ambulance was on the way to take him to the hospital. Arlen was escorted to the police station, and though the cops had to do their job, Arlen had found them to be a mostly polite bunch with a screwed-up sense of humor. They said Arlen should apply to join the force. Leon had been giving them hell for a long time.

The next day, Eula came to the house again with a Tupperware container full of homemade tomato soup and a batch of cookies. She was sweet as sweet could be, making small talk with his mother, explaining that Arlen hadn't started it, painting a picture of Arlen as the great defender of women, children, and small animals everywhere. Arlen wasn't sure his mother bought it, and he didn't care. He'd fought for what he wanted. That evening, when they sat watching the sky go dark and Eula kissed him, Arlen would have fought a thousand more battles for her to have her kiss again.

It was only later, when he was sitting in the interrogation room at some police station in a city he didn't know very well, that the true price of winning Eula's affection had become clear. The detective told him: *Tell us about the guy you beat up down in Virginia two years ago.* The cops stood looking at a folder that Arlen wasn't allowed to see, smirking at one another and saying, *You put this guy in the hospital*, and, *Really did a number on him.* Arlen hadn't known how to defend himself. He was the stranger who had shown up in town just when the senator's wife had turned up dead. And someone in the building where Arlen's cousin lived swore she "recognized" Arlen from the police sketch that had been running on a perpetual loop on the local news. The cops called Arlen's tiff with

Leon a *prior*, which Arlen knew was not a good thing because to say he had a prior meant that they thought of that fight as *the crime prior to the current crime*. Slowly, the notion of being innocent until proven guilty was revealed to be untrue in countless little ways.

Once he was firmly entrenched in prison life, Arlen thought back to the fight, to the smell of summer earth, grass, popcorn, and car exhaust. To the way Eula had looked at him when they sat together on his mother's porch, her girl's eyes wide with apology and pleasure too. He got to spend two years with Eula, got to make love to her for the first time and hold her afterward, got to marry her, got to move their few belongings into an empty and waiting house. And he knew if he had to choose between not having Eula or having the fight all over again, he would roll up his sleeves a second time, knowing full well where it all would lead, but thinking of nothing besides how badly he'd wanted her to love him.

The cops picked up Arlen walking through Jackson Ward with an open bottle of Wild Turkey in his hand. He hadn't even bothered to wrap it in a brown paper bag. When they asked Arlen where he lived, he'd said, *Nowhere*. But he gave them Will's name.

Now Will stood begging the police officer, a guy who was friends with one of his brothers but whose name he could no longer remember, for a little mercy. They were standing on the sidewalk. The darkness was yellowed with porch lights and streetlamps. Around them the people of the neighborhood were staring out from their stoops and windows. Will reasoned: Yes, Arlen had been drinking. But he hadn't been bothering anyone. He hadn't been driving. It was no big deal.

The officer seemed unconvinced.

"You do know who this guy is, right?" Will pointed with his thumb toward the cop car, where Arlen sat hanging his head.

"Should I?"

"You hooked yourself Arlen Fieldstone—the guy they just let outta prison? Nine years he was in there, without having done a thing wrong."

"*That's* the guy?"

Will nodded. "Yeah. Poor bastard."

The cop crossed his arms. "Man. Talk about the short end of the stick."

"There's gonna be a lot of questions if you bring him in. Lots of reporters, I mean. Asking questions and such."

"I hate reporters," the man said.

"Think you might cut him a break?"

"I shouldn't." He glanced about as if he expected someone to be watching him. "You taking responsibility for him?"

"Yeah," Will said. "I am."

The officer clasped Will on the shoulder. "You're a good man."

Will nodded solemnly. "Arlen is too. When he's sober."

"Aren't we all," the man said. "Get him home. And tell your brother I was asking about him."

"Sure thing," Will said, and he hurried before the officer changed his mind. He collected Arlen from the backseat of the squad car, steadying him with a firm hand, and then he walked at Arlen's side slowly, so slowly, as if they were taking a leisurely evening stroll. Arlen smelled of sweat and whisky, and the way he shuffled along in his wrinkled clothes and wouldn't meet anyone's eye put Will in mind of a homeless man.

Will helped Arlen into the passenger seat, then shut the door. The smell of sweat and alcohol was strong. Will had to hold his breath until he could roll down the window. The hot night air offered no relief.

"So on a scale of one to ten, how plastered are you?" Will asked.

"Eighty proof." Arlen laughed a little. "You mind stopping at the drugstore on the way back? Cop took my whisky. I need a replacement."

Will grated his teeth together and started the car. "And what money are you gonna buy it with?"

"Oh, right," Arlen said brightly. "Course I'll pay you back."

Will sighed and drove through the tangle of University of Richmond buildings, dark now except for the occasional flash of a security light and campus phone. People more shadow than flesh slumped along the sidewalks, lingered outside of doorways, or sat nodding off at bus stops.

"Here's all of it," Arlen said, and he reached awkwardly into his pocket and pulled out the wrist-sized wad of money from Will's cashbox. He tossed it on the bench seat between them. "Minus the Wild Turkey."

"What were you gonna do? Take off with it? Skip town?"

"Where would I go? Disneyland?" Arlen snorted. "To see if Eula's gonna put me up for the night? Pull the other one."

Will shook his head. In the glare of the passing streetlights, his knuckles against the steering wheel had gone pale like eight little moons.

"And how'd *you* do today?" Arlen flapped Will's chest with the back of his hand. "Get any action?"

Will glanced over to see Arlen's face—a white, white smile that reeked of sneering. "Course I didn't get any action. Wasn't looking for any."

"No?" Arlen's chuckle was low, slightly menacing. "You think I don't know why you dragged that girl out with you today?"

"Arlen—"

"Don't you *Arlen* me. Sound like my momma. I might've been in prison for the last decade, but I know that look a man gets when he's talking about a woman. And I seen it on your face."

"You're not making sense," Will said through clenched teeth. Arlen was dangerously close to the truth. And if Arlen knew it, Lauren knew it too. The thought was unnerving. He didn't want her to have any more pull over him than she already did.

"You do know that woman ruined my life," Arlen said, his voice sober now. "And here you are going on pleasure trips with her when I can't even bring myself to leave the shop—"

"Hold up. You didn't do such a bad job getting out of there today."

"Hmm." Arlen looked out the window. They'd just about reached the apartment in Carytown. "Guess you're right about that. Guess I did get out, didn't I?"

"That's right. You did. And now it's time to take the next step."

"Which would be . . . ?"

"Putting this whole prison business behind you."

"You mean I gotta make nice with your pretty lawyer."

"I don't think she works as a lawyer anymore. And no—you don't have to make nice with her. But you've got to do *something*. And far as I can tell, talking to her and hearing what she has to say would be a good first step."

"I ain't interested."

Will pulled the car up in front of his building and put on his hazards, double-parked. "I'm just trying to help you."

"Ain't nobody can help me," Arlen said.

"Then I'll make you help yourself."

Arlen sighed, so deep and heavy that Will could feel the very weight of it pressing down on his own chest.

"Lauren's not going away until you see her."

"Well, in that case, you shouldn't be trying so hard to get me to call her up."

"I don't follow," Will said.

"Once me and little Miss Sunshine are square, she's gone."

"Not important."

"Right," Arlen said.

The car idled but Arlen made no move to get out. The street was quiet. The vintage clothing shops and gift boutiques were silent and dim. Even this late in the evening, the air was oppressively hot and the hum of air conditioners was the street's only sound.

Arlen put his hand on the door, then seemed to think better of it. He turned to Will, his face awash with streetlight. His pupils were red. The skin around his eyes was puffy and blotched. Will knew then that he'd been crying.

"Sorry about this," Arlen said.

Will took off his seat belt, leaned over, and hugged him. His brothers had always been tough guys—not much for brotherly contact except on the rarest occasion. But Will couldn't even begin to understand how much Arlen had likely starved for affection of any kind. And so he held him close and tight longer than he normally would have—no matter that Arlen smelled like booze and armpits—before Arlen sniffed and let go.

"Wait." Will picked up the wad of cash on the seat. "Take this back in with you?"

Arlen glanced down at the money for a moment, then back up at Will. "Sure thing," he said. And then he walked his slow and somber walk back inside.


Lauren hadn't needed her brother to tell her over the phone about the latest letters to the editor that had popped up in online versions of national papers. She'd already seen them. She regularly punched her own name into search engines to see what people were saying about her, as if she might have some control over their chatter simply by knowing what it was. She read the letters with all the compulsion and sourness of a jaded detective, hunting herself down.

*Dear Editor: What happened to Arlen Fieldstone is an atroc-
ity, and someone should pay. The city's case against Arlen was
full of holes—anyone with half a brain could have seen that.
And the defense attorney appointed to Arlen was a joke. Why
hasn't the media picked up on the fact that she quit lawyering
and started teaching elementary students not long after the
trial? Seriously—why did justice have to take so long?*

*Dear Editor: This just goes to show that lawyers and murder-
ers are both after only one thing: the thrill of the kill. And
damn the consequences for an innocent man.*

*Dear Editor: I get that it's the prosecution's job to convince
juries of crime. But all I'm saying is, if Lauren Matthews is
supposed to be this great people-reader, how did she not know
Arlen was innocent? Was it that she didn't care?*

From his room in Rhinebeck, Jonah seemed to enjoy reading
the latest complaints against Lauren and what she'd done. He liked
to laugh at the letters to the editor—to poke fun at bad spelling, at
illogical arguments, at the zany and bombastic things people said
when they had an audience. To Jonah, the letter writers were igno-
rant, spouting off like fountains in the town square—knowledge
without comprehension. He flipped through the latest diatribes
with the same kind of joy as when he played Skeeball at the shore.

Lauren, on the other hand, had no fondness for seeing herself
lambasted from coast to coast. Before she'd fled Albany for Richmond, her colleagues and bosses had seemed to be wondering if
she was a liability, if there was something about her that they'd
failed to see. Her promotion was in jeopardy. So was her reputa-
tion as an expert and a professional. What company would hire a

firm where she worked—she who had sent an innocent man to prison? She'd held her head up as best she could—until Sunday night, when she'd decided to make the trip to Virginia. She didn't consider it running away from the problem, but toward it. And when Jonah found new clippings that mentioned her name, she'd said, *Yes, read them to me*, if only to prove to herself that she was strong enough to hear.

"Look at it this way," Jonah said. "Have your book sales spiked?"

Lauren was embarrassed to admit they probably had.

"Controversy sells," he said.

"I'm not exactly interested in selling Arlen's controversy."

"You haven't thought of doing a book about the trial?" Jonah asked, incredulous. "You're smack in the middle of one of the greatest legal controversies of the decade, and nobody's offered you a book deal?"

"Oh, they've called," Lauren said. "But I've ignored them."

"Are you crazy?"

"Probably." She scrolled to the next page on her search engine, scanning for her name. She sat on Maisie's spare bed, leaning back on a pillow, her computer on her lap.

"I think you should write another book," Jonah said. "People need to know what happened. Plus, you can donate a portion of the money or something like that."

"It's not my story to tell."

"You can't protect him, Laure. You do know that, right?"

Lauren stretched her neck to the side, working out tension. When she and Jonah were young, they'd had a dog that went missing, and all that long night, Lauren had suffered the strange sense of having misplaced herself, so that her thoughts kept flying out to the marshes, out to the stands of oak and elm, to the edge of the river where the train tracks rusted under electric wires, to all the places her lost dog could roam. She had the same sense about Arlen now—that half her mind was here, obsessing at her computer, and half was out there with him haunting the town. She hadn't realized he was so volatile—leaving and taking Will's cash. She told Maisie: *If the doorbell rings tonight, don't answer it. It's for me.*

"Can you stand to hear one more?" Jonah asked merrily. "You'll like this one."

"Where's it from?"

"*The New York Times.*"

"Okay." She braced herself. "Let's have it."

He read, " 'Dear Editor: Everyone is pointing at Lauren Matthews for Arlen Fieldstone's wrongful conviction. But here's the truth: She's not a cop, so she didn't gather evidence. All she could do was interpret it for the jury. If you want to blame someone for Arlen's mistreatment, blame the jury that convicted him. Blame the cops who botched the evidence. Blame a weak defense. But don't blame Lauren Matthews for doing her job.' "

"Wow," Lauren said after a moment. Editorials in support of her were so few and far between. She wanted to keep this one, to read it again when she was feeling down. "Oh. That's . . . Will you save it for me?"

"Of course I will."

"Who wrote it?"

He laughed. "Do you have to ask?"

It took a moment before the truth set in. "You did."

"Yep. And they published it too."

Lauren smiled and relaxed into her pillows. "Thank you, Jonah."

"Anytime," he said.


Later that night—so late that the commercials on the television had switched to advertising nine-hundred numbers and singles party lines—the ringing of Will's phone smashed the silence of his dark house, and his heart jumped into his throat.

He sat up on the couch—he hadn't realized he'd fallen asleep—and he groped for the receiver among pillows and cushions. His hands were clumsy, and his brain, too, seemed to be tripping over itself. He thought: *Was it the police? Had Arlen gone again?*

But when he pressed *talk*, he heard only the soft sound of Lauren's voice, saying his name like a question. "Will?"

"Yeah." He cleared his throat. "Hey. What's going on?"

"Shoot. I woke you up. I'm so sorry."

He didn't bother denying it. With her, there was no reason to lie. "You're up late for an early bird."

"I couldn't sleep. I was worrying about Arlen."

Will turned down the TV show he'd been half watching while he nodded off—a middle-aged couple was renovating a converted barn—and he shifted the phone from one ear to the other. "We found him."

"Where?"

"Jackson Ward. They were gonna arrest him for public drunkenness."

"Oh no."

"But they didn't arrest him. The guy let me take him back to the apartment. No harm, no foul."

"You were good to do that."

"Naw."

She paused a moment. "You and Arlen are really close."

"We were," Will said. "And—yeah—I guess we still are."

"How'd you meet him?"

"You know I don't remember?" Will laughed. "He's one of those people that you've known for so long that you can't remember meeting them. He moved to town when we were both thirteen. And I don't recall introducing myself. It was more like he was always just there."

"I'm glad he has you. Not everybody would do what you've done."

"Well, I knew he wasn't guilty," Will said.

For a while, there was nothing on the other end of the line, so that Will nearly wondered if he'd lost the connection. The dark of the living room and the hiss of the phone line gave Will a sense of intense intimacy: there was Lauren's voice, and his, and nothing more. Pervert that he was, he had the urge to ask her what she was wearing. Not that he needed it to be sweet scraps of ribbon and lace—he couldn't quite picture Lauren in girly and frivolous lingerie—but he wanted to be able to see her, wherever she was, to know what she looked like when she wasn't looking at him.

"Lauren," he said, "Arlen didn't disappear because of you, if that's what you're thinking."

"I'm worried that taking me out with you today set him off."

"If it did, that's not all bad."

"How do you figure?"

"We got him to leave the building."

"Leave the . . ." Lauren's voice was soft with astonishment. "Oh. I didn't realize . . ."

Will put his feet up on the coffee table. The flickering light of the television licked between his bare toes. "He had to do something to get himself back into the world. It was probably like his first day of high school all over again—except a thousand times more intense."

"I probably would have gotten a little drunk for that too," Lauren said.

"See? That's why I think having you in the picture isn't such a bad thing. Even if you piss Arlen off, at least he's engaging. He can direct all that energy toward something, instead of bottling it all up."

"You don't think he's dangerous, do you?"

Will let his eyelids fall shut in the semidarkness. He could picture Lauren's wide-set eyes, big eyes that seemed to always be
taking in everything at once but that also seemed to obscure her.
She favored clothes that were rugged, serious—so that there was
something slightly combative in her carpenter's shorts and sneakers, something challenging even when she wore a dress. She was a
strong woman—physically and emotionally too. She seemed to
thrive under pressure. But some part of him wondered if she was
more vulnerable—more human—than she made herself out to be.

"You're safe," Will said. "Arlen's angry. But he's not violent."

Lauren sighed. "Maybe this wasn't a good idea. Maybe I should
have just left him alone."

"Whether you were here or not, Lauren Matthews, you
wouldn't have left us alone."

"Us?"

"Either of us," he said, not caring—for the space of a moment—
if she knew how she'd fascinated him over the years. "Better you're
here now, and we can help Arlen deal with this once and for all,
than have waited until it was too late. If anything, I'm glad you're
here. And even though he doesn't know it yet, Arlen will be
glad too."

When she spoke again, he could hear the smile in her voice.
"There's not too many in the world like you."

"I bet you say that to all the guys," he said, and inwardly he
thrilled. Lauren, who had once looked out of the television set at
him with her unseeing eyes, saw him now. At least a little bit. He
liked her more than he had just eighteen hours ago.

Something about the late hour, the darkness, and not being
able to see her made him brave. "How come you're not married? I
figured buying a mansion and popping out a couple of kids would
have been on your to-do list."

"Who says they're not?"

"But you're single."

"I'm considering my options."

"It must be hard," Will said, thinking to himself. "To see every little last secret a person carries around. I don't know how you could be with someone if you were always trying to get into their head."

"It can be difficult," she said, her words clipped.

"You probably spend five minutes on a date and already know whether or not you're going to stay for dessert."

"Sometimes."

"But other times . . . ?"

"Other times I *can't* see anything. I'm completely obtuse . . ."

"Why?"

"Lots of reasons." She laughed a little, and Will found himself savoring the sound. "Expectation. Chemistry. Stubbornness. And—and love. Love blinds a person. Knocks out all reason. All the people-reading I do, and I'm completely illiterate when it comes to love."

"Are you in love with someone?" he heard himself ask.

She took in a breath, hard and fast, as if she wasn't sure of when she might get to breathe again. Now he could picture her. She would be in a small room in her friend's house, with the street-light shining in through the blinds and the air conditioner humming. She would be leaning back against her pillows, her pretty legs stretched before her and crossed at the ankles, bare except for flimsy cotton shorts.

When she didn't answer, he knew. She was in love with someone. And whoever he was, he probably didn't deserve it. Silence so thick didn't happen when a woman was confident that the man she loved was in love with her too.

"Will?"

"Yeah?"

"I should go."

"Sure. No problem," he said lightly. "I'll pick you up around noon or so tomorrow. Okay?"

"I'll look forward to it," she said.

When the sun rose again on Thursday morning, Lauren was awake and ready to greet it, but she'd just barely beaten it to the punch. With the first light in the sky, she headed outdoors for a brisk walk to clear her mind. She had no idea where she was headed, but she had her cell phone on her and she didn't think she would get lost. As she walked down Monument Avenue, figures of Confederate heroes and modern scholars looked down their noses at her from their perches. She turned, guessing she was headed south and west, until she found herself in a cramped little area of boutiques and eateries. As owners lifted metal grates and set out chairs and flowers, shop after shop seemed to open its eyes.

With brick as far as the eye could see, Richmond steamed and sweltered, a giant kiln with its denizens baking inside. Heat like that—it did something to people. Even now, in the relative cool before the morning, the pace of life was slower—cats ambling across empty roads, clouds rolling across the sky, even the streetlights seemed to yawn long and yellow before brightening to green. *A person could get used to this,* Lauren thought. She couldn't remember the last time she'd taken four days off in a row.

Her phone rang in her pocket and she reached for it. To her surprise, she felt an unexpected pang of annoyance. Usually, she welcomed her ringing phone. No matter what she was doing, a phone call was never an interruption—but right now, at this moment, the ringing startled her like an alarm.

She glanced down at the number and saw that it was not work, but it was her assistant's home number. She picked up quickly.

"Rizzi? Everything okay?"

"Hi, Lauren."

"What's going on?"

"I only got a minute," Rizzi said. "I'm trying to get the kids off to school and then get myself to the office, but I wanted to check in with you."

"You're calling me from home."

"I didn't want anyone to overhear me at work."

Lauren was walking faster now. "That doesn't sound good."

"When do you think you're coming back?" Rizzi asked.

"As soon as I can. I'm trying. Things are . . . complicated. Why?"

"Well, they're getting complicated here too. Bryce has really started bitching about having to take on your case with Dautel Pharmaceuticals."

"It's a difficult case. I'm sure he is."

"You don't understand. He's questioning your character. Your values. And he's being snaky about it. Trying to get the board to rethink your candidacy for partner. And I think he's lobbying to get them to vote while you're away. I just thought you should know." A pause, and Lauren heard the sound of children squealing in the background. "I told you . . . no fingers in the fish tank!" Rizzi yelled.

Lauren pulled the phone away from her ear.

"Look, I have to go," Rizzi said. "I'm doing my best to keep pumping positive energy into your cause, but we both know I don't have any clout here. Please tell me you're coming back soon."

"It's not like I've been gone a month. It's only been four days."

"But it feels like a month," Rizzi said. "An important month. I really have to go."

"Okay, thanks," Lauren said. She shut her phone, her mind racing. Bryce was trying to move in on her territory. He had ammunition: her publicly embarrassing involvement in Arlen's case, her absence from work at a critical time. She loved her job, but she hated its politics. Over the years she'd become reasonably good at dealing with big egos and high competition. But she couldn't guard her position against her enemies if she wasn't there to defend it. She needed to get back home.

She slowed, passing mannequins dressed in vintage cotton sundresses and plastic beads, a gift shop with lead mermaids on concrete pedestals, a bakery that smelled of chocolate and yeast. Though no one thing stuck out as familiar, the neighborhood as a whole had a familiar vibe. And when she looked around, she was startled to realize she had walked herself to the neighborhood of the antiques shop. It wasn't long before she stood in front of the building. There was a sign out front: APPOINTMENTS BY PHONE OR BY CHANCE.

She stopped walking, thinking of the job she'd come here to do and her job back home. Burt needed her; she knew that. He needed her to be there while he helped support her run for partner, and he needed her to handle her caseload. She'd planned on being gone for one day—two at the most. And yet here she was, the morning of her fourth day in Richmond. She'd told Burt that she was having an emergency—she gave only the vaguest description of her appointment at the cardiologist—and she'd promised to be back. She didn't know how she could buy herself any more time.

As far as she could tell, there was only one option. She had to compel Arlen to see her. Today. Her heart in her chest felt like a leaf on a branch, flipping over before a storm.

She crossed the street, heading toward the antiques shop, the double yellow line passing beneath her sneakers—and just in time, she saw the door to the shop fly open, the glass sending a shard of sunlight her way so that she had to shade her eyes, and then: *Arlen*.

He held a small doormat, and he let it go so it flopped on to the sidewalk with a puff of dust. She stopped walking, not quite out of the street, but almost. He looked up. He was thinner now than when she'd last seen him. He wore a tired T-shirt that had faded from years of wear. White tube socks were pulled halfway up his calves, interrupted only by the straps of the sandals on his feet.

"Arlen . . ." She'd stopped a few feet away, said his name.

The recognition came instantly. She supposed her voice gave her away. And no sooner had surprise flared across his face, than it was gone—burnt out like flash powder—and anger set in. He pulled himself up straight, his wide shoulders flexing.

"What do you want?"

"I . . ." Words failed. Lauren had thought she'd wanted to give something to Arlen: her apology. Her willingness to step up and take some responsibility for what had happened to him. And yet, he wanted to know: *What do you want?* And she realized that he had far more to give her than she could offer him.

She swallowed hard. "I was hoping we could talk."

He pulled himself upright. "I got nothing to say to you."

"Please, if you could just . . . for a few minutes—"

"I got nothing to say."

He held up his hand. With his head tipped back and his eyes squinting at her in the dawning sun, she knew that he'd made himself into the kind of man who was master of his kingdom—and his kingdom was anywhere he happened to be standing at the time. His upper lip drew back in disgust. And then he shut the door behind him and was gone.


When Eula opened the paper the next morning, her ex-husband's face was staring back at her.

*Jackson Ward—Yesterday evening, residents reported that famous ex-convict Arlen Fieldstone was seen wandering through the neighborhood while intoxicated; however, police did not make an arrest. Fieldstone made headlines when he*

*was exonerated of the charges of murdering the wife of then
senator Juan Raimez.*

Eula cursed, pulled the About Town section out of the paper,
and punched it down into her recycling bin. She supposed she
shouldn't have been surprised when, that evening as she got home
from work, there was a reporter waiting for her on the front lawn.

"Excuse me. Eula Oates?" The man was carrying a handheld
voice recorder, and his smile was stretched as tight as leather. "I
was hoping you wouldn't mind if I ask you some questions."

"You can ask anything you want," Eula said. The man was following her across the lawn, to her front door. "Don't mean I'm
gonna answer."

"Has Arlen Fieldstone been in contact with you?"

Eula dug her keys out of her oversized purse. "Not too many
men bend over backward to get in touch with their ex-wives."

"After he was found guilty, you divorced him. You'd only been
married for a few months at the time. How does it make you feel
to know that the reason you divorced him was all wrong?"

Eula held her head high. "My mistakes are my business.
Nobody else's. Now, if you'll kindly excuse me . . ." She turned her
key in the lock and opened the door.

"Wait, wait," the man said. His bald head gleamed as waxy
and pink as Silly Putty in the sun. "What if Arlen still loves you?
What will you do?"

Eula closed her eyes, and to the reporter, it probably looked like
no more than a blink. But for an eighth of a second, Eula could see
Arlen again—see him exactly as she'd seen him that day, when he
got down on his knee right in a puddle in the storm-soaked parking lot outside the Chinese restaurant. When he opened the box
and showed her the tiniest stone she'd ever seen. He was beaming
with such perfect, boyish love that he might have been offering her

the Hope diamond. She saw herself reaching out—for him, for the ring, for everything he was offering, and they stood together under the streetlight, holding each other and kissing and crying happy tears for a very long time.

By the time Eula's eyes were open again, the world was back to normal. "You go on, now," she told the reporter. "Get off my lawn."

"But—"

"Go!" she said. And then she shut the door in his face, and locked it, and slid down along the wall until she was sitting on the floor. She rested her face against her hands.

**Lesson Six:** Eye contact is key in people-reading. It tells. There are accepted normal behaviors for eye contact in everyday conversation: a speaker will tend to watch or stare a bit more while she's listening, glance away when she begins to speak, then glance back again at certain points in her sentences. Break the pattern—hold eye contact too little or too long—and people will say, "I don't know why, but that person makes me uncomfortable." Luckily, most of us acquire the language of eye contact so naturally that we can't even articulate what that language is.

There are certain times, though, when biology compels us to specifically break the usual rules of engagement. Prolonged eye contact releases hormones in our bodies. And when you see two people holding eye contact long enough to catch your attention, you know it's only a matter of time before that contact is broken—by either a kiss or a fight.

# CHAPTER 6

Lauren was working a case in Phoenix when she first saw Edward. He was across the courtroom, leaning with his palm flattened against a desk, reading some papers, his red tie hanging down from his chest like an arrow pointing to the ground. She watched him. She liked his stern navy suit, his perfect white teeth, his flourish of dark hair. And the moment he looked up, his gaze honed in directly on her without vacillation, as if he knew where she would be standing even before he raised his head. He didn't look away, but he smiled his heartbreaking smile. There was a certain challenge in his stare, and it called to her in the way that mountain peaks call to climbers, or clouds call to men who like to jump out of planes.

There were a million stories Edward's eyes could have told to her then, though he didn't say a word. If his gaze had traveled over her, unseeing, she would have known that he had things on his mind and no room for her among them. If he'd looked at her for a significant moment, then glanced back to the paper on his desk, she might have known that he was interested in her, but not prepared to act.

But from the other side of the courtroom, he'd spotted her, and if he'd pointed his finger at her and then crooked it to say *Come here*, he couldn't have been more obvious in the message that his stare communicated. And yet only the two of them heard the conversation, though to Lauren it had seemed as loud as if the very walls around them had fallen down.

She'd gone that night—alone—to the watering hole that she'd been told was the hangout of the judicial set. The night had been chilly, so she'd pulled a light sweater over her shoulders and walked the half mile down the road in the violet Arizona dusk. She sat at the bar, reading the crowd like a book—all the fascinating stories— waiting to see if the man who would turn out to be Edward would show.

But he never came. And in hindsight, she supposed it was silly to think that he might somehow know where she would be, *and* that she would be waiting to see him. For all she knew, he had a girlfriend, a lover, a wife. And yet, she simply couldn't believe that she'd misread his glance that was more than a glance, the thing in his eyes that was more than passing flirtation.

Later that week, on her last day in Arizona when she'd given up on him, he found her. He stopped her with a hand on her arm while she stood at the clerk's counter. His grip was firm, almost possessive, as if he—a stranger whom she'd spoken to only without words—had some preexisting right to touch her.

"Lauren," he'd said.

And she'd been startled because he knew her name.

"You're the one everyone keeps talking about. The one who reads people."

She smiled, flattered. "And you're . . ."

"Hungry," he'd said. "I'm heading out to lunch. I'd love for you to join me."

His boldness had taken her aback, sent something electric and charging up her spine. And yet she'd expected it. Her instincts had been right—at least in that one small thing—before he turned her certainty about him completely upside down.

In the afternoon, Lauren followed Will and a man named Abbott through shin-high grass. The earth looked arthritic, gnarled with rocky lumps and scarred with seams of old walls. They traipsed through tangles of outbuildings, crisscrossing paths that may or may not have once been roads, and it occurred to Lauren that the clusters of old buildings—part sheds, part cabins—might have been slave quarters. At the far end of the field stood an old farmhouse that was once painted a color but had now turned the dull gray-brown of neglect.

"How long you owned the place?" Will asked.

"Lord." Abbott took off his tractor-green hat and rubbed the gray remnants of his hair. "Since before the war."

Lauren glanced at Will, uncertain.

"The Civil War," he explained.

"Ah," she said under her breath. Then, to Abbott: "It's been in the family that long?"

"Yes, ma'am. And we got plenty of stuff here worth some pretty big bucks. Stuff I got to sell."

"That's why we're here," Will said cheerfully. "With cash."

They came to one of the larger outbuildings; on second glance, it seemed that it had once been someone's house, in the bungalow style of the twenties. It was crooked on its frame, with a bamboo rake and a shovel leaning up against the side. The door was half-open, dappled in sun and shade.

"Here's as good a place to start as any," Abbott said.

They followed him single file into the falling-down house. As Abbott began to look around the piles of stuff that had accumulated over the decades, Lauren stole a glance at Will. She liked to watch him work; his face was a mirror of the things he saw. A look of barely contained excitement came over him as he scanned the heaps and piles that, to Lauren's eye, were merely old junk. She liked that these things—so dilapidated and without function— thrilled him. Looking at him made her share some of that thrill.

"Here we go." Abbott cleared an old lamp and a kid's racetrack off a big, solid-looking dresser. "This here's an item I think you'd be interested in."

Lauren moved closer. The dresser was a warm, chestnut brown. The handles were so simple they almost couldn't be called *handles*. And the lines were smooth and clean—not an embellishment to be seen.

Abbott leaned a hip against the dresser and crossed his arms. "My granddaddy worked the dockyards in Massachusetts, round about 1910. His buddy come from a family of Shakers, and before they parted ways, the guy gave him this."

Will pulled out a drawer and peered inside. "It's in perfect condition."

"Sure is," Abbott said. "It's a family treasure. But I'm fixing to clean out the place now. So it's got to go."

"Do you have kids?" she asked him.

"Two sons," he said. He sounded tired. "They don't live around these parts anymore. Both moved up north to New York City."

She kept him talking about his sons and listened closely, all her senses attuned. Beneath the faint scent of engine oil on his skin, there was something else—vitamins. No, more than that. A medicinal sweetness. She wondered if he was sick.

Will, who was on his knees with his face nearly pressed to the floor, redirected the conversation back to the old dresser. "Got anything to prove the provenance?"

Abbott looked down at him. "Just my good word."

"How much?"

"Fifteen hundred."

Will laughed. "I meant how much for the dresser."

"Twelve hundred," Abbott said.

"This isn't worth eight hundred bucks . . . even if it is what you're saying it is."

"You got reason to doubt me?"

"Where did you say your grandfather worked?" Lauren asked.

"Marblehead, Massachusetts. But then he come back to run a theater in Fredericksburg." Abbott slanted his eyes at her; his expression wasn't suspicious, just resigned. "I'll let you think it over. I'm going back in the house to watch the race. C'mon in when you decide what you want. Then we'll talk."

Lauren watched as Abbott left. And then she was alone with Will. The quiet of the room settled between them.

She started forward.

"Let me see—"

Her ankle turned. She felt herself losing balance, the moments stretching out long. Will moved fast, two hands jutting out to steady her. They gripped her hard enough to hold her up. In a split second she'd glanced down to see that she'd tripped on an old toy fire truck. And by the time she'd raised her eyes to his, her equilibrium had returned.

"Thanks," she said.

He looked into her face, holding her arms above her elbows. His eyes—his face—filled up her whole field of vision. Heat flashed through her. Her cheeks burned.

"Are you . . . *blushing*?" Will asked, mystified.

Her face grew hotter. "It happens."

"Why?"

She tried to tap into her most clinical poise. "Scientists aren't sure exactly. Maybe we blush to show apology—so our bodies prove that we mean what we say. Or maybe we blush because we're angry at ourselves for something we did wrong. There's lots of theories."

"But you blushed 'cause you almost just fell."

"True," she said.

"God knows I'm the last person you should ever feel embarrassed around." His hands were warm on the bare and sticky skin of her arms. "I like when you blush. You look . . . well . . . you look real. Not like how you look on TV."

"How do I look on TV?"

"More fake." His gaze wandered over her face, her neck, her shoulders. "I like you better this way."

He let her go, and she felt a new kind of vertigo at the loss of his hands. She'd always embarrassed easily—since she was a child. She was even embarrassed by her embarrassment. But Will was right—he wasn't the kind of guy who judged a woman for being what she was.

"Anyway . . ." She tucked her hair behind her ear. "I think the chest's a fake."

"You know about Shaker carpentry techniques?"

"No. But I know about people. And I don't think Abbott's telling the whole truth."

"Okay." Will crossed his arms. "Spill."

"You first. How did you know it was a fake?"

"Well." He crouched down and ran his hands along the old chest of drawers. "There are a couple of signs here. First, there's the wood. Wood warps and shrinks as it gets older, especially if it's been left out in an old house like this. But here the joints aren't raised at all, so I can tell the body's the same now as the day it was made."

Lauren looked closer. He was right. The wood was perfect. Too perfect—not a warped grain in sight.

"Second, it's distressed, all right, but the distressing is a little too uniform for my taste. When furniture wears down, it happens in certain spots—not all over, all at once. This looks like somebody dirtied it up on purpose, but they didn't think about *how* a thing gets dirty. The places that wood wears and doesn't wear."

Lauren crouched next to Will, her ankle giving her a slight pain. She was only beginning to realize that for all her skill in reading people, Will had spent his life learning to read objects. They talked to him, told him things they didn't tell other people. Lauren was fascinated, not by the old dresser, but by the man.

"What made you get into antiques?" she asked.

He stood, and she thought he sneered slightly. "You mean you can't just read my thoughts and know it?"

She straightened beside him. "You're avoiding the question."

"True."

"Why?"

He paused for a long moment, then turned to look at her. His eyes were not accusing, not at all mean. But when he spoke, he hurt her—whether he meant to or not. "I'm not sure I want you to know."

She kept her face as still as possible. She'd thought, over the last couple of days, that she and Will had been . . . establishing something, if only because they were spending time together and working toward one common goal: Arlen's rehabilitation. Last night on the phone with him she'd told him things about herself that she'd been embarrassed to remember in the morning. But now she realized what a fool she'd been—to think that sharing a goal could make them friends. Will was civil to her, but he didn't *like* her.

"How about you tell me something," he said. "What exactly do you do these days? Because you're not a lawyer, right?"

"Yes and no," she said, and to her surprise her breath was shaky. She wanted to be as honest with him as possible. Any question he asked, she would answer. He deserved that much. "Obviously I tried Arlen's case. But after that, I got offered a job as a jury consultant. I help other lawyers pick juries and construct arguments."

"What do you mean, you pick juries?"

"I guess it's not really picking the ones we like so much as rejecting the ones we don't. I research potential jurors. Then we reject the ones that we think might be biased against our clients."

"You research people? Like a private investigator?"

"It rarely comes to that. Hiring a PI is the hard way of doing things. I like the easy way."

"Which is?"

"The Internet," she said. "We gather all the information we can from various social networks—you can tell a lot about people by who they follow on Twitter or what groups and organizations they 'like' on Facebook. Then I put the pieces together based on the composite profiles. Nine times out of ten, I can predict how a juror will vote even before the trial begins."

"That's why I used to see *you* on TV every six months, as opposed to some other jury consultant."

"Yes. But I don't really do TV spots anymore. It seemed—I don't know—gross after a while. I didn't get into people-reading for the publicity."

He leaned against the dresser, crossing his arms. "So why did you get into it?"

She was quiet.

"Tell me the biggest reason."

"The biggest reason?" She dragged a fingertip along a dusty mirror beside her, leaving a clear swirl. She understood now why Will had been so hesitant to talk to her about his love of antiques. Telling him about the facts of her job was one thing. But telling him why she did it . . . that opened a door she wasn't sure she was ready for him to walk through. And yet, after everything she'd done to Arlen, she had no right to hide. "Part of the reason is probably because of my brother."

"Go on."

"He's got BPD. Borderline personality disorder. He spent some time in jail before we knew what was going on with him, which—of course—made the whole thing worse. Then when they let him out, my parents insisted he go into a private care facility for a while. But these days he's doing okay."

"Why was he in jail?"

She toyed with a clothbound book perched on a pile of boxes; it was soft with dust. "My mom got in a car accident with him the year he turned eighteen. I think I was twenty at the time. Anyway, he was fine except for a couple scrapes and stuff, but my mom was in pretty bad shape. My brother beat up a medic when they tried to put her in the ambulance."

"Couldn't they have used an insanity plea?"

"He hadn't been diagnosed at that point. Plus, people often think that insanity means being crazy. But that's not true. A schizophrenic can be declared totally sane. *Insanity* just means whether or not you can tell the difference between right and wrong."

"In that case, I think we all have moments that we're insane."

She smiled bleakly. "They locked my brother up for five years. Five years of his life, gone. Wrong jury, wrong lawyer, wrong crime. It was the perfect legal storm—and my brother took the brunt of it."

"And that's why it hurt you so much to find out Arlen wasn't guilty. Because of your brother."

She rubbed her forehead. She thought of how strange it was to hear Will explain her to herself. And how strange it made her feel to know he wasn't wrong. "All right, I confessed. Now it's your turn. Are you going to tell me why you got into picking?"

He shrugged and smiled—a smile that didn't entirely reach his eyes. "I'd tell you 'I do it for the money,' but you know that's not true."

She smiled. "But the money's not bad."

"It's helpful," he said. "When I was in high school, I started picking and trading real hard. I made some lucky finds. I saved up enough to buy my building at a foreclosure sale. And that's all she wrote."

"That's all?"

He shrugged. "I like old things."

"I can understand that," she said. He seemed uncomfortable, so she let it go. She felt pleasantly exhausted—refreshed, even—as if she'd just run a few miles. Talking to Will had felt good.

She walked back to the dresser and touched the smooth wood. "I hope you weren't planning on buying this."

"And why not?"

"Because I'm going to," she said.

"But it's not real."

"I know. But I like it. And besides . . ."

"Besides what?"

"Abbott needs the money."

Will peered at her as if he couldn't quite make out what was right in front of his face. "You just keep surprising me."

She smiled. "What's eight hundred bucks between friends?"


Arlen had seen the lawyer from his trial—his first trial—standing outside his building looking like a lost puppy, and since that moment, he'd been wrestling with a kind of surliness that had clenched him like an alligator doing a death roll with his mood between its teeth. Customers came into the store, one by one, and Arlen wasn't the friendliest to them—the fact of letting them through the door struck him as friendly enough. He thought he must have had on his death-row face, because a few people who wandered in made halfhearted attempts to bargain, then left with empty hands.

Now Arlen was alone in the shop—thank God. Men in suits were talking about sports on the television that Will had jury-rigged to sit on a platform near the ceiling, but Arlen hardly listened. The antiques store bored him; he preferred to be actively working, doing something or fixing something—as opposed to babysitting a pile of junk. He didn't like being surrounded by so much stuff—so much of the past—as if the tide of clutter was growing and growing and would one of these days drown him.

He had to get out of here—he knew that. He needed to pick himself up. To get a job that wasn't a handout. To start paying some rent. But now his name had been in the paper for last night's unfortunate incident, and he'd be hard-pressed to find work outside of Will's antiques store.

He was half watching a commercial for toilet bowl cleaner when the door opened and who should walk in but a preacher. He didn't have the white collar or the getup of a minister or priest, but Arlen could tell right away that the guy was a man of God because of the way his eyes didn't so much as touch any of the junk in the store, but instead landed right on Arlen and then lit up like Christmas morning. Arlen braced himself.

"What'd you want?" he asked.

"You must be Arlen. I'm Pastor George Scott."

"Do I know you?"

"No. Well, not yet. Do you have a moment?"

Arlen sighed. "You don't need to convert me or save my soul. I already believe in Jesus."

"Glad to hear it." George's laugh was a little self-conscious. "But I'm not here to save your soul. Actually, I wanted to offer you some assistance. Of the financial variety."

Arlen picked up the remote control and turned off the television. "I'm listening."

The preacher walked up to the counter. He had sandy-colored hair that was thinning, and friendly, hazel eyes. His skin was pale white and had only just started to show its first wrinkles.

"We've got a fund," George said. "Our parishioners are good people—generous people. And we've got a fund that helps convicts get back on their feet after doing their time. It's wrong the way the system just drops them after all's said and done."

"The whole system's wrong. What do I gotta do to get this money?"

"Nothing."

"I don't have to come back to church?"

George laughed nervously. "I mean, technically you wouldn't have to. But you're certainly welcome."

"And how much you gonna pay me to go to your church?"

"It's not like that," he said. "But . . . a hundred bucks a week. For a limited time. Our funds aren't exactly infinite. But we hope it helps."

Arlen scratched an itch on his chest. It was a lot of money that the preacher was offering. He knew he'd be crazy to turn it down. But the idea of owing somebody something . . . of being in somebody's debt . . . It felt like prison all over again. He didn't let himself think it through any more before he heard himself reply.

"Well, I thank you for the offer. But I'm afraid it's not gonna help."

George's face went slack with surprise. "Well . . . why? What do you need?"

Arlen couldn't help but think of his mother, who had encouraged him to go to church with her every Sunday from the time he was a baby to the day they put him away. Some days he'd hated it—the smell of pew wax and old ladies. Everybody always making such a fuss: *And how's little Arlen doing in school? Are you being a good boy?*

But other days, he'd loved it. The choir singing at the top of their lungs and clapping their hands, the wood of the pew vibrating with the sound of the organ—it made him feel like God was never so close to the people who loved Him as when they were singing. In the back of his mind, Arlen could hear his mother's voice, speaking to him from her years in the grave. And she wasn't happy. *This man will help you,* she said. *Don't be a fool.*

"What do I need?" Arlen took in a deep breath. "What I need's a job."

George looked a little surprised, as if Arlen had asked him to procure a hooker instead of a line of work. "I'll certainly see what I can do. What are you good at?"

"Not a damn thing," Arlen said.

Will parked in front of his house and pulled open the back of his van, where Lauren's new dresser was tipped on its side and fastened with nylon straps. A sturdy quilt was folded beneath to keep the wood from being scratched. Lifting the boxy piece of furniture into the van had been no problem, in part because Lauren was stronger than she'd looked like she would be. Will was certain that hauling it out wasn't going to be a problem either. They worked well together, with none of the bickering, doubt, or uneven laboring that sometimes annoyed Will when he brought in a new picker. When Lauren focused on the job at hand, she was patient, thoughtful, and efficient—as long as she wasn't on her phone.

"Thanks for letting me store this at your place," she said. "I'll pay you to have it shipped up to Albany as soon as I get back."

"It's fine."

Will climbed into the back of the van and began to loosen the chest of drawers. He tried to give his full focus to the job, but Lauren was standing just a few feet away, framed by the door of the van, her hand on her hip, her shoulders slouched with fatigue, her clothes spotted with dirt and sweat, and the narrow road behind her trailing like a ribbon. He absorbed all he could of her out of the corner of his eye, taking a snapshot in his mind. He liked her this way, slightly more casual and relaxed. So distant from the corporate-America superlawyer who had walked into his shop a few days ago. He wasn't so arrogant as to think that being with him had changed her. But she made more sense to him now.

"Nice house," she said. "I like the color. What do you call that? Mushroom?"

"Tan."

He worked the straps on the chest.

"Owned it long?"

"Six years," he said.

His house was a work in progress. It fronted a road so narrow and obscure that cars had to pass one at a time. Holsteins grazed behind a barbed-wire fence across the street. He'd bought the old Victorian fixer-upper for next to nothing about two years after he'd opened the antiques shop and started turning a profit.

The house had come a long way since he'd first stepped foot inside. The first floor now had refinished hardwood flooring, custom shelving and lighting, a kitchen full of stainless steel and granite, and a few of Will's favorite and most prized antiques on display in curio cabinets or on the walls. The first-floor bedroom, bathroom, and laundry were all decked out with the best appliances and most interesting collectibles Will could find. But the upper floors, they weren't ready for public scrutiny. And they sure as hell weren't ready for Lauren.

"It's a big house," she said. "How many bedrooms?"

"Four on the second floor. One on the first."

"That's a lot of bedrooms."

"I got a good deal. And it's not too big."

He pushed the dresser toward the back bumper. All day, he'd been aware of a tension between them—a slight frustration, a block that kept him from fully relaxing around her. He didn't like that her phone rang once an hour, and she always dropped whatever she was doing—or whatever she was holding in her hand—to move out of earshot and take the call. Occasionally, he got the feeling that even when she was standing next to him, she was apart from him, not fully present in the place where she was.

She had him edgy and twisted up—more now than when she'd simply been the face who looked out at him, unseeing, from the television screen. More than once he'd caught himself looking at her breasts, which were small and high, and unmanageably intriguing. In another life, she might have been a gymnast, and at one point Will had actually found himself wondering how flexible she was—a thought that led to other speculations and an immediate need to remove himself temporarily from her company.

He shimmied the chest into a better position to lower it.

He told himself: a quick lay was not on the table. Or the bed. Or the kitchen floor. He liked Lauren: he admired her strength, her determination, and even—he had to admit it—her sense of right and wrong. But when he tried to see himself through her eyes, even he had to look down.

"Ready?" he asked.

She flexed her arms hero-style. "Bring it on."

He pushed the dresser to the edge of the van, then balanced it and tipped it carefully down. She grabbed the bottom lip with both hands, and a moment later, he heard her hissing and saying, "Ow!" under her breath.

"What happened? Catch a finger?"

"No." She let the corner of the dresser down onto the ground.

He saw her glance at her hand, then drop it fast. "Nothing. Just a pinch."

He hopped out of the van. "Let's see." She didn't move. "Come on."

She rolled her eyes and extended her hand, knuckles down and palm open to the sky. He took it and held it closer to his face. A dozen or more little brown splinters peppered her skin like freckles.

"When did this happen?"

"When I grabbed that falling board back at Abbott's."

"Doesn't look good," he said.

"No?"

"I think we'll need to amputate. It's the only way."

She laughed.

"No, really," he said. "I've got an old Civil War medic's kit out back. Long as you don't mind the rust."

"No gangrene for me today, thanks."

Will watched her draw her hand to her belly; she stiffened when her palm brushed her shirt. He ran a hand through his hair, looked at the door to his house. He didn't want to invite her inside. He was afraid to have her in his home, among his things. He'd taken great, exhaustive pains to make his house inviting for guests—but still. He didn't want Lauren, who saw everything, poking around.

But he also didn't want her to suffer longer than she needed to or get an infection. He steeled himself.

"Come on," he said. "I got tweezers inside."

"I can do it myself. When I get home."

"Aren't you right-handed?"

"Damn. I guess so." She looked at her open right hand. "I can get Maisie to help later tonight. I'm sure I can keep from passing out with pain until then."

Will looked her over: Her tight clothes that she probably wore to the gym but which had served her well at the old farm today.

Her skin that was tanner now than when they'd met. Her legs that were deceptively long despite her short stature. He shook his head at himself. He was as red-blooded as any man; privacy or not, he actually wanted to invite Lauren inside.

"Let's just do it now," he said.

Lauren waited in the kitchen while Will bustled about his house to collect the things he needed to operate. And though she knew she shouldn't, she couldn't help but look at the African masks, jade tea set, and vintage metal Coke signs on the walls. Will's taste was impeccable: his counters and appliances were practical with a sleek modern edge, but his love of whim and charm rescued the room from overly modern severity. Will's house was so neat and tidy and organized, so much the opposite of what she'd seen at the antiques store, that it was almost more like a showroom than a home.

She wandered through the kitchen door and into the living room. She saw a wooden square the size of two doors nailed directly to the wall with fat iron spikes. It drew her attention—the whole room had been arranged to direct the eye toward it. She stepped closer and understood what she was looking at: dozens of keys, keys of all shapes and sizes, hanging from brass brads in the wooden board.

"You like it?" Will asked.

She didn't turn, but she could feel him approaching her. He stopped just behind her shoulder, looking with her at the collection of keys.

"They're beautiful," she said. She lifted her hand, then hesitated. "May I . . . ?"

"Sure," he said, and to prove the point, he reached out and slipped one of the prettier keys from its nail. He placed it in her hand. It was a fat black skeleton key, the top shaped like a four-leaf clover. "I found this one when I was cleaning out an old funeral home."

"Some good luck," she said.

He chuckled.

She reached out and ran her fingers along the bottoms of the keys, so they tinkled a little like muted bells. Her hand stopped at a particularly long key with chunky teeth and a fat handle. "What about this one?"

"I don't know what it's to," Will said. "I bought it off a guy who picks old shipwrecks as a hobby. He said this came from a wreck at the bottom of Lake Champlain. Probably from the Revolutionary War. But I can't know for certain."

"Oh wow," she said, and she touched it gently. "How long have you been collecting keys?"

"Here was my first," he said, lifting a small skeleton key from the corner of the board. "I found it in the attic of my mother's old house. It's nothing fancy. Just your basic skeleton. But it just . . . I don't know . . . I had to keep it."

"God—you're right. I never thought about it before. These are beautiful."

He smiled. "Careful. It's easy to fall in love with them."

"And you have no idea what any of them go to? What they open?"

"The usual things. Doors. Cabinets. Jewelry boxes. Safes."

"But you don't know anything specific about *these* keys."

"For the most part, no." He reached out to touch one. "Every one of them has a story. I just don't know what any of them are."

She turned away from the board to look at him. She wanted to touch him, to lay her palm against his face. Will collected keys because they were beautiful and they meant something to him. Each key had a purpose. They gave privacy: they locked people out of rooms. They gave punishment: they locked people in.

"Pick one," he said.

She looked at him, disbelieving.

"Pick one. It's yours."

"Oh no, I couldn't."

"Really," he said.

She looked over the keys on the wall, all of them beautiful in their own ways. A rush of greed swept over her. But she didn't reach out her hand. "Thanks," she said. "But—"

"You don't have to decide now."

She bit the corner of her lip, trying to convey her apology with her eyes.

"Come on," he said. "The ER bills by the minute. And the operating table is ready to go."

He led her back to the kitchen. They sat together at the wooden table, where he had set down a plate, ice cube, paper towel, and tweezers.

"Ready?"

Her heart skipped—not the big and terrible gurgling she'd felt sometimes over the last few days, but instead a quieter kind of tremor. She'd never done well with needles or stitches. It wasn't pain that made her nervous, but the sense of not being able to control it. "Could you . . . um . . . ?"

"What?"

"Would you mind coming to sit next to me instead of across from me? I don't want to see what you're doing."

"No problem," he said, and he slid his chair close to hers. Even after the day's work, his scent appealed to her—something soapy not quite masking the smells of earth, sunshine, and barn.

She slipped her right hand across her body and he took it. He pressed the ice cube into her palm—the cold stung. She held her breath and squeezed her eyes closed. She sat as still as possible. His shoulder touched hers.

"Okay?" he asked.

She opened her eyes. "Fine," she said lightly.

He laughed. "You had your eyes closed. I haven't even done anything to you yet."

"Just tell me you're as good at surgery as you are at antiques."

"This? Surgery?" He moved the ice a bit lower in the valley of her palm. "This is nothing."

"Oh, so you do this kind of thing all the time," she said. She wanted to keep him talking, to train her mind away from his closeness and heat.

"I've patched up my fair share of injuries. Sprained ankles. Hornet stings. I even delivered a baby once."

"No way."

He nodded, moved the ice again. "Scout's honor. It was a little girl."

She glanced over at their hands, hers resting in his, the faint sheen of water from melting ice. As he told her the story of delivering the baby, she let herself look at him. His hair had been sun-lightened and kissed with the slightest undertones of strawberry. His eyes were the most unusual shade she'd ever seen. They were the kind of gray-green that could go unnoticed in casual conversation, but when she looked at them—really looked—their color was shimmery, elusive, the color of a river on an overcast day.

At some point, she'd stopped listening to his story—and started listening to the story between the words. She saw his rapid blinking, his dilated pupils, his almost imperceptible fidgeting. It was only after she spoke that she realized she'd interrupted him.

"Will, what is it?" she asked. "What's wrong?"

"What? Nothing."

"Are you sure everything's okay?"

"Why wouldn't it be?"

She looked away from him, anchoring her gaze to the table before her. "I always do that. I'm sorry."

"Tell me why you think something's wrong."

"Your breath. It's more shallow than usual. Plus, you're blinking more than six to eight times per minute."

"You're counting?"

"No. I can just tell." She curled her fingers closed. "Is my being here making you nervous?"

Will sighed heavily. When she ventured to look at him again, she was taken aback by the firmness of his stare. "*You* don't make me nervous, Lauren Matthews."

She felt the blood rising to her face. Heat that had been tucked safely away, just out of her mind's reach, now flashed sweet and sharp though her whole body. "Some people are uncomfortable around me. You know—because of the people-reading thing."

"I'm not some people."

"But you wouldn't be the first guy who didn't know quite what to do with me."

"If you've met a guy who didn't know what to do with you . . ." His voice trailed off. He lifted the ice from her palm, put it back down again. There was grit in his voice when he spoke. "Fine. I admit it. I am nervous right now. I'm worried that I'll hurt you. With the splinters."

They were quiet a long moment. Lauren's head was spinning. Her blood felt hot. Will's shoulder pressed against hers, unrelenting contact. Her focus had narrowed to that single distracting spot. She cleared her throat. "Why don't you have a wife and a brood of kids living here with you in this big house?"

He laughed a little. "So now you want answers."

"I can guess them," she teased.

"No need." He lifted the ice from her palm, set it down on the plate. "I was seeing someone for a while, off and on. But then we ended up more off than on. Which was okay by me."

"What else?"

"Nothing else," he said. He squeezed her hand; her skin tingled. "If the patient is properly anesthetized, I'm going to operate now."

She tensed up.

"Don't worry. I'll be gentle."

She laughed, and then she turned her head away, to look out the window and watch the cows across the street ruminating on their dinners. He began to work the slivers of wood out of her skin—a slight pinch and sting. She couldn't bring herself to watch, but she knew from his focus and grip that he was efficient and not at all squeamish. When she tried to draw her hand back—an involuntary gesture—he clasped it more firmly. She tried not to wince.

*"Ouch!"*

"Sorry." He eased his grip. "Having trouble with this one. It's deep."

"No worries," she said, but her toes curled inside her shoes.

She sat quietly while he worked. She closed her eyes, gave in to the unpredictable sensations. When at last she heard the sound of the tweezers hitting the plate, she didn't open her eyes right away. Beside her, Will made no move to get up. She felt him trace a slow line from the top of her middle finger all the way down to the heel of her palm. Heat—heavy and wet as a summer afternoon— burned through her. And when she opened her eyes, Will's face filled her vision.

He, too, seemed to be caught in a question. But he didn't lean forward, didn't make good on the promise his eyes told. Instead, he recovered, curled his hand around her until her fingers were closed in a fist, and then he drew away. On the plate between them, the ice cube had melted. He picked up the dish and carried it to the sink.

"That wasn't so bad," he said.

She barely heard him. Frustration was a tightening knot inside her. Will had wanted to kiss her—she'd wanted him to. But even though he might have been physically attracted to her, he didn't *like* her enough to want to kiss her. The understanding stung far deeper than a splinter under her skin.

She pushed out her chair and went to her purse, which she'd dropped on the countertop when she came in. She pulled her phone from its designated pocket to glance at her new messages. To her dismay, there were none. She opened an e-mail she'd read earlier and perused it again.

"We have to put the dresser away," she said as she scrolled through the images on her phone's screen. "I'm assuming we're bringing it into that old barn out back?"

"It's okay. I don't need your help. I can do it myself."

"Why? What's out there?"

"Nothing. A barn."

She shrugged. "Okay. I really need to get back. I'm going out with Maisie tonight."

He wiped his hands on a towel, then started across the room. His car keys had been hooked to a loop of his jeans with a carabiner; they jingled when he pulled them off. "Then what are we waiting for? I'm not keeping you prisoner here."

"Will . . ."

He stopped in the doorway that led to the foyer.

"Can you ask Arlen if he'll see me tomorrow?"

He glanced at the phone in her hand. "Work bothering you again?"

She nodded.

His sigh was both impatient and resigned. "I'll ask him. Again. But—look—why don't you write him a note or something? In your own words, so he'll know what he's expecting if he does agree to see you."

"Thank you. I will."

He pointed at her before he walked out of the room. "Next time we do this, you wear gloves," he said.

**Lesson Seven:** When reading a person, whether someone you know well or a complete stranger, it's important to keep in mind that there is more to talking than just truth or lies. There's a spectrum of truthfulness, ranging from hard fact to statements made without perfect confidence to blatant fabrications. Most people know the difference between the truth and a lie. But it's the in-between—those words uttered between truth and lies—where you can gather the most information.

# CHAPTER 7

When the mail carrier came to the antiques shop in the evening, the cardboard envelope she'd dropped on the counter had been stuffed full nearly to bursting. The woman, who had dark skin and darker, mirthful eyes, rapped her knuckles against the counter a few times and smiled. "Hey, Arlen. Looks like you got yourself some fans."

He opened the envelope when she was gone, pulling the cardboard tab like the cord of a lawn mower. Among dozens of envelopes, big and small, a letter from his lawyer was inside. It was printed on soft cream paper. The language was thick as molasses and about as straightforward as a figure eight, but Arlen managed to piece out the basic meaning. The lawyer was sending photocopies of documents pertaining to Arlen's application for compensation with the State of New York. He hoped to hear something soon. The lawyer knew Arlen needed the money (that he had *uncommon need for financial restitution, given the extremely damaging repercussions of an unjustifiable conviction*). But in the meantime—this part Arlen understood with no problem—the law office had received some letters from the public, enclosed herein.

One by one, Arlen wedged a pen into the envelopes to open them. There were some drugstore cards scrawled with phrases of encouragement. A bundle of drawings done in crayon, children's hands traced to look like birds. There was a sheet of lined paper written in the beautiful, flowing penmanship of a schoolteacher. Some were sealed with stickers, others with tape and fuzz.

He leafed through.

*. . . writing to let you know that I think it's terrible what happened, and I'm using your case in my intro to criminal law class . . .*

*. . . would think that this kind of thing is something out of the Dark Ages . . .*

*. . . you're an inspiration to us all . . .*

*. . . enclosed please find a check for a collection taken up at our synagogue . . .*

*. . . wishing you all the best . . .*

At one point, Arlen had to stop. He couldn't read the words. For more than a decade he'd thought he was forgotten; but here he was, remembered again.

One man, a student, was going to put Arlen's story up on his Web site, and he wanted to know: did he have his facts straight? Arlen lowered his head and read:

*The trial: Arlen Fieldstone's case shows us just how easily wrongful convictions can happen—that they can happen to anyone who's in the wrong place at the wrong time. The "evidence" presented against Fieldstone was stacked like this:*

- *A lead from a woman who lived in the building where Fieldstone was staying and who wrongly identified Field-*

*stone as the man in a police sketch, followed by positive*
*identification from the victim's housekeeper, although*
*she admitted to not having had a clear view of the man*
*she saw near the property the night of the murder*
- *Unreliable forensic evidence based on dog scent identifi-*
  *cation when Investigator Derek Hoffman indicated that*
  *his scent-decimating dog "Rusty" had found evidence of*
  *Fieldstone having been in the victim's home (which the*
  *defendant categorically denied)*
- *Political and social pressure to successfully prosecute a*
  *criminal, any criminal, quickly*
- *Weak legal defense counsel and strong prosecution*

Arlen put the paper down. He thought: *So this is how they're gonna tell it.* It all looked so easy on paper. The tale needed a better ending—something more dramatic and meaningful than *He got out of prison: The End.* And while some part of him was glad that this student wanted to make his case into a banner against wrongful convictions everywhere, some other part of him didn't want the story to be told at all. He wanted his life to be everything that was going to happen from here forward, not everything behind. But was that possible?

He gathered up the letters and tucked them back into the envelope. They barely fit. He went to the door, locked it and turned the sign, then climbed the creaky stairs to his apartment alone, the comforting voices of strangers in his mind.


When the sun set in Richmond, the alleyways darkened long before the avenues did, long before the windows of tall buildings stopped reflecting the melon haze of evening. Stoplights at intersections began to stand out brighter and brighter against the dusk, reds growing redder, greens deepening. Good people and bad people and all the people in between stood waiting at bus stops for their ride home or sitting in traffic with their heads propped on their hands.

Lauren showered, cool water and hibiscus refreshing overheated skin. Evenings when she did not stay in to work were rare. But when she did manage a night out with friends, getting ready always verged on sacred—the last glance in the mirror, the fastening of buttons and clasps. She slipped on a black sundress made of cotton so soft and clingy it might have been ink. She hid the circles under her eyes with concealer, she darkened her lashes to a thick black, and she put on the reddest lipstick she could find in her bag.

She thought of Edward, then Will, then Edward again. She looked good and felt even better. She wished that Edward could see her like this, just so she could flaunt the fact that she didn't need him and was going out for an evening without him. And she wished that Will could see her like this too, because maybe he wasn't planning to put a move on her anytime soon, but she wanted to make it damn hard for him not to.

She picked up her earrings from the dresser, slipped them in.

She supposed it was natural to compare Edward and Will to each other, if only because they were so very different. Her interest in Edward had been easy, maybe even a little bit expected. It was perfectly ordinary and right that she should be attracted to a man like him: he was good-looking, powerful, moneyed, sure. He was all the things she was. Early on she'd felt that there was a kind of unspoken etiquette between them, rules to guide the dance of courtship, so that she knew what to do and he knew what to do, and there was never any doubt.

Unlike Will, Edward had never once asked her why she got into jury consulting, and she'd never thought to ask him why he practiced law. His admiration had not been easily won; though he made a habit of charming everyone, he respected few. His high standards both terrified her and made her proud. But he'd never asked *why* she did what she did: it was Will who cared about that. Will, with his worn-out boots and soft heart.

She walked down the stairs, her high black heels clicking against the old pine, one hand trailing along the sturdy banister. Maisie was waiting for her on the couch, watching a sitcom rerun on television.

"Wow." She clicked off the TV and threw the remote control onto the coffee table. She was wearing dark jeans and a black tank top; her hair was in a ponytail. "You look hot."

"Thanks."

"So what's the deal?" She grinned and reached out to ruffle the bottom edge of Lauren's dress. "Are we on the prowl? Tell me we are."

"I think I just need a pick-me-up."

"In that dress? I'm sure you can get some nice man to pick you up."

Lauren laughed.

"Why do you need a pick-me-up? Hard day?"

Lauren thought back over the afternoon—watching Will count out cash as fast as a bank teller; hearing for the first time a peahen calling in the top of a tree, the sound raising goose bumps on her arms; and then—that heated flash in Will's eyes, so taut and elemental that a person didn't have to be a body-language expert to recognize a desire that raw.

Science wanted to turn sexual attraction into mathematical calculation. Studies showed again and again that facial attraction was based on symmetry and proportion. Men wanted a woman's waist to be seven-tenths the width of her hips. Women wanted a man's shoulders to be broad, his voice low. Chemistry, too, got in the mix. People disliked scent profiles similar to their own—hardwiring to ensure genetic diversity. Women were usually repulsed by the smell of raw male pheromones, but found themselves loving the smell if they were near ovulation. And men who could make logical judgments about facial attractiveness lost that ability—their analytical skills completely boggled—when exposed to imperceptible amounts of female scent.

The science was fascinating, but Lauren had no use for it. If sex appeal was a simple equation of $1 + 1 = 2$, people would simply *know* when they were compatible the moment they met—and that would be that. But she was becoming increasingly attracted to Will by the day, more aware of the way he moved, the way he casually touched her, the strength of his body and hands. She liked his smell, his smile. She liked his face—masculine without being overly hard. Seeing his house had changed something inside her too. The house *was* a bachelor pad, but it wasn't just a place he lived: it was his home and he cared about it. It turned her on.

More and more, she liked him. And more and more, she wanted. Yet, when he could have kissed her today, when he'd held her suspended in the question of whether he'd wanted to kiss her or not, he'd backed down. He was attracted to her, but he didn't want to be. It hurt to think of it. She tried to push the thoughts away.

"I guess 'hard day' isn't the right wording," she told Maisie. "It was a nice day, really."

"Then why the sexed-up heels?"

She shrugged. "Why not?"

The doorbell rang and Maisie excused herself to answer it. Her friends would arrive soon, and Lauren was looking forward to meeting them. She couldn't remember the last time she'd spent an evening with a group of relaxed and happy women who were not sitting in lotus position and wearing yoga pants.

She glanced at herself in the mirror over the old fireplace and adjusted her bangs. She straightened when Maisie returned—

alone. Her friend walked with her two hands linked in front of her belly button, her steps small.

"Lauren?"

"What's wrong?"

"There's a reporter at the door. He's asking for you."

"For me?" Lauren asked, though she knew the question was ridiculous the moment she spoke it.

"I'm sorry. I didn't know what to do."

"It's okay. Did you tell him I was here?"

"I didn't really tell him anything. I'm sorry! I clammed up. I think the most information he got out of me was *hold on*."

Lauren ran her hands down the front of her dress, looked at herself in the mirror. A reporter. When she left Albany, she hadn't told anyone where she was going—not even her parents. And yet, here was a reporter at the door, asking for her. Her mind ran through the possibilities and landed quickly and firmly on the most obvious one: Bryce was trying to sabotage her. He wanted to rattle her cage, to let her know she was being watched. If he'd talked to Burt or even Rizzi, he would have known where she was going. Apparently she could leave the Albany city limits, but Albany politics were not so easy to shake.

"I wasn't sure if you wanted to talk to him or not," Maisie said.

"Not a big deal." Lauren crossed the room and put an arm around Maisie's shoulders to give her a quick squeeze. "I'll take care of it."

She steeled herself before she went to the door. She pulled herself up straight inside of her black dress. She could handle reporters. She was used to their scrutiny. Some were thoughtful and conscientious, but others were full of hot air.

She put on her game face and yanked open the door. "Can I help—"

She stopped.

No one was there.

The street was busy, young men and women going about their evenings together or in groups. The trees that had been planted in the sidewalk whispered a little in a warm wind. She closed the door.

"That was quick," Maisie said when Lauren came back into the living room. "Did you threaten to slap him with a lawsuit?"

"I would have, but he was gone. I guess he changed his mind."

Maisie frowned. "I don't like that."

"Well, I do. Did he say what paper he was from?"

"No. I don't think so. Or, if he did, I didn't hear it. He just said he was a reporter. That was all. How do you think he found you?"

"I have a hunch. The guy at work who picked up my caseload isn't my biggest fan right now. I'd put my money on him."

"Well, can I pretty please with a cherry on top listen when you call him up and ream him out?"

Lauren laughed.

They heard the door click open at the same time. Lauren hadn't locked it behind her. Instinctively, her weight shifted to the balls of her feet, her stance softening. Someone had come in.

"Hellooo?"

Maisie's face went slack with relief. "Corina."

Lauren relaxed.

"That's just Corina. You're gonna love her. Ready to go?"

Lauren's breath, which had jumped into her throat, was now settling back into her chest. Her heart was slowing. The tension in her muscles eased. "Let's go. I'm so ready for some fun."


Will finished moving the old dresser out to the barn, then locked the door's heavy padlock behind him. It thumped the old boards when he let it go. The sun was nearly gone now, and the crickets were singing from their hidden perches on blades of grass. In the soft dusk, Will's house stood two and a half stories tall, the down-stairs windows gleaming gold, the upstairs windows dark.

He put the barn key in his pocket. As usual, Lauren's observations about him were right—his house was too big for him. And he felt sometimes that he rattled around in it like a kid walking in his dad's shoes. He started across the lawn toward the sliding glass doors he'd had installed six months ago.

Over the years, he'd gotten very good at being a bachelor. Of course, he had his family: his brothers and sister, Annabelle, who, together, could make as much noise as a block party. He also had his mother and her husband, who always needed something to be repaired, hauled, or assembled—and who always repaid him with a home-cooked meal. And he had friends as well, good guys who didn't require much attention or maintenance except for the occasional invitation to watch a football game or grab a beer.

But fundamentally, he was alone—the only person on the planet who truly knew what he was. Annabelle had her suspicions; she'd asked him once in an absentminded way, and he'd told her he was storing some things for a friend. And there had been close calls with ex-girlfriends as well, until he'd finally decided that the risk of discovery (which inevitably led to well-intentioned intervention, which led to failure, which led to irritated or maudlin break-ups) wasn't worth the opportunity for semi-regular sex.

Normally he didn't have trouble being alone. Life was good. But something about the evening tonight was *off*. A certain shift in the shadows. A certain thinness of light. The ache of loneliness, so hard to define, made him feel as if he'd been filled up to the brim by empty space—as if it was possible to be filled by nothing. He walked across the drought-brown grass of his yard, slid open the door, and went inside.

In his kitchen, he got things ready. He put out bags of greasy potato chips and fatty white dip. He stocked the fridge with silver cans of beer. He had two fresh decks of cards, wrapped in plastic, in the center of his heavy kitchen table. And he fiddled with the dial of the radio station until he found one that played guy songs, most of them from ten years ago.

Arlen was first to arrive.

"Come on in," Will said. "Any trouble getting here?"

Arlen was holding a case of beer. "Naw. No problems."

"You didn't let the cabbie overcharge you?"

"I think he undercharged me. But anyway—I got my own money now."

"How's that?"

"Fella from a church came by. Said he'd give me a hundred bucks a week and try to get me a job."

"That's great."

"There's good people out there yet."

Will led his friend into the kitchen. Arlen wore jeans that he'd probably bought from the thrift store not far from the antiques shop, and a button-down shirt of light cotton—burgundy and green plaid. He was clean-shaven and smelling so strongly of aftershave that he'd probably killed a couple dozen mosquitoes on the way in.

"Ready for some cards?" Will asked, bringing his hands together with one quick, loud clap.

"Yeah, you bet." Arlen stopped in the middle of the kitchen and looked around. "Looks like you did okay for yourself."

"Not too bad."

"This is just how I pictured it would be. Just what you always said you wanted." Arlen smiled. "I'm glad for you. I'm real glad."

Will nodded. Visions of the past, of tattered backpacks, of car parts magazines, of beer cans cooling in the clear water of the creek, flashed vividly through his mind. Since Arlen had been released from prison, he hadn't so much as mentioned their past—the time they'd shared together as boys. He seemed to live only in the present moment, completely absorbed by its joys and problems. Now, to hear him talking about how things used to be, no matter how obscure the reference, made Will's chest swell with satisfaction. Arlen, the Arlen he used to know, was still there.

"Something missing, though," Arlen said, peering around.

Will knew he was being set up. "What?"

"The wife. The rugrats."

Will shrugged. "Not exactly the kind of thing you can pick up at a pawnshop." He mimed writing a note in the air. "Memo to self: Look for comic books, wall art, wife and kids."

"Come on, now. Don't get all defensive on me."

"I'm not defensive."

"Uh-huh."

"I'm *not* defensive. And I'm not exactly a senior citizen yet. I've still got some time. We both do."

"You never know how much time you got."

"No, I suppose you don't," Will said. And he saw that Arlen had a look in his eyes as if he were drifting away inch by inch on a raft. It was a moment before Arlen returned from whatever place he'd gone to, but once he did fight his way back into Will's kitchen, his expression turned clear and bright.

"So who all's coming?"

"Couple of my brothers. The guy Rourke who does antique lures—you met him. My buddy Donnie from across town might come later, but I'm not sure."

Arlen made a slow circle of the room, looking at Will's collection. He had to clear his throat before he spoke again. "How'd it go today picking?"

"Fine. No problems."

"Watch that girl doesn't get hurt on the job. She'll sue you."

"I don't think so." He thought of her hand in his. The terribly erotic little sounds she'd made as he'd worked on her splinters. He forced his brain to change direction. "She's serious about talking to you. I think, even if you wanted to yell at her, to stomp your feet and scream, she would welcome it. She knows she had a part in putting you in prison."

"So that makes her a saint," Arlen said.

"I don't see anyone else here to apologize. Where's the lawyer who didn't defend you? Where's the senator? The judge?"

"Well—"

"Nowhere. That's where they are. The only person who's here and who's willing to take some responsibility for what happened to you is Lauren. And that counts for something."

Arlen was slack-faced for a moment; then his cheeks drew up in a horrible, over-wide smile. He began to laugh. "Wow." He shook his head and put his hands on his chest. "She really got to you, didn't she?"

Will went to the fridge, got himself a green beer bottle from the bottom drawer. He took a long breath before he shut the door and turned to face Arlen again. "She's not who I thought she was."

"You do know she can manipulate you. She can read you like a book and get you to do what she wants."

"I don't think that's what she's doing."

"Course you don't."

Will bristled. "Careful."

"I'm just saying."

The front door swung open—no ringing doorbell, no knock—but there was the noise of it hitting the doorstop and then the loud bickering of Will's two oldest brothers as they came inside. Will went to the foyer to greet them. "Guys. Welcome." They carried plastic grocery bags filled with pretzels and tubs of spreadable cheese. Farther behind them, Will's friend Rourke was coming down the front lawn, where the grass had been worn to hard-packed dirt in a line to the door.

"From our dear sister," Scoot said, pushing his bag into Will's hands. Scoot was a big man with a linebacker's shoulders and a beer drinker's belly. He wobbled side to side even when he was walking forward and straight. "She told me she wanted to fatten you up."

Will laughed.

"And these are from my wife." Will's other brother Hank handed off a plate of brownies. He rubbed his belly. "But apparently I'm not allowed to eat them."

His brothers went into the kitchen without being escorted, talking loudly and making a big, rowdy fuss over Arlen. Will was filled with unspeakable gratitude for them. The terrible oppression he'd felt earlier in the evening seemed to be lifting; their loud voices drove the demons out of the dark corners of the house. He waited as Rourke walked the last few steps to the door.

Rourke nodded. "Hey. What up?"

Will swung his arm around for a brisk handshake. He left the front door standing open, then showed Rourke inside. His brothers were already opening Will's refrigerator and cabinets, grabbing for pint glasses and arguing about the best way to avoid Richmond rush-hour traffic. Arlen stood looking pleased but awkward, not quite sure how to join in.

"Rourke?" Will gestured for his friend's attention. "I want you to meet Arlen Fieldstone. Arlen, Rourke."

"Heard so much about you," Rourke said, and Will thought he saw a little glint of wariness darken Arlen's eye. "I mean . . . I heard about you from Will. Not— I didn't mean the newspapers."

"Nice one, Rourke." Will's brother Scoot kicked out a kitchen chair and dropped into it. "Arlen's used to it by now. He's a regular celebrity."

A bitter noise caught in Arlen's throat.

"So what's next for you?" Rourke asked. "Writing a book? Getting a reality TV show? The offers must be pouring in."

"No offers. And no TV."

Will clasped Rourke on the back and smiled. "How 'bout we quit the gossiping and play some poker?"

"Fine by me," Arlen said.


The Mexican restaurant was the color of cantaloupe, with flamingo-pink accents and a teal ceiling painted with clouds. If there was an air conditioner in the building, it was either completely broken or exhausted of all cool air, and everything Lauren touched—the door, the lip of the bar, the stool when she pulled it out—was sticky. Revelers sat jammed in elbow to elbow, and the noise of the crowd was deafening—people struggling to be heard, each laugh louder than the next. But the margaritas were cheap, the nachos were piled sky-high, and a wall covered in pictures of Elvis and pinup girls ensured that no topic was prohibited for a night among new friends.

Lauren was enjoying herself. At first, a pesky and useless feeling of anxiousness had gripped her. She kept thinking she was forgetting something: an appointment, a phone call, an e-mailed document that perhaps hadn't gone through. But as the minutes passed and the surface of her red-pink sangria descended into the bottom of her glass, she began to have fun.

Laughter flowed, sweet and full. The conversation wasn't exactly challenging—discussions of shoes, television shows, husbands' bad habits—and Lauren adored it all. She *missed* this. As undergraduates, she and Maisie had shared a close group of girlfriends who got together in their pajamas to watch movies and drink wine. But once she'd moved back to Albany for law school—and Maisie had moved to Richmond—Lauren had thrown herself body and soul into her career. Her friends dwindled to a number that she could manage, which was not much of a number at all. It made her wish she had more time to give to others—and more time to give to herself.

"So how long are you here for?" Maisie's friend Corina asked.

"It's a little up in the air. Not very long."

"You seem so familiar," she said. "But there's no way I've met you before, right?"

"I come to Richmond to visit Maisie as often as I can. But no, I don't think we've met."

Corina nodded and lifted her highball for a quick sip. She had long brown-black hair that was flat and parted straight down the middle like an open book. Her face was narrow and her eyes were big. She'd smiled at Lauren with real gladness when they were introduced, but now her mouth was slack and her gaze tipped to the ceiling. This was Behavior 101: the tendency to look up when recalling a visual memory.

"I remember where I know you from," she said, lifting her hand, then dropping it on the bar with a smack. "You were on the news."

Lauren smiled.

Corina was delighted, her face lit brightly and her smile wide and white. "Why did I see you on the news? I can't remember for the life of me . . ."

"Lauren has a book out," Maisie put in. "She gets called to the news stations because she's an expert on body language."

"No, I don't think that was it." She leaned her wrist against the bar, her brow furrowed with thought. "No—it was . . . Oh. You're that lawyer . . ."

"Was," Lauren said. "Now I do consulting work."

"Wow." Corina picked up her mojito, swirled the ice and mint around in the glass until it began to fizz. "It's crazy what happened. About that guy being innocent and all."

"Yeah," Lauren said. "Crazy."

She drained the last swallows of fruit-laden wine from her glass. Since she'd come to Richmond, there were moments when she almost felt as if she were on vacation—a break from daily life. But there was no getting around the reason she'd come down to Richmond in the first place. She wondered if it would always be like this, if she would always have to feel like the past was jumping out at her from dark corners or stalking her in a crowded room. If everyone in the bar simultaneously fell silent and pointed their fingers at her, she wouldn't have felt any less guilty than she did now.

"Excuse me," she said to Maisie.

She shifted on the bar stool, pulled her phone from her purse as if it had been vibrating. It hadn't—but she did have a number of unchecked messages. She'd never before realized how often she used work as a retreat or excuse, and yet, here she was reaching for her phone as a refuge for the second time today. She wondered if those days and weeks when she was floating in work—when there was so much work to be done it felt like wading into water over her head, and stretching every bone in her body to keep a toe on the very bottom and her nose an inch in the air—were those entire, exhausting days nothing more than a kind of escape from life, as opposed to life itself? Did her passion for work mean she lived *more* intensely than the people around her? Or did her passion for work mean she lived *less* hard—because of all the experiences that she'd sacrificed in the name of her job?

She glanced through her messages, feeling Maisie's eyes on her. She felt not as if her messages were an infringement on the present, but rather that the present was the aberration, and her many voice mails and e-mails and texts were the persistence of her real life poking through.

"Everything okay?" Maisie asked.

"Oh, yes," she said. "But I'm so sorry. I've got all these messages in." She held up the bright pane of her phone; the blue and white pixels gave Maisie's skin an alien glow. "I have to go."

She offered a few more polite sentences—excuses, apologies, insistences that she didn't need a lift since she could get a cab—and then she was out of the bar, and she could breathe again. She was heading for the street, for the friendly gray and white of her laptop, the glass of sparkling water she liked to keep beside her while she worked, and the silence that was so companionable and understanding of her need to get things done.

Often enough, there were cameras at the Albany courthouse. White television vans. TV anchors with expensive jackets and comfortable shoes. Loitering reporters who threw their cigarette butts on the ground. For Lauren, all of this was expected and usual on any given day at the courthouse. And so on the afternoon that Arlen's conviction had been overturned, she hadn't realized right away that the two reporters at the bottom of the stairs—who were flirting so heavily with each other that they'd nearly missed their opportunity—had been waiting, in part, for her.

She'd meant to walk past them briskly, to avoid catching someone's eye. She'd perfected the art of brushing off reporters with no more thought than if they were wearing cardboard placards and handing out summonses about the End of Time. But that day, she hadn't been able to make herself invisible. A man with a microphone and a woman with a camera came after her. They blocked her path.

*What do you have to say now that Arlen Fieldstone will be retried based on faulty eyewitness testimony and questionable forensics?*

Lauren had meant to keep walking—to brush off their question even before they posed it. But Arlen's name on the man's lips had caught her off guard. She'd heard a rumor that Arlen's case was being appealed, but she had nothing to do with the appeals process and hardly gave it a thought. Appeals were common; what convict wouldn't want to appeal, if only to assuage the boredom of life in prison? Appeals rarely changed a thing. But to hear that Arlen's appeal had ended with a judge throwing out the previous verdict— *her* verdict—she'd barely managed a reply to the reporter before he fired at her again.

*How do you feel about the accusation that government misconduct and bad lawyering also played a role in his conviction?*

She could only remember stuttering.

*Do you hold yourself to be personally responsible for his wrongful incarceration?*

For a moment, she thought of her brother, then of Arlen, until they both seemed to swirl together in her mind so one was indistinguishable from the other. And in that moment, which felt as if time had been skewed and drawn out like a lengthening shadow, she did something foolish: she let her guard drop.

For days, the networks replayed the clip: the reporter's question, the slack-jawed look on Lauren's face—such naked shock— then a tactless dodge. The image of her face recurred like a familiar nightmare, replayed again and again, for a full twenty-four-hour news cycle before it finally went away.

She'd given the reporters some rote answer; she couldn't remember it now. Something trite about "just doing her job" and "we'll have to wait for the results of the retrial" that didn't even get replayed because of how jumbled and ridiculous it had been. Her mouth was saying some words, but in the back of her mind, she was thinking of her brother. The prosecutor who'd bagged Jonah had also been "just doing his job."

She'd hurried around the reporters as quickly as she could,

trusting that they wouldn't follow her. After a time, they didn't. The sounds of shouted questions died down. When she was out of sight, she stopped and leaned against the wall, forcing herself not to think about Arlen Fieldstone—the man, not the case—and pushing him back into the furthest recesses of her mind, as if she could seal him, brick by brick, safely into the prisons of memory, where she'd done nothing wrong.

Around one a.m., Arlen was starting to get sleepy. A haze of cigar smoke hung in the air. Colorful plastic bowls held only greasy shards of salty snacks. The radio station had changed from music to talk. And yet, Will's friends seemed to have no interest in packing up. The lighthearted banter of early evening had faded, and it left in its wake the surly, resolute silence of weary men who had nothing to do but prove one last point to one another—though what the point was Arlen couldn't say.

Now he and Rourke were the only two guys left in the game— the last hand, Arlen hoped. He hadn't won a round all night. Five hours of poker and not one single hand had gone to him. He'd begun to get angry—frustration strangling from the inside out. He'd learned many lessons about anger, but the most important one was that a person who wasn't angry at one specific thing found himself being angry at everything. A dangerous state of mind.

Now, though, his luck was turning around—and just in the nick of time. Though they played only for pretzels, he wanted desperately to win. He had a full house: twos and eights. He'd barely been able to hide his excitement—it threatened to come bursting up out of him like a geyser. He was sure everyone at the table knew exactly what he was holding, as if they could see the reflection of the numbers in his eyes. He trembled to anticipate laying his cards down, a win that felt as if it had taken lifetimes to earn.

Over the fan of his cards, Rourke eyed him. Will's kitchen was dim except for one bright light that shone over the center of the table, and it reflected off Rourke's angelic blond hair. "I'm all in."

Arlen nodded and tried to stay cool. Then, as slowly as he dared, he lowered his cards to the table. He didn't even bother pronouncing the obvious. The hand spoke for itself.

Rourke's face fell. He folded his cards up, tapped the bottom edges on the table, then tossed them so they landed with a skid. "Well, I'm cooked. You win, Arlen."

"About time," Will said.

"Hold up." Arlen didn't move to grab the pretzels in the center of the table. He had no interest in making a big show of pulling that pile toward him as if it was a heap of gold coins. But the cards . . . those he wanted to see. "What'd I win against?"

"What's it matter?" Rourke asked.

Arlen leaned his forearms on the table. "Gloating rights."

"Gloat away," Rourke said, waving his hand. "Weren't nothing but a couple pair."

"So let's see." Arlen reached out for Rourke's neat stack of downward-facing cards.

Rourke put his hand over Arlen's, pinning it down. "It ain't necessary."

Arlen's stomach soured. "I should say it is." He held Rourke's gaze with all the power he'd learned he had in himself one day when a man tried to jump him in the showers. "Show me the damn cards."

Rourke drew his hand back.

Arlen turned over the cards and spread them out, one by one, to see. Four perfect little tens were looking back at him. Four tens and a six.

He started to laugh—laughter that rose up from some black and burning place within him. The anger rolled over his body in waves; he felt as if a demon had climbed up from some awful place inside him, making him nothing more than a puppet of bones and meat. He stood up so fast his chair hit the floor. And then hands were reaching over the table to grip the front of Rourke's shirt. Fear clouded the older man's eyes.

"What the hell was that?" Arlen demanded. "You think I need to be babied? Like I'm some kind of charity case?"

"Naw, man. Easy. Let go."

"You don't *let* people win," Arlen said through his teeth. He heard Will calling to him as if from a great distance. He gripped Rourke tighter, and when he spoke, his spit flew in the other man's face. "You only let somebody win if you feel bad for them. Do you feel bad for me? Huh? Do you?"

Panic had set into Rourke's face—a wild, grasping, searching look. He held Arlen's wrists in his two hands. "I said, let go—somebody—"

Will picked up the edge of the table and dropped it so it slammed the tile floor, and Arlen came to. He had the odd feeling of just having been woken up from a vivid dream. Will was looking at him. His eyes were harder than Arlen had ever seen.

"Let him go," Will said.

Arlen didn't move. He felt like he was shrinking.

"Let him go."

Reluctantly, he released the other man, giving him a slight jerk for good measure. "Letting me win. Jeez."

"I think you'd better let me drive you home," Will said.

"Call me a cab." Arlen straightened his shirt. He still had some money. "I'll be outside."

He managed to hold his head high as he walked toward the door. He tried not to let himself hear Rourke's complaining, the brothers asking if he was okay, the peeved murmurs as he left the room. He tried not to care that he'd been looking forward to playing poker tonight, to meeting Will's friends, to having a normal evening with a bunch of guys who weren't convicts and didn't care that he'd done hard time. He let himself out. And then, when he was at the far, dark edge of the lawn, he let himself cry.

**Lesson Eight:** Sometimes when we rub our eyes it's because we're tired or we've got an itch. But other times, rubbing, covering, or closing our eyes can be an unconscious gesture to block out things that make us uncomfortable or that we don't want to see. It is a retreating inward, when the world within is more acceptable than the world without. Think of it: People rubbing their faces in long meetings at the office. Parents taking a little "break" from their unruly children by closing their eyes while they wait for the traffic light to turn green. Our body language mirrors our thoughts about our surroundings—how they are and how we wish they would be.

# CHAPTER 8

For a long time after he left her—after she told him, *Go*—Lauren thought of Edward. She thought of him when she was at the grocery store, because he'd loved cashews and she'd fed them to him one by one on a rainy afternoon. She thought of him when the evening news came on, because he'd once insisted that she not put her clothes on for the rest of the day so that when he called he would know she was naked. She thought of him when she opened a bottle of wine, when the torque and twist of pulling the cork made her think of the way he'd made love to her on the ice-cold tile of her kitchen floor.

They'd made love so often. Lauren should have realized that was *all* they did, all they were doing, even when they weren't engaged in the act. When they went to dinner it was a precursor to making love. When Edward called her in the afternoon, whispering words that burned with audacity, it was to tempt her toward making love. When they watched a movie on her couch, never his, his hand inevitably found its way to the drawstring of her pajamas.

She'd thought he was romantic. That sex was bringing them closer and closer. And yet, it was all smoke and mirrors—an illusion of intimacy that disguised a gap a mile wide.

As the summer slogged on, thoughts of him were being squeezed into oblivion—she had other things to occupy her. But she'd yet to shake him completely. In the morning light on Friday, she sat up in bed and realized how late she'd slept; it was almost seven. She knew from the soreness of her body, the hypersensitivity of her hot skin, that she'd dreamed of Edward. The feeling of his presence was as strong as if he'd just gotten up for a glass of water and would at any moment come back to her bed. She leaned over her bent knees and ran a hand through her loose hair. Already, the blurred memories of the dream were leaving, swiftly carried off by the current of consciousness. She could no more grasp the details—the mathematics of a bent elbow, the music of a gasp—than if she were to try to catch a ghost with her bare hands.

She padded down to the kitchen in bare feet, still reeling with the aches and pains of longing. It irritated her, how a dream she could not remember could be so troublesome. There had been heat, of course. Skin. Sweat. Sex that was not like some race to the finish line, that was not the athletic coupling of two competitive people, each striving for perfection. Instead, in the dream, sex was a path she and he walked together, and now the memory of that tenderness—so unusual that she wondered if she'd ever felt it at all—was a wish of her heart as bitter as it was sweet.

She grasped at the edges of fading images as she pulled a tin of coffee from Maisie's cabinet. She fished out the requisite grinds, then ladled them into the filter. The smell perked her up. She filled the coffeepot with cool white tap water, willing the ache of need to subside like water swirling down the drain.

It wasn't until midmorning, when Maisie called and asked where she was headed and Lauren heard herself say Will's name, that the shock came. The dream—skin and sweat, heat and greed. Lauren closed her eyes. It hadn't been about Edward at all.

Arlen sat in Will's office on a ripped green leather chair that might have been from the fifties and that made his back cramp. Will's office was as cluttered as his store—knickknacks, an old-fashioned radio that didn't work piled up on a heap of old-fashioned other things—stoplights, fans, typewriters—that also didn't work. Will picked among and moved around his treasures like a kid on a jungle gym, easy and free. But Arlen wasn't so comfortable. He sat among the stuff, thinking, and waiting, swiveling the chair from side to side.

The computer beeped, and he spun to face a monitor the size and shape of a small fish tank. His experience with the Internet was little more than anecdotal. From other inmates, the ones who came and went, he heard about screens that let you look at the person you were talking to, like a videophone. And from television shows, he heard new words and acronyms that made no sense and might have been an alien language: *emoticon, gravatar, jpeg* . . . Even innocent words, like *window* and *wall*, had turned slick in his grasp.

Now that he was out, he saw that everyone was caught in the Web, whether they liked it or not. Only recently was he beginning to understand how dramatically the world had leapt forward into the future while he'd been made to stand still.

He watched the computer turning on—the shimmery graphics and friendly little beeps and chimes. Will had given him a crash course in Web surfing, and now he worked the mouse with the awkward concentration of a child learning to use a fork for the first time. With two fingers he typed G-O-O-G-L-E, a stupid name for a company, and waited until the page came up. There was nothing but a rectangle, waiting like a slit in a door that had the universe on the other side.

He clicked. The cursor blinked.

*Eula . . .*

His skin prickled as if he were about to hack into the FBI or rob a bank. Did he even know his ex-wife's name anymore? Had she remarried? He felt something deep within him trembling, though his hands seemed steady as ever. Here he was, an ex-convict afraid to do something that wasn't even breaking the law.

He cracked his knuckles, then typed her name, her name that was his too: *Eula Fieldstone.*

When nothing familiar came up but some old articles about his trial, he tried not to feel defeated. And yet, to not find her on the first try had stung. It made him wonder if he wasn't meant to find her. He didn't know if he had it in him to try again, and he sat for a time, staring at the computer screen, waiting for courage.

His fingers had strength his heart did not.

He typed, this time using her maiden name. He plodded awkwardly and uncertainly through the maze of links and text that was the Web. And when she finally did turn up in a white pages listing, buried so far in his search results he nearly missed it, what he found made him feel as if someone had cinched a belt around his lungs.

The Internet told him everything. Her name, her age, her phone number. And the location of her house—the house they'd bought together, the house where she still lived.

She hadn't moved.

She was still *there*.

He leaned back in his seat, closed his eyes, remembering. She hadn't wanted to buy that house—the one she still lived in. She'd said it was too big for them. It had patchy grass, a little garden along the back fence for tomatoes and herbs, a birdbath in the stamp-sized front yard, and five small bedrooms on the second floor.

"What on earth do we need five whole bedrooms for?" she'd asked.

Arlen's answer had been fast. "For four kids."

They'd bought the house with money Arlen, Eula, and his in-laws had scraped together. His mother had helped too, as best she could, though Arlen hadn't wanted her to since cash was so tight. Their families had celebrated the closing with a big dinner of deep-dish pizza, and they ate it sitting on pillows and blankets on the dining room floor. That first night, when their families had left and the sun had set, Arlen made love to his new wife on the grass in the middle of the yard, with Eula whispering and laughing and saying, *Don't you dare*, until she stopped saying any words at all.

They'd been in the house for only two weeks before Arlen left. "I'm going up to Albany to see Cousin Joe," he'd said. He promised her: "A few days. That's all."

*A few days . . .*

He put his elbows on Will's beat-up desk, dropped his face into his hands. *Eula.* She was still there. What did it mean? Had she remarried and settled her family into that house—the family that should have been hers and his? Or was she alone?

His teeth hurt and he realized he'd been clenching them. Anger was such a constant companion that he noticed it no more than he might notice his own bones under his skin. But he never let himself be angry at Eula. Not in all this time. He didn't hate her when she stopped coming to his trial after the eyewitness had said, *Him*, didn't hate her when she never visited, didn't hate her when the divorce papers arrived. In his heart, he'd had trouble accepting that Eula was not still his wife. Though the shape and nature of his love was quieter, more reserved and almost paternal now, how much he loved her had not changed.

"Hey." Will poked his head into the office. Arlen tried to act as casual as possible as he closed down the Internet search before Will could see.

"Doing okay?" Will asked.

"Fine, just fine," Arlen said. "You should see what they get women to do on this thing. Hoo, boy. Seriously hot stuff."

Will laughed. "Just don't get a virus."

"Virus? I can't even touch these girls."

"I mean, my computer can get a virus," Will said. "A bug—"

"I know what a virus is," Arlen said, though in fact his idea of it was vague. "I was kidding around."

"Ah," Will said, but he seemed to be thinking of something else. Since Arlen had gone to jail, Will's face had gotten older. Lines had formed around his eyes from too much time in the sun. His hair had thinned slightly. Despite his age, something boyish still tinged his smile now and again. But now, none of that joy was visible at all—only a serious and somber stare.

"Look, man," Arlen said, "about the poker game—"

"Forget it," Will said.

"Naw. I can't forget it. I lost my temper. Wasn't right."

"Hey." Will held out his hand, palm open, and Arlen took it with a firm clasp. "We're cool? Right?"

"Are we?"

A funny smile snaked across Will's face. "We're cool." He let Arlen's hand go. "I had no idea Rourke could squeal like that."

"Tell him I owe him a beer. Or something stronger."

"Will do," he said. And when he glanced down, Arlen did too. He saw that Will was holding something in his hand, paper pinched loosely between two straight fingers.

"That for me?" Arlen asked.

"Yeah."

"What is it?"

Will held out the piece of paper.

Arlen took it, though he wasn't sure he wanted to.

"I'll just leave you to it," Will said. Then he patted the door-jamb twice the way a person might pat a sick dog, before he ducked out of the office, leaving Arlen alone with a knot in his belly and the notion that he could not stand one more thing to go wrong.

*Dear Arlen,*

*I'm writing to you because I don't know what else to do. I'm committed to staying in Richmond as long as I possibly can, to see you. But I'm under some pressure from work and family to get back to Albany. I hope you'll understand.*

*I owe you an apology. And you deserve one. I'd like to think that it might give us both some peace.*

*I won't take up much of your time, and I probably don't deserve a moment of it. But I've never been timid, so I'm asking. Please.*

*Lauren*

Jonah didn't call often. Normally, Lauren phoned him. He always seemed glad enough to talk to her, and if she let too much time pass between phone calls, he sometimes acted funny. But rarely was he one to initiate a chat.

So when her cell phone rang and Jonah's name appeared on the screen, she answered it immediately—with a quick apology to Will. He'd been talking about dating old furniture by the shape of the nails, and he stopped, mid-sentence, when she turned away.

"Are you okay?" she asked her brother.

"The better question is, are you?"

She glanced at Will. Above them, the wind was blowing the leaves of the trees this way and that, so the pattern on the forest floor danced like sunlight on the bottom of a pool. Will had stopped talking, speckles of sun and shade fluttering over his face and chest. His heather-gray T-shirt was slightly frayed around the neck; his jeans were ripped at the knees, faded nearly to white. He was looking at her with an expression caught between concern and uncertainty—whether he should stay or leave her alone.

She held up a finger, apologizing with her eyes and mouthing, "One minute." Then she began to walk away. Last year's oak leaves crunched under her feet.

"What do you mean, am I okay?"

"I know about your heart," Jonah said. "The palpitations."

She stepped around an old green sink that had been tipped on its side and left to the elements. "Oh, that. It's no big deal."

"Come on." Jonah's voice was pinched with annoyance. "Think about who you're talking to for a second here."

She came to stand under a tall tree, and when she turned around, she saw that Will had wandered in the other direction to give her some privacy. She thought: *I really do like him.* She watched him bend down, pick something up off the ground, his whole body tense with focus and deep thought. Even as Jonah spoke, she continued to watch him, the lean bend of his torso, the lift of his shoulders and neck.

"Why didn't you tell us?" Jonah demanded.

"So my heart is giving me a little trouble. It's not a big deal."

"You know I'm the last person to get on anyone's case, but there could be serious consequences if you don't get this under control. Unless of course you *want* to have a stroke and lose all feeling in the left side of your body."

"Don't be so dramatic."

"If you think this is bad, wait till you hear from Dad."

She leaned against the old tree with its thick ribbed bark. Fifty feet away, Will was leaning with his foot propped on a stone, his head bent reverently to whatever he held in his hand. "How did Dad find out?"

"Burt called and asked how you were doing."

"Crap." She turned and picked a fleck of dried bark from the tree trunk. "I wouldn't have told Burt about the heart thing— except that the alternative was worse."

"What was the alternative?"

She laughed at herself. "The alternative was trying to explain that I had a 'nervous breakdown.' Don't tell."

"They still have those?" Jonah said.

"Apparently."

"I thought they were called panic attacks now. Sounds more edgy and hard-core that way. You know, *panic attaaaack!*"

"Call it what you call it—I might as well have told Burt I couldn't work on the Dautel case anymore because my dog ate my homework."

"You're right. Dad wouldn't understand a nervous breakdown. You know I've been supportive of your going down there, right? You know Dad went stomping out of here the other day because I told him to leave you alone?"

"I didn't know that," she said. "But thanks."

"The thing is, I'm worried about you. I'm worried you think that telling Arlen you're sorry might somehow . . . undo what happened to me."

"Of course I don't think that."

"Well—I didn't mean you thought it *literally*. I more meant, in a cosmic way."

Lauren leaned her head back against the tree.

"You should come home," Jonah said. "If Arlen doesn't want your apology, then you can't torture yourself over it. Come home, and let's get you healthy."

"It's only been five days. And besides, I wrote him something. A letter. It could make him change his mind."

"But you can always go back down there if he decides he wants to see you."

"I'm sorry, but I have to do this. If I thought there was any real danger to my heart, I wouldn't be here right now. But I talked to my doctor about trying to, um, deal with my stress levels on my own, and then we can go to plan B."

"Please?" he asked. His voice was sweet now—that tone he took when he wanted her help. "Lauren, if something ever happened to you, I . . . I don't know what I'd do."

She wished she could see her brother, to reassure him. And yet, she understood just how he felt because after his car accident, and after he'd been arrested, she felt as if she'd lost him—and a part of herself with him. When they were kids, Jonah had always been her best friend. He'd understood her when no one else could because—like her—he could see the world beneath the world.

"Jonah, listen to me," she said in her courtroom voice. "I really believe that if I can just . . . get things under control down here, then my stress level will go way down and I won't have any more episodes. My heart will be fine."

"*Fine?* Fine like when Dad was *fine*, when he had that cough he ignored and ended up in the hospital for a week?"

"It's not like that at all. I'm already feeling better. Actually, come to think of it, I haven't had any *big* episodes since . . . since last Monday. I really think that coming down here for a while is what's helping. And I've got to follow my heart on this one."

"I'll pardon the pun, but only because you're not in your right brain these days." She heard Jonah sigh. "Just tell me this isn't about me."

"It's not," she promised. She heard the beep of her call waiting, and when she glanced, she saw that her father was on the other line. "I've got to go. Dad's calling."

"Ignore it," Jonah said. "He is not good for your stress level."

"Nice thought. But he loves me. So he's got as much right to lecture me as you do."

"Fine, fine. Call me later."

"I will."

Above her head, a squirrel was jumping from branch to branch, shaking the limbs like an animal twice its size. The sun had taken on a gold-green hue in the underbelly of the woods, glinting off rusty car motors and porcelain. Will was sitting on a tree stump some distance away, his head tipped back as he drank from a vintage canteen.

Though she knew she was about to be yelled at by her father—not only for being sick, but also for embarrassing him in front of a colleague who knew more than he did about his own daughter—it occurred to her that it was actually a very nice afternoon. And that she was glad to be outside. In light of—and in spite of—everything, she felt strangely optimistic.

She clicked over to the other line. "Hi, Dad," she said.

Will had never been squeamish about garbage. He spent more time than most thinking about the concept of trash—of *keeping*. And while he'd met other people—like the long string of his almost-but-not-quite girlfriends—who turned their noses up at thrift stores, he personally had never cringed to pull a gently used sweater over his bare shoulders on a fall afternoon. Most often, he merely felt grateful to have a sweater at all.

Back when Lauren had been a public figure—rather than a woman who had dozed off in his car this morning—she'd seemed like the kind of person who would be squeamish about garbage. But she'd surprised him. Now they worked together inside a building that had once been a mechanic's shop but which had been turned into a giant storage shed. Through glassless windows, the sky had turned the same gray as the cinder-block walls, and moss had begun to grow in the cracks of the concrete floor. He paused a moment to watch Lauren work. She was sifting through a tangle of plastic beads and costume jewelry that swelled over the sides of a large cardboard box. Necklaces were knotted with bracelets, jewels, and pins, but she dug through patiently.

"I didn't know you were into antique jewelry," he said.

"I'm not. But my niece is four, and she is all girl. Anything pink or sparkly. She'd go crazy for this stuff."

"I'm guessing your niece is responsible for your bracelet there?"

Lauren laughed and plucked at the threads around her wrist. For weeks she'd been wearing a bracelet that Dakota had made for her. "Not exactly professional. But I love it."

"Do you see her a lot?"

"Not as much as I'd like. But as often as I can." She held up a handful of costume jewelry: a turquoise and red necklace, a gaudy stone bracelet, a giant owl pin. "Can we add these to the bag of loot?"

"By all means," he said.

She straightened up and tucked the jewelry into a cotton tote. "It's amazing what people hold on to."

"Yeah," he said.

"Me? I don't keep anything, hardly."

"You must keep some things."

"No," she said. "I go through my condo about once a year. And if there's a thing I haven't used or appreciated in the last twelve months, off it goes." She looked around, hands on her hips, at the sprawl of *things* around her. "All this stuff, though . . . it's like treasure and garbage at the same time."

Will murmured an agreement. Then, in silence, they went back to work, turning over picture frames and opening boxes to see what was inside.

Lauren seemed to enjoy picking, more each day. She'd tackled the job with real enthusiasm and even hunger—Will guessed she approached everything that way. And yet, her enthusiasm would probably wane once she got back to Albany. The unexpectedly pleasant days he spent with her would be condensed into a few anecdotes to tell to friends at dinner meetings or bars. This—the cobwebs and mouse poop, the sunburn and sore muscles, the picks and pans of new finds—this was a diversion for her, a detour from life in the fast lane.

Will bent down and halfheartedly lifted a board to see what was underneath it. He wasn't usually so glum. In fact, he normally considered himself to be a cheery sort of guy. But, funny enough, the more interested Lauren became in picking, the less his own heart was up to the task.

Watching her reminded him of when he'd first started going through other people's things, when his mother would take him back-to-school shopping at the local thrift store. He would stand among racks of musty-smelling clothes, hangers scraping metal rods as he pushed them from side to side. One year, he'd picked out an oat-brown sweater that had looked good as new except for a hole near the hip. The sweater had pleased him; he thought it gave him a shot at looking trendy and fitting in.

But the day he wore it for the first time, a classmate recognized it—hole and all—as the sweater he'd donated last year *to the poor*, and soon the whole school knew where Will Farris got his clothes.

He'd had a choice that day: He could embrace other people's

things, commit himself fully, publicly, and unapologetically to loving their castoffs. Or he could be embarrassed, for himself and for his mother, who worked so hard and who wanted him to be proud.

He began to spend more time at the thrift store and even got a job there over the summer, to show he made no secret of his affection for recycling stuff. And he began bringing in fun finds to show off to his friends—skull-shaped lighters and old movie posters with aliens and buxom heroines. As long as he offered a steady stream of curiosities, he could sometimes pass for marginally popular despite being dirt poor. Gradually, he forgot the point he was trying to make, and what had once been a decision about what he stood for started to become who he was.

He picked up an old alarm clock, which might have worked or might not have. He'd been accused on more than one occasion of thinking too much about thrift, about waste. But sometimes, he walked into a store—a dollar store, perhaps—and he was overwhelmed by the notion that what he was looking at was little more than an organized landfill. At some point, each purchase—a toothbrush, a book, a frying pan, a wedding dress, a lamp—would make its way to a garbage can. The only difference between one person's garbage and another person's bargain item was a matter of time, place, and semantics.

When Will drank too much with friends who indulged him, he tended to go off about the inherent *wrongness* of it all—how the instant a person purchased a new car, its value plummeted simply because it was no longer considered *new*. *Used* did not necessarily mean *soiled*—as if a person's decision to purchase an object fundamentally tainted it. He knew his ideas made people uncomfortable, and so around strangers, he kept them to himself.

But now, with Lauren standing not a few feet from him, bent down and looking with absolute focus at the box full of plastic trinkets, he found himself thinking again about those old convictions, and he wondered what she would say if he showed her who he really was.

"Oh wow. Look at this!" She stood up from the box. Her eyes were bright with pleasure.

"What is it?"

"It's a ring!"

She was holding a huge, red glass ring—a fake stone so big it was the size of his thumb. It caught the light and sent ruby sparks flying against the walls. Lauren held it and laughed, delighted as a child hunting Easter eggs.

"What kind of person would wear a ring like this?" she asked, turning the fake gem back and forth. "Good Lord. Talk about ostentation!"

He smiled. "Does it fit you?"

She glanced up at him as if she'd heard something in his voice she didn't quite know how to gauge—and he realized: she knew what he was thinking even before he did. She loved the ring, and so he wanted her to have it, naturally.

She stuck her index finger through the ring band. "Looks like it's a no-go."

"That's because it's a man's."

"I don't know any man who would wear a ring like this. Unless he was a drag queen."

Will laughed. "In the early days, it was usually men who drove the cars."

"I'm afraid I'm missing something here."

"It's a blinker," he said. He couldn't help it: he reached for her hand and gently slipped the ring from her finger to try it on his. It was a better fit. And then, to demonstrate, he mimed moving his hands on a steering wheel, then putting his left hand out an imaginary window and flicking the ring so it caught the light. "See? At night, the ring would reflect so you could let other drivers know you were turning."

"That's amazing," she said. "But . . . what if you're turning right?"

Will laughed. "You make three lefts." He handed the ring back to her, basking in the warmth of her gold-taupe eyes, her sincere delight. "You have a nice smile."

She ducked her head, not quite a blush. "Thanks."

She slipped the ring back onto her finger, but her gaze stayed on him. She was considering him, thinking. And instead of shying away, as he'd originally done, he stood for it. He had the sense of being an artist's model, waiting to learn what he looked like through another person's eyes.

"I can see why you like this. Picking, I mean."

"It's addicting," he said.

"I just don't know how you part with all this cool stuff once you find it."

He shrugged and prayed he didn't give anything away. "It's like with you and reading people. You read a person, think: Oh, that's interesting. Then . . . it's over."

"Well, that's one part of it," she said.

"What's the other part?"

She laughed nervously. "I don't know. Self-preservation?"

He said nothing, but watched her.

"I don't see anything else in here. We should go—"

"No. Wait." He kept himself from reaching out and taking her elbow. He didn't want her to move, not even to turn away. "What do you mean, self-preservation?"

Her lips pressed together. "You learn to read people because you have to, when people don't really say what they mean."

He looked down at her face, and what he'd once seen as sharp angles and a kind of haughty blankness was softening now. "Why are you here?" he asked gently.

"You mean in Richmond?"

"No. I mean, why are you here with me? Today. If you'd told me you weren't coming anymore, you know I would help you anyway."

"I know," she said. "Because—"

"Right. I have a tell."

She smiled shyly, bent her head, and walked a few steps away from him. When she looked back, even he could see that she'd decided to tell the truth.

"I like picking. And, also, you're good company."

He warmed under her compliment, but the feeling ebbed quickly. "Good company compared to your guy in Albany?"

"I don't have a guy in Albany."

"So you say," he said. She might not be seeing anyone officially, but she was hung up on someone. It annoyed him. "Come on. I don't think we're gonna find anything here."

He stepped over the threshold of a doorless frame. When he turned around, Lauren was still standing in the old garage, half in a slant of sunlight and looking down at the ring in her hand.

"You want that or not?" he asked.

"What would I do with it?"

"Not everything you love has to be practical."

She turned it over, considering. "My brother would think this is really cool."

He felt some slight disappointment, though he couldn't say why. "Suit yourself," he said.

Arlen carried Lauren's note. All day long and well into the afternoon, it burned in his pocket like a hot coal. He knew that what he was about to do was wrong, but after Will had left for his latest expedition, Arlen had closed up the store and hopped a bus out of town.

Now he was tired. The bus ride had taken hours. He walked

the long, dusty roads through western Virginia, Lauren's note heavy as if he were dragging an anchor along the ground. The gravel road crunched under his sandals, and startled chipmunks scurried into thickets of brown leaves. He walked until he couldn't feel the ache in his feet anymore. He walked until he got hungry, and he thanked God for the first good luck he'd had in a while, when some local farmer had put a wooden bucket full of apples out on his front lawn with an honor box. He walked until the ache in his heart got to be so big that he felt as if the sun was going down inside his chest instead of the sky.

Finally, he came to his mother's house—the house he grew up in. Its severely angled roof was still pointing like an arrow to the clouds, its two second-story windows arched as if surprised to see him. There was a calico cat sitting on the stairs, blinking sleepily. A wide porch swing caught the breeze. On it, someone had placed a book, the pages open, facedown.

His mother's house. He'd inherited it when she died of uterine cancer, about four years ago. She and Will had been the only ones who hadn't given up on him—Will had gone to her funeral but Arlen hadn't been allowed. *Too dangerous*, the facility superintendent had said. And maybe he was right. Arlen had been angry that his mother was dying, but he was even angrier that he couldn't be there to take care of her. He was the one who should have been changing her sheets and making her fried eggs for breakfast. If they'd let him out, they would have had a hell of a time getting him back in.

In lieu of a funeral, a lawyer had come with a document saying that Arlen was going to get everything—which was mostly just the house. And for a few weeks, Arlen had thought it was a dream come true. He had somewhere to go. The idea that his mother's house was waiting for him to move back into it made his little cell more bearable—at least for a while.

Then came the notice about the taxes—that nobody was paying them, that money was owed. He realized he couldn't keep the house; either it would fall to the ground waiting for him to be released or the bank would take it back. He didn't want to sell, but he had to. It seemed more respectful of his mother's memory to sell the house than to lose it. He tried to find a Realtor to help him, but being in prison made the task daunting. Nobody wanted to work with a convict. In the end, the bank took the house away.

And yet, now, in the heat of a Friday night, he stood before it again—windows and shingles, posts and walls. Here was the house that he and his mother had called their own—where she had let him sift the flour when they were baking, and where she'd gone at him with a broom when she caught him smoking cigarettes in the old chicken coop out back. He knew he didn't have much time—that if he didn't move on, the house's new owners might see him hanging around for no reason and call the police.

But he didn't go. He'd come looking for answers—his mother's advice. In a certain way, he hadn't known where he was since the day he was set free. Of course, he knew he was staying at Will's apartment. In Richmond. But he still didn't know *where he was* in relation to things, to his old life. He wanted to see some part of it again, if only to prove to himself that it had happened.

The woman who let the screen door bang behind her was wearing a pink apron and flip-flops. She put her hands on her hips and scowled at him. "You here to see John?" she asked.

"No, ma'am," Arlen said.

"What's your business?"

Arlen put his hands in his pockets and slumped his shoulders. "Nothing, ma'am."

"What's that?" The woman walked to the edge of the stairs. "Speak up. I can't hear you."

"Nothing, ma'am. I just used to live in this house, is all. When I was a boy. Me and my mom."

"Well, you don't live here no more," the woman said.

"No. I don't."

Arlen knew that this was when he was supposed to turn and go. But his feet were like lead, and his heart was chained to the spot.

"How'd you get here, anyway?" the woman asked.

"Walked. From the bus stop."

"You walked? All the way from Heyger's corner?" The woman glanced up at the sky and shook her head, as if asking God to commiserate. But then, when she looked back to Arlen, her eyes had softened some. They were dark and almond shaped; her black hair was tied back under a colorful headband. She put her hands on her hips and sighed. "Well, my grandmother would turn over in her grave if I didn't at least give you a glass of water before you head back. C'mon up here, now. We'll take a quick walk around the place; then you'll be on your way."

"I appreciate it," Arlen said. Then he held the door open for her before he followed her inside.

**Lesson Nine:** Sometimes facts—the way a woman does her makeup, the way a man carries himself—aren't enough to clue you in to people's inner workings. In truth, facts can get in the way, leading you down dead-end streets and circling paths.

Some people believe intuition isn't miraculous; it's just the workings of the unconscious mind telling the conscious mind what to think—like a person whispering instructions in a dreamer's ear. But others believe intuition is a higher sense, no different from any other of our five senses. It's intuition that compiles facts and interprets them. It's the sense of rightness that you can't put your finger on. Without intuition, facts are meaningless. Trust it, whatever it is.

# CHAPTER 9

Most of the apologies Lauren had made in her lifetime were forgettable. When she stepped on someone's foot in a crowded movie theater, she said *sorry* with the same instinct that made her say *bless you* when a person sneezed. If she accidentally swore in front of her mother, she followed up with a swiftly murmured, *Oops, sorry*, as her mother rolled her eyes. And when she was talking to a colleague in a crowded train station or conference room, she said *sorry* when she couldn't quite make out what she'd heard.

It struck her that to say *sorry* was a kind of currency—a barter or trade. If she accidentally stepped in front of someone in a line, *sorry* would fix it, a little offering or sacrifice, before she moved to the line's end. But she wasn't entirely certain that the power of apologizing was a fair trade for what Arlen had endured. Prison life was no life at all. Arlen would have learned things he hadn't wanted to learn. Seen things he never wanted to see. While other people grew into adults by worrying about their jobs, their finances, their good friends—Arlen had not.

Lauren was looking out of the van's window as Will drove her back to Maisie's house. Today was Friday, and she'd missed five days of work. The more she thought of what it meant to make an apology, the less meaningful her offering began to seem. Perhaps Arlen was right not to see her. Perhaps she should take her cue from him, and simply go back home.

And yet, she still felt she had some business in Richmond, some reason for staying. She turned to glance at Will, and he smiled warmly. Her heart filled up with lightness and all her self-pity evaporated. Will was such an unlikely ally. He made her feel better. He showed her a different world—a place where castoffs were beautiful, where a person could stop for a milk shake in the middle of the day for no reason at all, where no amount of knowing which restaurants were trendy or which politicians were inviting her to their fund-raisers could ever impress him.

That was when she realized that *sorry* had an opposite—a balance.

Will glanced at her. "What are you thinking?"

"Nothing," she said. "Just . . . *thanks*."

The house looked like Arlen's old house, except not at all. There was the kitchen that connected to the parlor that connected to the living room where his mother had sat mending his clothes and watching game shows. And some of the furniture was even in the same place—the table in the dining room, the sofa against the wall—simply because the floor plan naturally dictated the position of certain things. But upstairs, Arlen could hear children playing and the sound of loud video games rumbling the floorboards. The woman's husband had lingered for a moment, quizzing Arlen to see if he really had lived in the house, before deciding he believed him and going back to the TV.

Now Arlen stood in the kitchen, drinking a glass of water and half listening to the woman complain about her neighbors, folks Arlen didn't know. This house was alive, vital. A family lived here. A family who knew nothing about him. He wished with all his heart that he could still be meaningful in some way to this house— that there was just one small thing he could claim from it as his own. But all traces of himself in this place were gone. And the boy who'd lived here, dreaming that one day he'd get so rich he'd buy his momma a new car—he was unrecoverable.

"Hey, now. Doing okay?" the woman asked.

He was embarrassed when he realized he'd begun to cry, tears that slipped so silently down his cheeks they could almost go without notice. He'd been so weepy lately, so completely consumed by his feelings. The only other creatures he'd ever seen that had emotions as raw and uncontrollable as his were infants. He finished his glass of water and set it down in the sink, as easy as if it had been his sink from all those ages ago. "Yes. Thanks."

"You come a long way on foot to see this house," the woman said, her voice gentle. "How long you lived here?"

"Until I got married. When I was twenty."

"Pretty young to get married."

"Sometimes a man just knows what he wants," he said.

The woman smiled. "Me and my Shawn been married going on fifteen years now."

"And you like this house."

"That's right," the woman said. Arlen watched a cloud pass over her face. "They said the lady who lived here died."

"My mother," Arlen said.

"I'm so sorry." She reached out and squeezed Arlen's hand. He held it for a moment, glad for the touch, then pulled away to wipe his eyes.

"Oh, hold on, now. I got something you might want," the woman said. "Wait here."

She disappeared, and when she came back a few minutes later, she was holding an old watering can, galvanized metal worn to dullness by dirt and age. She handed it to him.

"We found it on the property," she said. "Was it yours?"

Arlen turned it over. There were a hundred little dents on the bottom from when he and Will had decided to use the watering can as a snare drum. He'd caught a lot of flack for that.

"Yes, it was my mother's." He turned it upright. "You don't mind if I keep it?"

"It's had a good life while you were gone, but it's yours. Fair and square."

"Thank you," Arlen said.

In his hands, the watering can felt just heavy enough to remind him that he was holding it. He walked back out to the porch, to the flat front yard that was covered with patches of crabgrass and clover. The sun was gone, but there was still an hour's worth of light in the sky.

"You don't have to walk back," the woman said. "I'll get my husband to give you a ride over to Heyger's. Won't take but a minute."

"Thank you," Arlen said. "But I'd like to walk, if it's all the same."

The woman shrugged and looked at him a long while. She was about fifteen years older than him, and her eyes were full of wisdom. She held his gaze strongly, with resolve and quiet intelligence—as if she had something very important she wanted to say.

"You take care of yourself, hear me?" she said. "I know your momma's gone, but that's what she wants you to do. You're her child, and you've got to take care of yourself. Body, mind, and heart."

Arlen nodded, cradling the watering can in his arms. Then he set off down the road, with the crickets chirping in the underbrush and the frogs singing in the treetops, and the watering can swinging at his side.

On Friday evening, Lauren and Maisie took a drive to Hollywood Cemetery so Lauren could tour the old, old stones of people famous and not. The sunset cast a strawberry glow over the granite and marble headstones. Maisie linked her arm through Lauren's, and they strolled past tall obelisks and statues of angels and dogs.

"Here we go," Maisie said. She stopped before a little mausoleum that had been carved like a cave into a grassy hill. Marble columns stood on either side of a gated doorway. "This is the one where the Richmond vampire lives."

"Oh." Lauren peered through the bars but saw nothing in the fading light. Maisie had told her the story of the railroad tunnel accident that had birthed the legend of the Richmond vampire. One survivor, who had emerged from the rubble of the collapse with scorched skin and broken teeth, had given way to decades of vampire stories. "Well, we had Italian for dinner," Lauren said.

"Yeah. All that garlic bread. So we're fine."

They walked on in companionable silence. The evening was thoroughly still, so still that Lauren could feel the stillness in her bones. And as they walked, it struck Lauren that the headstones were antiques in their way—that a monument was a token that people kept to remember, not different from a locket or a photograph. She'd never been especially sentimental, but spending time with Will had been slowly and steadily altering her perspective.

She was beginning to see what she hadn't before: how fiercely people needed proof of the past.

Richmond itself was a city that seemed conflicted with its history. The capital of the Confederacy had not shaken off its antebellum roots—and it did not necessarily want to. As one of the major ports of the triangle trade before the end of slavery, monuments of the past took on many forms: here, a proud statue of a Confederate general on horseback; there, a replicated crate in which a man had hidden for days to escape life as a slave. In the middle of a striving and modern city of many races, some residents still referred to Jefferson Davis's mansion as "the White House" without needing to distinguish it from that other White House near Capitol Hill. Maisie, who had not been born in Richmond but who had moved there after college, explained it like this: When there were no answers, a person learned to live with the questions.

"I don't know if I like it," Lauren said. "But I guess I see what you mean."

They walked on. When her friend spoke again, her voice was soft, as if she didn't want to disturb the peace of the evening. "Did you give Arlen your note?"

"Will did."

"Are you sure he did?"

Lauren glanced at her friend, whose eyes were narrowed in suspicion. "He'll deliver it."

"It just seems odd to me. That he's making you work for him. If he's such a great person, why is he making you help?"

"He's not *making* me. Maybe at first I thought he was. But not anymore."

"So you're hanging out with him voluntarily?"

"Looks like."

"Hmm," Maisie said. "Interesting."

Lauren laughed. "It's not like that."

"Oh no?"

"What else will I do all day while you're at the office?"

"Knowing you, I'd say work compulsively and worry about your newest case."

"Exactly. So you should be happy for me that I'm hanging out with him."

"I am happy. I just think there might be a little love-connection thing happening."

Lauren turned away as images of the morning's surprising dream flashed through her mind. She could remember more now—the way the mattress bent under Will's elbows, his body like a shadow moving over her. The way he'd gripped her hair, held her face in two hands.

Will was not her type; she'd never dated a man like him. Instead, she dated only the men she regularly met: men with MBAs or JDs, good haircuts, and understated ties. She'd thought she preferred men who did gentlemanly things like buy her dinner or hold open the car door. But now she second-guessed herself. Given the fact that she was still single, perhaps she didn't know her type at all.

Although most of her colleagues were married and busy juggling a life of kids and careers, she'd never felt a desperate need to be romantically attached. She'd always figured that when the right guy came along, she would *know* it, fundamentally and perfectly, in the way that she knew things about people. But years passed, and this man—the one who was meant for her—hadn't made an appearance. Or, if he had, Lauren had been too focused on her career to see him. Most men were intimidated by her—she knew that. And while sometimes she enjoyed her own power, she also felt that it was a force field keeping people from getting close to her. She supposed she couldn't have it both ways.

Until she met Edward. Because he broke the mold.

For six months she'd cared for him. On their first lunch date, she was so overwhelmed by him—his intelligence, his movie-star good looks, his impeccable fashion, his taste for all things expensive, and his love of whatever was "the best." She started going to Phoenix as often as she could, and he would come to her hotel room late at night. Or he came to Albany. The conversation was light; the sex, heavy. They made love with the passion that they brought to their work, as if the conversation of naked bodies was a kind of debate or argument. She'd been so, so sure. She would have sworn on her life that he loved her. And maybe he did.

She dragged the sole of her sandal along the ground. "Even if Will is attracted to me—and, I admit it, even if I like him—nothing's going to happen."

"Well, why not?" Maisie asked.

"Because I'm leaving soon. I've put everything on the line to come down here. My whole life. I've got to get back."

Maisie steered them down the newly paved paths of the centuries-old cemetery. They walked slowly. Lauren thought back over her day. Over Will. There was a mystery about him that she hadn't yet solved—and it intrigued her, energized her. Certain things didn't add up or fit what should have been a relatively straightforward profile. She knew his core values—that he was a good person who not only looked after the people he cared about, but who went out of his way for them. Generosity like his was rare, a treasure few people could find no matter how many old sofa cushions they looked beneath in a falling-down barn.

But aside from that, there were blanks. He was closed off about his background. She'd tried to ask about his family, his childhood, his life outside of picking, but he was even more guarded than she was—and that was unusual. She guessed he wasn't always so standoffish—that he was only like that with her—and the thought was disappointing. She wanted them to open up to each other, if only for a few days.

The old cemetery was beginning to darken, shadows growing and reaching among the stones.

"We've got to get back," Lauren said.

"Right now?"

"It's getting dark."

"We're fine. Nobody's gonna bother us."

"I know," Lauren said. "But I'd just feel better."

"Okay," Maisie said.

They started back over the undulating hills toward the car. Around them, the headstones glowed against the dusk, brighter than everything around them, each one a marker of the past. And though she didn't consider herself overly romantic, she wondered if she, too, held on to things, perhaps when she didn't realize. She wondered about her own symbols, the things she got attached to. She felt her phone bumping against her pocket. And then she knew.

While Maisie walked around to the driver's side of the car, Lauren flipped open her cell phone and scrolled. She supposed she'd been hoping Edward would call her. As if words could make it right.

She glanced up at the cemetery one last time. The fading sky had turned the white headstones a soft yellow pink. The grass was scorched brown in places where the sun and drought had taken their toll. Without letting herself think, she deleted Edward from her phone. She should have done it weeks ago.

"Everything okay?" Maisie asked through the open window.

"Great," Lauren said. "How do you feel about catching a movie?" She couldn't remember the last time she'd gone to see a movie in an actual movie theater. She found that she desperately wanted to.

"Now you're talking," Maisie said.


On Saturday morning, Will and his brother Scoot, who was *Scott* when he was born, stood out in Will's backyard looking hard at the sky. The land was flat—about one acre with a wide oak tree that dropped fat acorns in the fall, and a little shrub that flowered hot pink in July. A small barn stood at the back of the lot, serviceable enough but needing a coat of fresh paint. Will and Scoot pondered the dome of sky above them, paint cans close at their sides. The clouds were uniform and middling high, a yellowish gray that could have meant rain, or not.

"What do you think?" Scoot asked.

"I think we better hold off. No sense in risking it."

"Suits me."

They put down their cans on the concrete patio Will had poured last year; then they walked to the old barn. Will pulled a strip of white paint from it. It was brittle in his fingers. "I guess we can get to rearranging the inside. If you're up for it."

"Yeah, I'm game."

Will hauled open the door; it scraped the dirt. Behind him, his brother gave a soft whistle.

"Hoo, man. That is a serious lot of crap."

Will laughed and stepped into the dark of the small barn. It smelled of dust, and dry rotting wood, and a thousand mildewing things. His heart hurt a little to think of the way the years had worn down his favorite picks. Wood that wasn't regularly polished would split and bend. Iron that wasn't given a fresh coat of paint would rust. Rubber left to its own devices would sag and crack. But he loved this barn, and everything in it. All the forgotten, broken things.

"So what are we getting rid of?" Scoot asked. He was older than Will, and bigger around the middle. His head was large and bald, and while thinning hair might have made another man look aged and weak, the whole family agreed that Scoot hadn't started looking like his real, tough-as-nails self until *after* his hair had fallen out—as if it was baldness that was his natural state and his years of having had hair were the anomaly.

"I don't have a definite plan," Will said.

"But we're getting rid of *something*."

Will looked around the barn, piled high with his finds—the ones he couldn't bear to put in the store to sell. "I suppose we are."

They got to it. Scoot began digging through the first-floor's worth of stuff, asking, "What's this?" and "What does this do?" and, "How about this goes to the shop?" Where the floor had been obscured, they climbed over piles—Will knew another person would think it was all garbage. Things snapped under their feet, wobbled when they reached out to steady themselves.

"What about this?" Scoot asked. He held up a tin car—flecked green paint and a missing tire.

Will shook his head. "That's a Dick Tracy cop car from the early thirties. I've got to keep that."

Scoot put it down. "Okay. This?"

Will mulled it over. His brother was holding a movie projector from the 1960s. It was broken, but Will had been meaning to fix it up one of these days to get it back to its former glory. He could probably sell it for a fair return. "Naw. I got plans for that."

Scoot put it down roughly. "You got plans for everything."

Will looked over his treasures—each one held stories within stories: the story of when he'd bought it, and the story of its life before it came to this barn. He felt bad that such amazing finds weren't getting better treatment in somebody's house, sitting in somebody's kitchen or living room, and inspiring endless conversations. In those situations, antiques like these came alive. But now they were dormant, collecting dust and years, waiting until they could wake to life again.

His collection had started innocently enough. When he'd first started picking, he'd sold almost everything he found, for as much or as little money as he could get. The point was just to make a buck. To get Arlen a better lawyer and to get out of poverty and his mother's house. But as the years went by, and Will saved up some money to open the shop and live in the apartment above it, he felt courageous enough to put his heart on the line and risk falling in love with some of his own picks. The organ from the old church in Fredericksburg. The rusty chassis of an Indian motorcycle that would never move again. And the keys—always the keys—that were so inexpensive to collect and yet endlessly intriguing.

When he fell in love, he fell hard. The items he picked seemed to draw from him a life of their own. And once that happened, Will was obligated, indebted, charged with the task of caring for the items because he knew nobody else would be able to care about them as much as he did.

He'd planned to use the old barn for a workshop, to refurnish, resurface, and repaint. But instead, as he allowed himself the leisure of collecting, the barn began to fill. And fill. And fill. And now there was no floor to speak of except for a patch, no loft except for a platform that was piled high with his things. The barn itself seemed to be growing tired of sheltering all these objects that Will had fallen in love with and promised to take care of. And Will was getting tired too.

"What about this?" His brother held up a little piano fit for a child. It was plastic, and not very old.

"That?" Will scowled at him. "Are you kidding me? Do you know what that is?"

"A kid's toy."

"*Your* kid's toy. It's the same one you used to bang on when we were kids."

"You saved it all this time?"

"Well, okay, technically it's not the same one. But it's the same *model*."

"So I guess we're saving it in case I decide to take up playing piano with one finger again?"

"I didn't think you could play that well." He took the toy from his brother's hands. Then he set it gingerly down on top of an older piano, a real piano, that hadn't played a note in fifteen years. He glanced around the barn and knew he wouldn't be getting rid of anything today. "C'mon," he said. "Let's get out of here."

"We're not done with this," Scoot said.

"Yes, we are."

Outside, the first raindrops flecked his shirt and skin. The sound of the padlock's muscular *click* when it closed was a welcome relief.

At first, Lauren didn't think she was being followed. She felt a noticeable strangeness as she walked through Shockoe Bottom, her yoga mat over her shoulder, her water bottle sloshing at her side. But she didn't think the pricking at the back of her neck was necessarily ominous. Instead, she'd written off the feeling as being residual guilt, a result of having slept in late on a Saturday morning. Not yet a week away from Albany, and already her routine was getting sloppy and soft. By the time she'd opened her eyes, her office had called twice and she'd had to put out two minor fires before she'd gotten out of bed. If she'd risen earlier, the fires would have been little more than match-sized flames.

So, as she crossed the street, she thought, *Guilt.* Guilt was giving her the unpindownable feeling of something not quite right. Rizzi had called to beg her to talk to Burt—to at least call and check in. And Lauren had said that, yes, of course she would. She'd meant to. She'd meant to again and again. And yet, there was always a good reason not to call him: like dinner with Maisie, like a hike through high weeds with Will, like a walk through downtown. She'd felt within herself a kind of loosening over the last few days—as if the heat had not only made her muscles slacken, but had softened her own definition of herself as a busy, productive workaholic. Each time she meant to call Burt, she thought of what it was that she really needed to say to him, and she found herself tongue-tied. So she did not call him at all.

Now she walked through Shockoe Bottom, through corridors of brick and mortar, past shops with tall bay windows advertising vegan sandwiches or massages. She passed big factories that had gone condo; stenciled white letters on red brick advertised flowers, rug making, and power tools. Some probably dated to the early twentieth century. Despite the pace of traffic and modern convenience, Richmond had an oldness about it—as if the present were happening on the backdrop of the past. Among the tattooed buildings, she thought of Burt, and work, and her dream of Will—and still the strange feeling of something she couldn't quite place lingered.

She stepped out of a patch of sunlight and into the shade of a small tree; then she shaded her eyes to look around.

Was she being followed?

She squinted behind her: women pushing sport utility strollers, men with canted heads talking on phones, children walking heavy-footed and pointing at things. No one was behind her. No one on the street looked dangerous. But still, the feeling lingered.

In all her years of getting the occasional threat of vandalism, she'd never once had a feeling of being followed. Not like this.

The thought occurred to her: *Arlen.*

She stopped walking, crossed her arms, and stood in the middle of the sidewalk looking around. In her chest her heart began to sputter, but she shushed it quietly—closed her eyes and exhaled. Arlen would have read her note by now; she wondered if he was looking for her—or, if not looking, then just being curious about her, to know what he was in for if he agreed to meet. Lauren stood motionless on the rounded tip of a street corner, exposed and in the sun. If Arlen wanted to see her, she wanted him to know that she was prepared for it. She waited, ready. She thought, *Come on.*

But if Arlen was following her, he didn't show.

The sidewalk was empty except for a few people, some walking Lauren's way also with yoga mats and towels. Some looked at her when they passed. Lauren stood until she began to realize how foolish it was to be putting so much faith in what was likely enough her imagination. Gradually, the feeling of being followed subsided, leaving behind it the strange sense of being completely and vulnerably alone.

She would see Arlen soon; she could feel it. She adjusted her yoga bag on her shoulder and walked into class.

Eula's mother didn't like to eat her vegetables. So twice a week Eula drove to the nursing home to make sure she did, coaxing her through swallow after swallow of corn, kale, and peas. Even mashed potatoes had become a problem lately, with her mother saying they were too mushy or too dry. Nobody tried Eula's patience like her mother—but she supposed it was payback. She'd never liked vegetables as a kid.

"Here we are, Ma." In the cafeteria, she set her mother's tray down gently before her. The room was quiet, soft voices not quite echoing but taking on the hollowness of a big space. Cheery pictures of lemons and oranges brightened the walls between the windows, and at plastic tables, senior citizens sat hunched over rectangular red trays. Eula straightened her mother's dinner before her. "Look. Lemon and herb chicken. And peas on the side."

Her mother gave a little frown but said nothing. They'd gone through this ritual so many times that she knew there was no sense in fighting. Eula picked up her fork and stabbed at the chicken. Thick globular sauces saved it from being dry as the napkin she used to wipe her mouth. She chewed slowly, settling into the rhythms of the room.

"I got a little raise at work yesterday," Eula said after a few minutes. "It's not much. But when I get paid next week, I can take us out to dinner. How would you like that?"

"I'd like it just fine," her mother said. "Will your husband be joining us?"

"What husband?" Eula asked carefully.

"Well, *your* husband, of course. Arlen. Is that boy coming too?"

Eula pushed her peas around her plate. She didn't want to eat them either. "I don't think so, Ma."

"Good for nothing," her mother said. "Men."

Eula sighed. For the past couple weeks, her mother had been imagining that Arlen was still a part of their family. Perhaps she'd been responding to the news that Arlen had been let out of prison. She might have heard his name mentioned by a gossiping staff member, and perhaps she'd seen him on TV. Either way, Eula ached every time her mother said his name.

She'd thought, when Arlen had first been let out of jail, that she wouldn't have any trouble coping. So he walked free. Big deal. What did that mean to her now that she'd gone on with her life?

And yet, she was living in a constant state of jumpiness—half fear, since she knew Arlen was furious with her and that he had every right to be—and half excitement, at the thought that she might see him again. At night, she dreamed he was in her bed, his arms around her as they both drifted off to sleep within sleep. And when she woke in the morning and he was gone, the pain of loss was nearly physical, as if he'd been convicted all over again.

The life they'd wanted had been snatched away from both of them by a court system gone wrong. Everybody felt bad for Arlen, wanted to help Arlen. But Eula? She was nothing more than the wife who hadn't believed in him enough. Who hadn't believed in her heart he was fundamentally good. The guilty verdict had ruined both their lives—but Arlen had been cleared of blame.

Some days, she made plans to go see him. Scenario after scenario flitted through her mind. She could hire a private detective, track him down. She would show up wherever he was—she always envisioned the confrontation would happen at a movie theater or a public park or some other place she could easily imagine—and she would hold her head up high and say to him, *If you want me, here I am.*

Sometimes in her mind he didn't answer. He stood looking at her with his gorgeous brown eyes, soulful and forlorn. Until she stepped backward foot over foot out of her fantasy and returned to wherever she happened to be—her desk at the bank office, the grocery store, watching TV.

Other times, when she offered herself, he kept her waiting a moment, as if the decision of whether or not to forgive her hadn't occurred to him until now. He needed a moment to watch her with hope and suspicion. And then he kissed her until they were both crying—because they were not too old, because they *could* still have it all, because the courts had taken everything from them, but not *this.*

The first scenario she could bear—the sight of Arlen walking away from her, the lonely feeling of disillusion as she came out of her dream and into the real world again. But the second fantasy— it caught her off guard. And when it did, it wrecked her. To think that he could still love her—and to know that he could not—was a torture no woman could stand.

"Let's not talk about Arlen," Eula said. "Let's talk about where you want to go out to eat dinner next week."

"Wherever it is, there won't be any peas," her mother said.


The Richmond coliseum on Saturday evening was so full of sights, sounds, and smells that it was almost too much for Arlen to bear all at once. Some concert was going on—thrash metal, and a band

Arlen had never heard of but whose music sounded like terrible fighting cats—and now excited stragglers were milling around the sidewalks, scavenging for action or drama.

In his regulation green shirt and cotton slacks that were too heavy for the warm evening, Arlen used a metal and plastic grabber to pick up paper cups and napkins. Someone had decided it was a good idea to hand out yellow "Richmond's hottest girls" fliers before the concert, and now they dotted the sidewalks like crumpled flowers. Some were wedged into sewer grates. He did his best to pry them out.

The church had come through for him, giving him money without asking questions and finding him a job. He liked the work. He liked the satisfaction of seeing a piece of garbage on the ground— and then seeing that it was gone. This was his third night of working at the coliseum, and he never quite knew what he was going to be doing until he got to work. His first day, his job was to amble around the concourses and clean up stuff as he saw it (he realized it was busywork, hardly work at all, but it felt good). His second day he was given a job that was more meaningful; he was loading equipment onto a truck—boxy black speakers and wires that seemed entirely mysterious and powerful. And now, his third day, he was outside in air that couldn't quite be called fresh, watching the kids in their early- and mid-twenties stand around looking for trouble. He felt a thousand years older than they were. And he looked older too, by how he was dressed and how he stood. Yet he was only five or so years away from the oldest of them.

He worked the street, cleaning. A handful of kids at the end of the road were laughing and monkeying around on a lamppost, playing at climbing. Arlen watched them. He felt a certain territoriality over the street now that he'd cleaned it. And he didn't like to see a bunch of hoodlums screwing around.

He made his way toward them. Though they were half in

shadow, there seemed to him to be something electric and pressurized about the group. They were laughing loud, calling out to strangers across the street, punching fists in the air. Arlen lingered a few feet from them, hoping that his presence as a person who looked semiofficial might be enough to make them settle down or at the very least move on.

But it didn't work. One kid, who wore an imbecilic winter cap despite the heat, mounted the base of the streetlamp and began to shimmy up with his two hands and feet wrapped around the pole for dear life. His friends called to him, laughing and cheering him on. Arlen walked over to the group and looked up at the kid who was by now halfway up the pole and wheezing.

"Get on down from there," he said. "You hear me? I said get down."

The kid slid fireman-style back to the pavement. His two feet landed at the same time, and he sprang up and sauntered toward Arlen. He was about the same size as Arlen, puffed up like a chicken and fuming. His jeans were two sizes too big. Behind the anger and testosterone in the kid's eyes there was something wickedly, dangerously pleased.

"You don't tell me what I can and can't do," he said.

Arlen laughed. "You ought to thank me. I saved you from having everybody find out that you're not strong enough to get to the top of that pole."

The kid tipped his head, his teeth pulled back in a sneer. "I know who you are. You're that guy who got thrown in jail."

"You ain't right in the head."

"You so totally are!" The kid turned to his friends. They were quiet now, sensing a threat. "This is that guy who just got let out of jail."

Arlen didn't say a word, hoping his glare was warning enough. His skin flushed with heat and his armpits itched.

"So—what—now you're all tough?" the kid said, his arms open wide in an exaggerated shrug. "Ten years of being somebody's bitch and you think that gives you the right to tell people what to do?"

Arlen threw down the plastic grabber and, in a blink, he had the kid up against a wall. In the back of his mind, Arlen considered that the group might try to come to the kid's rescue—then Arlen would be outnumbered. But none of them moved.

"Listen to me"—he pulled the kid toward him, then pushed him hard against the wall—"you little piece of shit. I say get down off that pole, you get off it. And I swear to God if you want to know about being somebody's bitch, I'll mess you up so bad you'll have to dig your balls out of your tonsils."

Arlen's teeth clenched. He didn't care that he spit all over the kid's face. He didn't care that people were behind him, telling him to stop. The kid was gripping Arlen's hands, his fingernails digging. His toes bumped Arlen's knees.

"Let me go, man. Come on. I didn't mean anything. Let me go."

Arlen blinked. He saw himself looking down on the scene, saw himself holding the kid by the throat, saw people gathered in a half circle behind them. As fast as the anger came on, it vanished. And when the blood in his eyes cleared and he could look at the kid against the wall, he saw that the boy was sniveling, that he was actually much younger than Arlen had first thought, sixteen or seventeen at the most, and that tears were gathering in his eyes.

Arlen gave him a little shove. "Son of a damn bitch," he said. He left his grabber and garbage bag on the ground, and he walked away.

**Lesson Ten**: The human face was designed for expression, and the human smile is especially expressive. We show smiles socially, as a kind of visual handshake. We smile to reassure. To convey understanding. To encourage. To laugh. We smile when we can't help it, sometimes through tears.

Take two pictures of a person smiling: one that is a nice, normal smile and another that is the same exact smile—except for being captured just moments after a joke. You'll know without a doubt which smile is the "real" smile (the Duchenne smile) even though the two are identical and even though you can't put your finger on why you know what you do. A truly happy smile comes from way down within the emotions: it lights the eyes.

Smiles have a practical function too. Smiles can be seen from great distances; they're big and recognizable. They were signals of peace from approaching tribesmen; they are still signals of peace across boardrooms and conference halls. Our smiles are banners we carry and hold high.

# CHAPTER 10

Lauren's heart pumped blood deep within her chest. Her heart was a miner that trudged down into the pits every day, rain or shine. It was the pistons and valves of an engine that operated by magic instead of gasoline. It was the heart that beat when she landed her first pirouette, when she learned to drive a car, when she day-dreamed about having a child, when she closed her eyes and slept. And Lauren believed in her heart like she believed in the earth under her feet—a thing taken for granted, a thing that would not change until the end.

But in the night, in the shadows caught between Saturday and Sunday, she woke in the film of a cold sweat, the sheet twisted tight beneath her. Her heart was a berserker, warring wildly against the confines of her chest. She put her hand on her ribs, wondering if this was it—if her heart would give up now. She panicked. She hadn't really thought her heart was in danger of stopping. Not like this. Not before she . . . before she . . .

*What?*

She lay awake in the faint red glow of a decades-old alarm clock, too afraid to reach for her phone. She waited, waited, hardly daring to breathe until her heart's wrinkled beat went smooth under her fingers and she knew that when the sun rose, she would too. She comforted herself: just a minor aberration. She'd over-reacted. She wasn't going to die. But still, if she was . . .

She rubbed her eyes to clear her head, decided to get a glass of water from the bathroom in the hall. She splashed her face in the sink. In the mirror, the woman who looked back at her was pale with faint crow's-feet despite an expensive skin regimen and a dedicated avoidance of the sun. She could see the past week on her skin—the days spent with Will in the hot sunshine. Last night, she'd passed out cold with her laptop open at her side.

She leaned against the sink. The frantic palpitations of her heart stopped as quickly as they came on. It beat normally now, but she minimized her movements. Just in case. All her life she'd handled stress, fatigue, pressure, and tension. She thrived on it. So what was different now?

Sometime over the last few days—when she'd been laughing with Maisie, or perhaps when she'd been digging up old farm equipment with Will, or rinsing the fine film of dust from the folds of her eyelids—a question had gripped her and not let go. There was, quite unexpectedly, the idea that she could be doing something different with her life. If she wanted to. But what? She'd dedicated her entire adult life to one singular and focused out-come: the reward at the end of the travails, her own private prom-ised land. And, since she'd so carefully laid down the tracks that would channel her toward a very specific kind of future, was it even possible to go in another direction now?

In the bathroom she stared herself down, patting drops of water off her face with a soft towel. And she wondered: If her heart was going to stop tomorrow, and she had to choose how to spend her last day on earth, would she get back in her Beemer and high-tail it to Albany to work on the Dautel case?

She held her own gaze and forced the question: What would she do if she wasn't locked into the life she'd already made for herself? The voice that answered came from someplace quiet and danger-ous: *You could do anything.*

The morning dawned muggy and hot, an early thunderstorm hav-ing swept through and made the earth steam, and already the bugs were flying frantically around Will's face as if tossed about in a small hurricane. At his side, Lauren occasionally waved her hands around to fight them off, sending the smell of sunscreen in all directions. Will had told her: *You get used to the gnats.*

They were walking down a long country lane—or, at least, a narrow clearing that had at one point been a lane but which no driver would dare run a car down anymore. The old road was thick with ridges of green-brown mud from ATV wheels. On either side of the lane, Will caught glimpses of promising old treasures in the overgrown woods—bits of rusty things he couldn't entirely see: an old refrigerator with the door cockeyed, a ladder that hadn't been climbed in twenty years.

Will stole a glance at Lauren beside him, and for once, he didn't think she noticed. She seemed distracted. She wore a black baseball cap; her hair was a tuft of ponytail that stuck straight out the back. She wore no makeup, and the sporty white sneakers she'd brought for her trip were now a healthy shade of eggshell. Each day, he found more to admire about her. She was tough in a courtroom and even tougher when she ducked beneath a porch or climbed a questionable ladder into an old loft. Of any partner he'd ever picked with, only she never seemed to complain. Not even when she was acting funny for a reason Will couldn't begin to guess.

"Why do you keep glancing behind you?" he asked.

She grimaced; apparently, she hadn't wanted him to notice. "We're so far back in the woods."

He laughed. "Right. If there's not a Starbucks within five miles, we've reached the outer limits of civilization."

She flicked his arm with the backs of her fingers, but she was smiling. "I'll have you know I don't drink Starbucks coffee."

"What do you drink?"

"Starbucks lattes."

He smiled. The woods were full of sounds, none of them mechanical. The air smelled green and loamy. He never felt safer than when he was walking down an old trail, with nothing but the sky, and the trees, and the occasional animal that lifted its head before running away. But a hint of nervousness shone in Lauren's eyes.

She glanced behind them again.

"Most of these picks are safe," he assured her. "We just don't want to sneak up on anybody."

"You ever get in any trouble on a pick?"

"Not really," he said. She glanced at him—the slightest narrowing of her eyes. And he laughed. He forgot he couldn't lie—or even fudge the truth. He confessed. "Okay, maybe a little trouble."

"Like what?"

He thought back on his past picks. Once, an octogenarian had run him off his property with a gun full of buckshot. The van still had a hundred little nicks in the paint. Another time, a man had come at him with a broken bottle—but that was before he realized Will had shown up with $1,000 cash, hoping to buy an old motor he'd heard was on the property.

But it wasn't always the men who were dangerous. Women, too, posed their threats. Some were reluctant to let him poke around on their properties—one had even called the police and then sicced her rottweiler on him. And occasionally he ran into women who wanted to barter with a commodity far older than the dollar bill. He knew what they wanted: he was a little built—enough to make it worth their while—and he knew they imagined *he* was the one who was dangerous. Only once had he taken anyone up on the offer, years ago, and that had been a mistake that left him hurrying out the back door with his fly down and his shoes in his hands. In some ways, he would have preferred the danger of a shotgun—at least with firearms, he knew where he stood.

Lauren was looking at him with that scrutinizing gaze of hers—he was getting used to it—and he patted her lightly between her shoulder blades. "Don't worry. It wasn't real danger. Just enough to keep things interesting."

"Define *interesting*."

"Biggest danger on a pick like this is raccoons. Little buggers are nasty."

She glanced at the woods around them. "So we're fine now. You know this guy."

"I know him," Will said. "Well, I know him some. We're okay." He saw her visibly relax. "Sorry. I guess I'm just paranoid."

"Any particular reason, apart from the obvious lack of sidewalks and pigeons?"

She fixed her gaze steadily in front of her as they walked, their reflections passing through the clouds that reflected in murky puddles. "Did you give Arlen my note?"

"I did."

"What did he say?"

"Nothing, really. He disappeared for a while. Don't know where he went. And he hasn't said a word about it since."

A muscle in Lauren's jaw tightened. "I thought he was following me."

"Really?" A bad feeling settled in Will's gut. In the treetops, a crow called, hidden by the dripping green leaves. "When? Where?"

"Shockoe Bottom. Yesterday around ten. I was going to yoga. And I don't know why—I just had this feeling that someone was following me."

Will took a deep breath. "Arlen was with me yesterday at ten. We were staining an old bookshelf."

"All right. Must have been my imagination."

He took her arm, stopped her. They stood in the middle of the forgotten road, tangles of Virginia creeper carpeting the ground around them. Will didn't hide his concern. Or his frustration. "If you thought someone was following you, why didn't you call me?"

"Because it was just a feeling. I'm sure I imagined it."

His grip tightened. "I'm no expert, but I'm pretty sure the first rule of self-defense is to trust your instincts. You should have done something."

"I did. I went inside."

He realized he was holding her; he let her go.

"You're angry," she said.

He took a deep breath. "What was your first clue?"

"Glabella wrinkles."

"Sounds sexy. What's that?"

She reached up and touched the spot between his eyebrows. "Here."

His eyes closed for a moment, and when he opened them again she was looking up at him, the rust-brown of her irises glinting like tiger's-eye. "*Glabella*," he said. "It sounds better on you."

She smiled.

"What else?" he asked. "What other parts have names?"

Her eyes sparkled. "The pad on your chin has a name. It's called the *chin boss*."

He looked at her chin; if she'd had a harder jaw, her chin would have made her face more soldierly than soft. He took a risk, reached out, and touched, pinched the nub of flesh with his thumb pressing the middle. It was firm and soft as a peach. "Hmm," he said quietly. "What else?"

She didn't smile this time. She was watching him, steady. "Philtrum."

"Where's that?"

"The small indent from the nose to the upper lip. Some mythologies say it's a mark left by the angel Gabriel, who touches his fingers to a baby's lip before it's born."

"Why?"

"To keep them from telling the secrets of heaven."

*Philtrum.* He touched her gently, and she let him. He'd never looked at a woman's face so closely before, and Lauren's held up to the scrutiny. Without makeup, she wasn't the porcelain doll she'd once appeared to be on TV. Her seemingly flawless skin actually showed freckles and lines. Beneath her beauty was her sleeplessness, her resolve and strength, all the pressure she put on herself—but also something hidden and tender. He wondered if, for all her studying the human face, she could ever put words to the way a person's features said so much in a way that was much deeper than superficial expressions of muscles and bone.

He dipped the tip of his index finger into the valley of her philtrum, the cradle of her upper lip. He wanted her mouth, wanted to trace his index finger along her lips and, if she would let him, push for entrance. Instead, he shifted his hand to her cheek. A safer terrain, with no name that he knew of to make his heart pound. He'd committed to drawing his hand away one split second before he thought she may have leaned into it.

"*Philtrum* is Greek for *love potion*," she said.

"Why?"

She looked up at him, eyes hazy. "They thought it was the most sensual part of the body."

"And to think I never gave it half a thought."

"Maybe you should."

He stilled. He wasn't so dense as to miss the challenge in her voice. But he had too much history with her—or at least, with the version of her that he'd found so compelling for so many years on TV and in books—to simply fall into bed with her. What did she want from him? A quick lay—a fling with a handsome redneck, like so many women he met on picks? Something that she could tell her friends about when she was back in Albany? A way to make her ex-boyfriend jealous? To up her chances of getting to Arlen? Or was it possible that she simply wanted *him* for no reason besides the wanting?

"Ho, there!"

He didn't have to come up with an answer. Hobo Jim had stepped out of the underbrush, and he stood in the middle of the lane waving his floppy straw hat around over his head and laughing in birdlike whoops.

"I got an old mattress back here," he said. "If you don't mind the mice."

Will pulled himself up straighter and he thought, *My God, I'm still fifteen years old.* He gave Lauren a nod, then held her eye long enough to tell her that he'd come back into the real world now, and that in the real world, things were different.

Hobo Jim's smile was as big as the moon from a hundred feet away, despite his long gray beard. He stood grinning like Lauren and Will were the most exciting things that had happened to him in a year.

"Oh wow," Lauren said under her breath. "Now, *that's* an antique."

"He'd probably let you buy him for a hundred bucks," Will said.

She turned back to him, and then she was laughing, and Will was too. If she'd thought for a moment that she might like to kiss him, she thought it no more. She gave him one last glance and then trudged through the mud toward the old picker who lived out on this property, the man who was shouting at her that she'd come to the right place if she was looking for a good time.


Nine years might as well have been an eternity. Nine years ago, Arlen had been a newlywed. He was going to night school for his nursing degree. Nine years ago, he snuck cigarettes outside when Eula wasn't there to catch him. He liked the band Pearl Jam. He got to a couple Redskins games a year, and he went home hoarse from yelling every time. Nine years ago, he liked when they had Christmas at his mother's house, instead of his in-laws', because his mother made better pie. He had no idea about things like prison tattoos, or gang signs, or what they meant.

Nine years ago, he had all his hair. The hardest day of his life until his arrest was when his father had showed up, asking for money, and Arlen had told him to go away. The best day had been his tenth birthday, when his mother had surprised him with a new bike and a cake shaped like a whale. Nine years ago, Arlen shone up his bowling ball once a week to meet Will and the guys, and once, he'd nearly bowled a perfect game. Nine years ago, the future seemed friendly enough.

Nine years was a long time.

Thirty-six *hours* ago, Arlen had walked out on his job. Last night, he'd fallen asleep in his clothes, rough cotton and hard buttons, and now his bed smelled like smoke and beer. In the refrigerator, there was the breakfast Will had brought for him; there was orange juice. In the bathroom, there was running water for a much-needed shower. He had all the accommodations of a good life around him now. No more armed guards. No more schedules and rules. Will had come through for him. The trouble was, he didn't think he could come through for Will.

He lay in bed, thinking. Was it worth it to try to explain to his bosses why he'd walked off the job on Thursday night? Were the police going to come looking for him after the boy filled out a report—*if* the boy filed a report? Was he going crazy, or did it seem that the longer he was out, the harder things got?

He rolled over, closed his eyes against the sunlight. He had no idea what time it was. He half remembered a story from when he was a kid, about a man who had gone into the woods for a nap and who came out twenty years later. Arlen had slept a long time last night. More than ten hours. He closed his eyes, listening to the sound of traffic outside the window, and then he slept more.

"So how long you known our Billy?"

Lauren sat with Will's mother, Jacqueline, out under the tiki torches that surrounded her white-limestone patio. Dinner had ended, and now the glass-and-iron table was strewn with paper plates, blue plastic cups of beer, and condiments. They'd had an impromptu picnic: two of Will's brothers, his sister, his mother, and his stepdad. Lauren knew Will hadn't felt completely comfortable bringing her along to his mother's house—his voice had betrayed his concern—but once his brother had called and found out Will was in the area, the troops had been rallied, dinner was assembled, and Will hadn't been able to tell them no.

Now Lauren was pleasantly sleepy, her belly full of carbs, meat, and beer. She couldn't understand why Will had been so reluctant to let her meet his family, or why he seemed so closed off to her at times. His mother and siblings were warm, funny people who obviously loved him. All evening long, they'd gone out of their way to make Lauren feel welcome—but not because they placed any great emphasis on formal manners: their affection was real. They cracked off-color and raunchy jokes, were suspicious of all politicians, and bought their potato salad from an old lady who lived down the road. The radio blared country music, the beer was sweet and light, and Will's brothers had made a big fuss over Lauren when Will arrived with her in tow.

Now the men had retreated to the garage to do something mysterious and manly—Jacqueline and Annabelle shooed them on their way—and Lauren sat together with Will's mother and sister, and the brand-new baby boy on Annabelle's lap.

"Will never said a single word about you!" Annabelle said cheerfully. "It's like you came out of nowhere!"

"Because he wanted to keep her all to himself," Jacqueline said.

Lauren laughed awkwardly. "I only met him on Monday. We're working together for a little while. Then I'm headed home."

"Where's home?" Annabelle asked, rocking the baby as she swayed gently side to side. Will's sister had bright, friendly eyes. Lauren guessed she'd gained some weight from her pregnancy, but she wore it well; she was healthy and glowing.

"Home is Albany," Lauren said. "It's at the top of the Hudson River. About three hours north of New York City."

"Oh, well, that's a shame," Jacqueline said. "Because it's been a long time since Will brought a woman to dinner—and certainly never as nice a one as you!"

"Are you an antiques dealer too?" Annabelle asked.

"No. I'm a lawyer. I don't practice anymore but I consult."

"You're a *lawyer*? What's Will need to be working with a lawyer for? He's not in any trouble, now, is he?" Jacqueline asked.

"Not that I know of."

Annabelle glanced up from the baby. "Are you my replacement? Helping him with the picks?"

"For a while."

Jacqueline looked at Annabelle with a crease between her eyebrows. "She didn't come all the way down here from New York State to go on picks."

"Maybe she collects antiques," Annabelle said.

"No offense," Jacqueline said, glancing at Lauren. "But you seem more like a modern type. Something tells me you don't collect antiques."

"No, I don't collect."

"Okay, then I'm stumped." Annabelle laughed. "You're not here because you're in love with Will. You don't collect antiques. You're a lawyer working with my brother but he's not in any trouble with the law . . . I know. You're Rumpelstiltskin!"

Lauren laughed. She wondered if Will was also getting the third degree about her. What she wouldn't give to know what he was telling them. "You found me out."

"Knew it," Annabelle said under her breath and smiling.

Lauren let a moment pass, then told the truth. "I'm here because I was part of the team that prosecuted Arlen Fieldstone. And I wanted to apologize. Will's been helping me get a foot in the door."

"Well, that's good of you," Jacqueline said.

"Very good." Annabelle got carefully to her feet, holding herself as if she was sore. "I always liked Arlen. How's he doing now that he's out?"

"I don't know. I haven't seen him."

"But I thought . . ." Annabelle's voice trailed off.

"I'm working on it," Lauren said.

Annabelle took a few steps toward her, until she was standing at Lauren's side. "Do you mind taking the baby? I've got to use the little girls' room."

"Are you kidding? I'd love to."

And then Annabelle leaned down to put the infant with tremendous slowness and care into Lauren's arms. "Thanks. Be right back."

Lauren shifted the weight of the baby in the crook of her elbow. She tried to think of the last time she'd held such a small child, but no memories came to mind. She watched him, fascinated. He had a slight rash on his cheeks, a flat nose, and fine, fine eyebrows. His eyes opened only for the briefest of moments while she settled him against her, and it seemed to her as if that small movement of his eyelids, opening them just long enough to recognize that he'd been moved, was a tremendous effort. His weight sank as she felt him relax.

"Mind if I smoke?" Jacqueline asked. She stood up from the table and made her way to the far end of the patio. Her hair was dull blond, dark at the roots but thin and fragile all around. Her face bore permanent worry lines, little horizontal ridges along her forehead. Her upper lip had the first feathery wrinkles caused by years of smoking. She lit her cigarette; it burned orange black against the dusk.

"We didn't always live like this, you know," Jacqueline said. She gestured with her free hand to the house, the property. The yard was worn in spots, punctuated by objects: a hot tub with a thick brown cover, a shed, a four-foot pool, a riding lawn mower, a horseshoe court, and a couple dozen concrete figurines of gnomes, geese, and bunnies.

"It's a nice place," Lauren said. "Comfortable."

"I didn't have any of this until I married my Robbie. And by then, Billy was already out of the house on his own."

"Will's very entrepreneurial."

"That's just a fancy way of saying 'desperate,'" Jacqueline said, laughing. "When Billy was a boy, we didn't have nothing. I used to send him and the kids down to the Elk lodge for dinner because I couldn't feed them. The horses in the neighbor's barn had better shoes than them. I worked my tail off—you bet I did. But we never knew where our next meal would come from or who might get stuck in the shower when the lights went out."

"Sounds tough," Lauren said. In her mind, she saw Will as a

boy—the young man whose photograph was on his mother's living room wall. He was skinny and knobby, a fishing pole over his shoulder. And he was smiling.

"Don't get me wrong," his mother said. "We were happy. Life wasn't easy, but I don't think anybody would have called it *bad*."

"Excuse me for asking," Lauren said. "But why are you telling me this?"

"Because my son won't."

Lauren looked down at the baby sleeping in her arms. She was conflicted to hear Will's mother talk about Will so candidly, especially given that Will had taken such pains to keep Lauren from knowing anything about his past. On one hand, she was eager to know more about him—to better understand—and Will's mother wanted to tell her. On the other hand, she respected Will too much to pry into his life. Because she didn't know what to do, she sat quietly. She brushed her finger over the baby's soft cheek.

"You know he dropped out of high school, right?" Jacqueline asked.

"No, I didn't," Lauren said, truly surprised. Will might not have been formally educated, but he could compete with any of her colleagues who had gone to Ivy League schools. He was as smart as he was intelligent—and all his knowledge he'd acquired on his own. "I guess he's more of a hands-on learner."

"Hell, no. He just about slept through eighth grade with all A's. Certainly didn't get it from his father's side of the family. He dropped out when he was a senior. Nearly killed me. But he wanted to work."

"I know what that's like," Lauren said. She'd begged her father for her first real job, a job that wasn't babysitting or shoveling snow. And he would have let her get a job too—if she'd been legally old enough. She was eleven when she'd written her first résumé.

"Once Billy decided to make money, he *made* money—know

what I'm saying? He didn't work at some five-dollar-an-hour job. He started digging around, selling old stuff. Used to pick through the trash dumps on some of the old farms, where the farmers used to throw the milk bottles. He'd shine them up with the garden hose and sell them in town. And it helped, you know. It helped me. He's always been generous."

"You must be proud," Lauren said.

"Yes. I am." She took a long drag of her cigarette, sizing up Lauren as she smoked. "You know he likes you."

Lauren was quiet.

"That's okay. You don't have to say anything. I just don't want to see him get hurt."

"And I wouldn't want to hurt him," Lauren said.

Annabelle came through the house's back door, and Lauren felt a shift in the air as she approached, a lessening of tension. She was glad for her return.

"He behaving for you?" Annabelle asked.

"He's perfect. An angel."

"I know I am," Will cut in. He came around the house from the garage, smiling cheerily. The wind blew his hair up in the back, and he pushed it down.

"You wish," Annabelle said.

The moment Lauren became the object of Will's attention, she knew it. She felt his awareness of her like a tightening from head to toe. He wore long jeans and boots—a uniform of sorts no matter how hot the weather, because of the perils of picking—but he'd changed into a clean shirt before dinner. It fit him snugly; it had some kind of scrolling design with words she couldn't read. She guessed he might have borrowed it from one of his brothers.

His face softened as he looked at her. "Can you stand to part with Louis and come with me for a walk?"

"Of course she can," Will's mother said, stubbing out her cigarette in an ashtray. "It's time Nona had a turn now, anyway, isn't it, sweetheart?" She leaned down to pick up the baby. "Yes, it is. It's time for Nona."

Lauren smiled. On her lap the baby had been a small furnace; now, as she got to her feet, the evening felt almost cool against her skin. "I could use a walk. Where are we walking to?"

"We'll know when we get there," he said.

Eula did not date regularly. Her friends who were still single seemed to date systematically and with a specific goal in mind, so that if a date did not promise to meet that goal or perhaps threatened to alter it, the contact was cut off. But Eula had no path she was carving for herself through the crowded and confusing world of dating. She'd been dropped back into the single life when—in fact—she'd had no intention of ever being single again. And now she was merely wandering this way and that, without enough love of dating to do it regularly and without enough hatred of it to quit.

She'd started seeing a man from her church, Mitch, a few months ago. She liked him a lot. His laugh was warm and his spirit was kind. His hair was flecked with gray squiggles, but there was a gold, youthful light beneath his dark skin that made his face glow. Her friends referred to him as "the doctor," not because he was one, but because he had a handsome, scholarly, thoughtful face like a kind pediatrician on a soap opera.

But Eula didn't think he seemed nearly that shallow; instead, it seemed to her that he had been gifted with the special kind of grace God bestowed on people who had known too much sorrow. If there was anyone she might talk to about her unending pain over Arlen—if she could force herself to bring it up to anyone—she thought it might be him. His wife had died years ago.

Eula's girlfriends kept telling her: the man was perfect. Why didn't she bag him up? And yet when he kissed her, she could not seem to stop holding herself away.

Tonight was their eighth date in half as many months. He'd invited her to his home. They ate on his screened-in porch, and though it wasn't a restaurant, he wore nice gray-green pants and a crisp white shirt. Tonight, he was obviously taking pains to impress her. He lit candles. He put on soft music. He cooked: spinach salad with raspberry vinaigrette and almonds. A few crackers with Brie. And a roast slow-cooked in coffee and soy sauce—a bit heavy for summer, but it smelled delicious.

She realized she'd been lost in her own thoughts for a few moments too long. The conversation had lagged, and she wasn't sure how best to pick it up again. She poked at her food. "The salad's fantastic."

"Oh yes. Pure decadence," he said, and she laughed. "It's funny. My wife made me eat so much damn salad. Hated the stuff."

"My mama hates salad," she said quickly. He knew about her mother, the dementia and the precancerous cells. She told him a story about her mother's refusals to eat healthy food, and he laughed where it was appropriate and nodded his head to encourage her to go on. He was easy to be around.

From the beginning, he'd made no secret that he was spending time with other women. She knew he wasn't having hanging-from-the-chandeliers sex with them, nor was he promising his exclusive love to any or all. He was simply fighting off the loneliness, just like she was. And she was glad to know she wasn't the only woman he was seeing. It removed some of the pressure to perform.

"Eula . . ."

Mitch put his hand out on the table. She knew he wanted her to take it, so she did. She smiled.

"Where are you tonight?" he asked.

"I'm sorry. I'm just a little distracted."

"Anything I can do?"

"No. I mean—thank you. That's sweet. But no."

She looked at her hand in his and then pulled away to drink the last sip of her wine. She tipped her glass toward him for a refill.

"I'd like to see you again," he said. He finished pouring her wine. "And . . . I want us to be exclusive."

She toyed with the cloth napkin on her lap. "I'm not sure I can do anything too serious right now."

"I'm with you there. That's why I like you. Believe me—five years later, it feels too soon for me too."

His brown eyes were warm and sincere. When she thought of what he'd been through—the shock of losing his wife, the wondering *what if*, turning to say something only to realize there was no one there—it was so familiar. In a way, she'd been widowed too. But her spouse had returned from the dead, and his never would.

She leaned forward a little bit. "If you want to see me again, I have to tell you something. Something about my ex-husband."

"I knew you were married before."

"But that's all you know?"

"People have tried to tell me things about you—all well-meaning people. But I told them I didn't want to hear it. I figure if something's important, it will come up in its own time."

"This is important," she said. "If you're thinking about getting serious with me."

"I'm not afraid of ex-husband stories. Or ex-husbands."

She took a breath. "The man I divorced was . . . is . . . Arlen Fieldstone."

He dabbed his mouth with his napkin and put it down on the table. "I see," was all he said.


The road leading away from Will's mother's house curved gently around steep hills and into the dips of shrubby ravines, so that

when Lauren got around one blind corner she found herself facing
another. She and Will walked by the light of the moon and the bar-
est glow of day left in the sky. There was no double yellow line
down the center of the road. No shoulders marked by white. The
trees and shrubs along the road's edge crowded in with such tenacity that she felt as if turning her back on them might give them
permission to swallow up the road.

They strolled along a steep curve, hugging the side of an overgrown hill. Fireflies lit up the underbrush, but Lauren hardly
noticed. She wanted to look only at Will, to better see what it was
that she was missing about him, the fundamental thing that she
didn't yet understand. She studied his profile: his high forehead,
the curve of his nose, his jaw that was neither strong nor weak.
Most of the men she'd dated had been of the devastatingly handsome variety, but Will's beauty was subtle, real.

She looped her arm through his and hoped the gesture came off
as friendly and comfortable. "So tell me," she began, and he interrupted.

"Oh, no. Why do I have the feeling I'm about to get the grilled."

"Is it profitable being in antiques? Do you make a killing?"

"Maybe not by some standards. But I do okay." They walked
for a while, slowly and without intention, Lauren's arm through
his. "The thing about antiques is that they don't go out of style.
With anything else you'd buy and sell, the stock goes out of date in
a matter of months, maybe years. But with antiques, the older they
get, the better. For the most part, anyway."

"Is that one of those recession-proof businesses?"

"When times get hard people start to sell things. Cheap. That's
when I can pick up a good deal, hold it for a while, and flip it for a
killing a few years down the line. That's how it's supposed to work,
anyway."

She heard something in his voice: he was talking as much to

himself as to her. She drew the logical conclusion. If he needed to reinforce his own rule, he was probably at risk of breaking it. "You keep many of your picks?" she asked.

"Course I do." In the near dark, she wondered if that was a blush creeping up his neck, or if they'd simply stepped into a shadow from the moon. "I like to hang on to the more interesting finds."

"What makes you keep something?"

He glanced away from the road before them, into the dark of the woods. "If something strikes me. Or if I know it's worth some money. Lots of reasons, really." She didn't miss it now: the way his jaw had clenched, then let go. "So how'd you do with my mom and Annabelle? Do I need to apologize for their interrogation tactics?"

"No waterboarding or stress positions," she said, letting him change the subject. She had no interest in making him uncomfortable. "Your mom wanted to know if we were dating."

The muscle of his arm tensed under her hand. "Did you tell her you're already seeing someone up in Albany?"

"I'm not seeing anyone," she said. She pulled her arm from him. "What do I have to do to convince you that I'm unattached?"

"You're hung up on the guy."

"I'm not hung up," she said. And it was true. She realized that even though she'd thought of Edward, she hadn't actually missed him in days. It was Will who took up more and more space in her mind now.

This afternoon on their pick, she'd flirted with him—or, at least, she hoped that was what she was doing. She'd never been very good at flirting. To flirt required a certain lack of directness, a willingness to hint and imply and be frivolous that she simply hadn't been able to perfect. Elusiveness was not a tool worth developing. If a thing needed to be said, she said it—without playing around. That was what she'd liked about Edward. On their first lunch date, he'd said, "I want to take you to bed." And the feeling that had washed over her was nothing shy of relief, because it was what she'd wanted too.

But today, standing on the road with her shoes getting soaked with mud, she'd wanted to flirt. To tease Will a little, to draw him out and see if she could make him want her. The trouble was, she hadn't thought much beyond that.

"It must be hard for you, in a way," Will said suddenly.

She stiffened. "Sorry?"

"I just think it must be a tough way to live. To see things the rest of us can't. To see the future."

"I can't see the future," she said.

"What I mean is, you can see a lot. Is that why it didn't work out with the guy in Albany?"

"It was more complicated than that."

" 'Complicated' is woman-speak for, 'It's not going how I want but we're having sex anyway.' "

"And you're the expert on woman-speak?" she teased.

"I do have a sister. And a mother, you know." He clasped his hands together behind his back. "You like my family?"

"I do like them."

"Read them to me," he said. "What did you see?"

"Oh, I can't do that."

"They're that terrible?" Will said, laughing.

"No! No, not at all. They're great. Really warm, nice people who are absolutely crazy about you and want you to be happy."

"Then what's the problem?"

She hooked her thumbs on her jeans. When she and Jonah were young, they used to do party tricks for their friends sometimes, just for fun. People would ask: *Does Kris Bronsen like me? Is Mrs. Dickerson really a lesbian? Could you go ask Mr. Oakley if we're having a test today, and then let me know?*

Most of the time, the errands and readings were harmless

enough. But when middle school girlfriends had started warring—Lauren still had no idea what had caused the rift—she'd been caught between two equally vicious factions, each demanding she scout information from the other side.

By the time she reached college, people-reading had become even more difficult. *What do you think of my new boyfriend, Lauren?* (She didn't want to say, *He's sleeping with you to piss off your sister.*) *Is my roommate telling me the truth about not taking the money I had in my closet?* (Lauren, as tactfully as she could, suggested getting a bank account.) *Lauren, do you think I should be worried that your father is . . . being unfaithful?* (She didn't know how to answer without telling a lie.)

Over time, she'd done her best to turn off her people-reading as much as she possibly could; she read only when she was in a courtroom or when she needed to know something. Between not reading Edward right and not seeing Arlen's obvious innocence all those years ago, she was beginning to wonder if she was in the wrong business.

She looked up at Will, and she understood he'd given her time to work through all the things she was thinking. He hadn't pushed her to reply until she was ready.

"It's okay," he said. "I was just curious if you see them like I do."

"How do you see them?"

"The same way I see a broken-down car that's been patched up with elbow grease and Hail Marys—and made to run again."

"Oddly specific," she said. "But I think I understand."

They came around a bend, and Will stopped walking, put a hand on her shoulder. "This is what I wanted you to see."

They'd stopped before a small pond—water so still and black it seemed to be less like water than sky. Stars were quiet overhead. Reeds and cattails gathered in, and a willow trailed its leaves on the surface of the pool. Fireflies in the rushes made the whole scene sparkle green. It wasn't a vista of a sweeping skyline or dazzling canyon, but it was beautiful—and Lauren loved that Will loved it, and wanted to share it with her.

"Wow," she said softly.

"Yeah." He stood at her side, looking ahead.

A firefly flew before them. Lauren wondered where it was going—what firefly errand it had to run—and Will reached up and caught it gently. He cupped it in his two hands.

"Look," he said. "That guy you were seeing, he was an idiot."

"You don't know him."

"Am I wrong?"

She thought about it. "No, I guess not."

"He'd have to be. To let things get . . . *complicated* . . . with you."

She smiled at him, something warming in her heart. His cupped hands were between them. The yellow-green flash of phosphorescence leaked between his fingers.

"Let me see," she said.

He stepped closer, bending his head over his hands as if in prayer, and she did the same. She reached to steady him for a better look, holding the orb of his cupped hands in hers, and when he opened his fingers a little, Lauren saw the lightning bug crawling around inside. She leaned close, peering into the hollow, and then the firefly opened its wings like a star unfurling and shot haphazardly back into the night. She straightened quickly to get out of its path, a little breathless with surprise and a kind of excitement she hadn't felt since she was a kid. She knew her eyes were wide when she looked up at Will and said, "Oh!"

She wasn't at all ready when he kissed her.

There was no gradual opening into desire. No slow-forming knot of arousal, no sense of the air going incrementally thinner, no bloom of heat like embers fanned to a brighter burn. Instead, she felt as if the black road had turned into a river beneath her feet, washing out from under her. Want and the feeling of something cracking apart came all at once, with a kiss that seemed to be over as soon as her sluggish brain caught up with her body.

Will pulled away, but not too far. He looked into her eyes and waited.

"I probably should have seen that coming," she said.

She hesitated, and she knew he did too—that he was second-guessing and wondering and thinking of doing it again.

"Will . . ."

She wrapped her arms around his neck, tugged him down to kiss him again. It was painful when she finally tore herself away. She straightened herself out—her shirt, her hair. Will watched her. She had no idea what to say. With Edward, it had always been so easy to know what came next—there was an understood direction. But she'd been so taken aback by Will, by the force of an attraction that had no predictable endpoint, that she was stymied.

He stood looking at her, his breathing hard. Frogs in the little pond chattered and splashed. There was no wind. Will had just made up his mind to say something—she saw the moment the decision flashed across his face—when blinding white headlights slid around the corner of the road, bright beams reaching into all the nooks and hideaways of the woods, and Will drew back.

They stepped farther to the side of the road, out of the way, and a red SUV pulled up beside them. Will ran his hands through his hair.

"Hey, y'all," Annabelle said in a loud whisper as the passenger-side window automatically rolled down. "I didn't want to go without saying good-bye."

Will walked up to the car, then leaned his arms against the bottom edge of the window frame. "Heading out?"

"Yep. Louis was hollering for sleep. Course, now that he's in his car seat, he's passed out cold." She glanced past Will toward Lauren. "Glad you could make it. It was nice talking to you."

"Thanks," Lauren said. She wondered if her lips were red, if her hair was okay.

Annabelle had a gleam in her eye. "I know you're going back up north, but I hope to see you again real soon."

"Great meeting you."

She refocused her gaze on Will. "You get her home safe, now, hear?"

"Yes. I'll defend her against the bears and wolverines. Did you drive all the way out here just to harass me?"

"It's a sign of love," she said.

Will backed away from the car.

"So long," she said, waving. Then she disappeared down the road, taking the noise and light with her. And when Lauren looked at Will again, she knew the spell was broken, that logic had set in, and that he would not kiss her again.

"Ready to head back?" he asked.

"As I'll ever be," she said. She rubbed her arms and, for the first time in days, she felt a little cooler, awash in night air. They walked the road they'd just come down, heading silently back.

**Lesson Eleven:** Practice people-reading long enough, and you'll probably begin to notice that it can be easier to get a read on a stranger than it is to get a read on someone you know. When we read strangers, we're willing to go out on a limb and make a wild guess. We have no emotional investment, so we're more open to seeing things how they are. But when we're reading someone with whom we've already established an emotional connection, the results of a read can be skewed.

# CHAPTER 11

*Dear Jonah,*

*A letter today, instead of a postcard. It's been a week since I've come down here. A whole week without being at work. Aren't you proud?*

*I have to admit: In between all the worry over Arlen, there are bright spots. Tremendously bright spots coming out of what I only thought was darkness. It's so much more than I could have wished for.*

*I might have come home today except for one thing: I think Arlen is getting closer to seeing me. I just have a feeling.*

*Also, there's another matter. A matter of the heart, I guess. No, not Edward. But I can't talk about it here. Suffice it to say, my obligation to apologize to Arlen feels like it's only the tip of the iceberg in terms the lessons I've come down here to learn.*

*Will I still be the same person when this letter reaches you?*

*Will you? I'm inclined to think we grow and change a little every day. Like I said: bright spots.*
   *LOVE so much and hugs and everything.*

*Lauren*


At certain times during his long incarceration, Arlen found himself conversing with Eula, telling her things in his head. He observed for her the way the light changed with the seasons—the texture, and color, and temperature shifting, a thing he'd never noticed before. He pointed out to her the guys to watch out for and the ones who were okay, and he described their stories. Sometimes, he imagined he was giving her instructions: *Here's how to get a jump on the lunch line. Here's how to plug your ears so you don't hear the guy sobbing at the end of the row.*

Now, sitting once again on the city bus, he wanted to tell her another thing: an observation that a bus was like a prison, with crowds of confined strangers, canned air, and people shuffling their feet down the aisle as if in chains. He told her: *I miss you worse now.*

After a short walk, he stood in front of her house. The neighborhood was imprecisely different. He could have taken before and after photos, then made a game of circling what had changed. Tree trunks had thickened. Driveways had been repaired or cracked apart. One house had been painted red. But the street itself, the black road baking in the hot sun, was still a gentle slope, a slight curve. And his house—*Eula's house*—was also unchanged.

He moved beneath the shade of a small tree, gathering strength. The house was large and white, with black shutters and striped awnings that put Arlen in mind of a domino. There was a brown package left on the front stoop—someone had ordered something; he wondered what—and a new pink shrub flowered next to the garage. The windows were all shut tight, opaque with blinds or curtains, as if they had been sealed specifically against him.

He could picture himself moving down the black asphalt driveway, to the front door with its half circle of window at the top. He could picture himself digging for a key, letting himself in—a nonevent. He saw himself coming home after work to this house, a bag of groceries on his hip, a little treat—chocolate ice cream or fresh strawberries—for Eula tucked inside. In his flannel bathrobe, he picked up the paper from the walk, tucked it under his arm—in his mind he could do those things so effortlessly, things that didn't matter at all.

*All right,* he thought. He coached himself. He bounced a little on the tips of his toes, like he'd once done in high school before a big game. He thought, as if there were more than one person in his head, *Let's go.*

But no sooner had he stepped off the curb toward Eula's house than the front door opened. A woman appeared.

She was small with wide shoulders, light brown hair that scrolled inward at her chin like curls of parchment. She was wearing a charcoal skirt that ended sharply at the knee. She was locking the door. She was picking up the cardboard box at her feet. She was talking on her cell phone. She was *Eula,* going about her day.

Arlen's throat locked. He felt weak with hesitation. In his mind, he called out to her, willing her to turn her head and see him. *Eula, please.*

She must have heard.

With the box under her arm, her keys in one hand, her phone in the other, she straightened up and looked in his direction. She glanced away, talking on her phone, then looked back at him again. He waited. Prayed. She raised her hand with the keys in them to wave at him, only a few fingers extending, before she nearly dropped the box. Then she was getting in her car. The engine turned over. Arlen made like he was walking somewhere. She backed out of the driveway, then disappeared down the road. The neighborhood grew quiet except for the sound of the interstate, roaring somewhere nearby.

*Eula* . . . She hadn't recognized him.

Arlen shoved his hands into his pockets. The sun made his neck sweat. The house stood straight-faced but pitying, watching Arlen go. He thought things through: there was only one conclusion to come to that he could see. If Eula didn't recognize him—and she obviously hadn't—it was because he wasn't himself anymore.

He wanted to know her again. And he wanted her to know him. But he needed to find the part of himself that was still worth knowing—the man he was before, the man she'd fallen in love with who held a job, who went to church, who cared.

He thought of Lauren Matthews, of what Eula would say if she knew he was no longer the kind of man who could forgive. When he did see Eula again—and he would see her—he didn't want anything bad hanging over him. Step by step, he made his way back to the bus stop, feeling like he was inching closer to Eula, to his old life, even while he walked away.

Maisie, who had the day off, insisted on taking Lauren down to the canal walk to eat their breakfast. They parked Lauren's car beneath a high overpass and headed down to the old canal, a slick of milky green water boxed in by white concrete. The sound of traffic seemed to come from everywhere, all sides and above. In the distance the floodwall loomed twenty-five-feet high, imposing and stately. It had been built to keep the James River from swallowing the southwest side of the city, and its surface had been etched to show the flood levels of storms from the past. Lauren shivered to see it—the impossibility of such high and raging water, when the only water here was the green murk of a two-hundred-year-old canal, lethargic as a dormant volcano.

They walked along the shoulder of the waterway, beneath low bridges and around angular walls, until they came to a few tables and chairs that had been set out on glistening white slabs. She pulled out a chair and opened her paper bag. Maisie waved when a canal boat full of tourists chugged by.

"So why did you cancel your trip with Will today?" Maisie asked, her elbows propped on the table and her bagel held between two hands. "Don't get me wrong—I love hanging out with you. But it seems odd."

"It is odd," Lauren said. "He kissed me."

"He did? When?"

"Yesterday. When we were at his mom's house."

"How was it?"

"It was . . ." She tried to think of how to describe the kiss: she thought of the feeling of the ocean surf pulling against the backs of her knees, hard enough to take her legs out from underneath her; she thought of the tug of gravity just as a plane's wheels come off the ground. She could not perfectly explain. "It was . . ."

Maisie threw her head back and hooted. "You're speechless? How do you like that? And we thought he *hated* you."

"Hate or not, he kissed me."

Maisie sat back in her chair. "So why in the world are you having breakfast with me instead of wearing his T-shirt and trying to find where he keeps the mugs?"

"I like Will."

"And?"

"Time's running out. I'm going to wait one more day, two tops. Then I'm gone."

Maisie shook her head, looking down. "You don't always *get* this whole romance thing, do you?"

Lauren was quiet. For all her research into human behavior—into courtship rituals—she simply hadn't had much real-life experience at all. Work had always seemed the greater priority; she'd believed that if she could establish a strong footing in her career, her love life would fall in line. It *had* to, after all. She'd imagined that love was a thing to passively invite and then to conquer. Once she was on top of the world, love would sit like a puppy at her feet.

At least, that was how she thought it might be. But all these years of working and working and working, and love had not fallen into line.

"It doesn't have to be so complicated," Maisie said. "What if Will just wants a quick little fling? Wouldn't that be fun?"

"Will doesn't *do* frivolous."

"How do you know?"

"His heart's as big as the moon."

Maisie put down her bagel, considering Lauren with speculation. "I think you're not telling me something."

Lauren laughed. "All right. Fine. I like Will. A lot. And I'm worried that what I'm feeling is just a rebound thing. Will deserves better than that."

"A rebound? From *who*?" Maisie asked.

Lauren looked down. "A guy I was sort of seeing. Edward."

"You were seeing someone?"

"*Sort of* seeing."

"For how long?"

"Six months."

"That's long for *sort of*," Maisie said.

"It wasn't like we were together every day."

"Because you work too hard," Maisie said—a statement, not a question.

"Because I have *ambition*. And because he lived far away."

Maisie reached out and took Lauren's hand. "Did you love him?"

"I thought maybe I did. Or maybe I *could*. But now, every day that goes by, I'm wondering more and more what the hell I was thinking."

"What happened?"

Lauren hesitated. There were many possible answers, all of them right. *I didn't pay attention. I saw what I wanted to. He didn't love me after all.* She thought over the past few months, the past few weeks of being without him, and it struck her that she could summarize all her complicated and unwieldy feelings about the situation in three little words.

"He was married," she said.

Maisie was speechless.

"He never told me. I didn't know."

"How is that possible? Nobody gets anything by you."

"That's what I thought too. But Edward did. We saw each other once every few weeks—I assumed he had trouble sneaking away from work to see me. But actually, he was sneaking away from his family, not his job."

"Oh God, Laure. I'm sorry."

Lauren nodded. "It's okay. It's probably better anyway. I always felt like Edward was in competition with me. I figured it was something we could work through over time."

Maisie crumpled her breakfast bag into a ball. "I think this is the perfect opportunity."

"For what?"

"For you to sleep with Will. Have a fling. Get this other guy out of your system."

"But like I said, I don't want to make things messy . . ."

Maisie stood. The frustration on her face was undisguised.

"Will's a big boy. He knows what's what. If you want him, Lauren, then why not go for it?"

Lauren took a sip of iced tea. Last night, the idea of going to bed with Will had been electric and imminent and thrilling—but here in the midmorning sun, the possibility seemed remote and much easier to consider in a logical way. Will was probably the only person she'd ever met who couldn't care less about what she did for a living. She couldn't impress him—at least, not if she was trying to. She would never be a trophy to him because of who she knew or how much money she made. And yet, when she dared to indulge herself, she thought maybe he liked her anyway.

"Well," she said, "if we don't have a fling, I have to do *something* about Will."

"Why?"

"Because. I'm thinking about him way too much. There's something about him I can't figure out—and you know I can't resist a challenge. Plus, he gives me this feeling of . . . I don't know, security? But at the same time, everything's up in the air."

"Oh, dear," Maisie said.

"What?"

Her face was drawn in concern. "That doesn't sound like a fling at all."


Will was having a showdown with an old lead glass lamp he'd found on the side of the road. The lamp shade was gone, but the clear crystal base was beautiful—really interesting and different. He loved it. He'd loved it so much that when he tried to put it in the corner of his shop where he stocked lighting, he found he didn't have the heart to leave it there, where someone might buy it and take it away. Now it sat on the counter and he felt that it was showing off to him, taunting him, since he could not let it go.

And yet, he *had* to. Some nights, especially when the wind was high, he listened to the old wooden boards of the barn creaking outside his window, and he worried that it was going to burst its joints. He'd packed so much in there. Each year, he promised himself that he would clean it out. That he would sell off the things that he really didn't need. And each year, he did not.

He looked up when he saw Lauren come in, and to his surprise, he felt *relieved* of a hundred worries he hadn't known he was carrying: the worry that she would avoid him, the worry that he'd insulted her, the worry that she would not show her face again. He hadn't meant to brush her off last night, but he hadn't meant to kiss her either. He was entirely out of control, and it scared him. He'd fantasized about her on and off for years, but that had been when she was more illusion than woman—when there was no actual chance of being with her. He hadn't thought it was possible for his feelings about her to be more complicated and convoluted than they were when he *hadn't* known her.

He walked around the counter to meet her. "Hey. What are you doing here?" He tried to keep his voice light. "I thought you were hanging out with Maisie today?"

"We did hang out," Lauren said. "We had breakfast."

"I thought you wanted a day off from picking."

"I do."

There was something different about her. She looked the same, but a little more conscientiously dressed. Makeup and nice shoes. She wore a black cotton shirt that looked so soft it seemed to drip off her. Her toenails were painted a color between plum and cherry, and her sunglasses were perched on the top of her head. She wore a khaki skirt that made Will's imagination flash: the hem of it riding his wrists.

He tried to put the image from his mind, and yet yesterday had brought a new intimacy between them that set his dreams crackling and spitting flame. All night he'd twisted in his sheets. He turned over the days and hours in his mind, appraising the minutes with scrutiny: the way she'd laughed at certain kinds of jokes, the way she stood up straighter when she was thinking hard, the way her arms had come around his neck. She'd opened up to him, more than he ever would have expected, emotionally and physically. During their travels, she'd told him about her family in the Hudson Valley, about her first year at her firm, about a pending promotion. She talked about what it felt like when her brother had been in jail, and how much she loved the judicial system—*believed* in it—but only if there were people who could defend as well as prosecute. Each day, she'd seemed a little more relaxed. Until now.

"Everything okay?" he asked.

"Oh yes. Everything's okay. No problems at all."

"Then what is it?"

She glanced toward his office. "I don't know if I want to talk about it standing in the middle of the store."

"Sure," he said. He gestured for her to follow him into his office where she would be more comfortable and they could both sit down. He tried not to imagine what she might think of it with its old couches and beat-up desks.

He gestured for her to sit on a love seat and she did; he dropped himself into his desk chair. "So what's bothering you?"

"Nothing's *bothering* me, exactly."

He considered her—how put-together she was. How cinched up. She'd been the same way when she'd walked into his shop seven days ago. But he knew enough about her now that he recognized the difference between real confidence and a reproduction.

"What do you want to talk about?"

She straightened in her seat with a little wiggle, as if she had an itch between her shoulder blades that she could not reach. "You kissed me."

He was ready. "I won't apologize for it. If that's what you're thinking. You kissed me back."

"I did," she said. She held his gaze, held it as if she'd taken his face between her two hands. He got up and went to sit beside her on the couch. He didn't think it was possible for a person's blood to hurt. But his did. It was an ache that had no precise location.

He risked moving closer. She was wearing perfume and he hated it. He hated her strappy black sandals and her mascara. All pretenses of the woman who had televised book signings and gave advice on morning talk shows. As far as he was concerned, her most honest moments were not when she was parading around in spike heels, but when she was standing in a beam of sunlight that made her hair shine the color of claret, when she turned to look at him over her shoulder, smiling, and calling for him to see what she found. He liked her better when she was sweaty and exhausted. He wanted to make her be that way.

"What do you want from me?" he asked.

"I want you to kiss me again. For starters," she said, her voice as even and practiced as if she were reading from a teleprompter.

He didn't like it. He didn't move. "And then?"

"And then I go back to Albany."

He hesitated. He supposed he should be happy. He knew he couldn't have a relationship with her, with any woman. The fact that Lauren wasn't looking for anything serious should have been a relief—he could have her and work her out of his fantasies, so that when she left, she *left*, and hopefully took his twisted-up affection with her. It was the perfect setup. And yet, he felt heavy to think of the road ahead: a few days, or even hours, of pleasure, and then—withdrawal. Some part of him cried out to protect himself. And yet, some other voice told him, *Now is all you have.*

He waited too long.

She stood. "Forget I said anything."

He grabbed her wrist. "Wait."

She was standing a foot to his left, looking down at him with a crease between her eyebrows. "Wait," he said again. He couldn't bring himself to stand, to embrace her. It seemed wrong—too intimate in some way. For a moment, he felt caught between desire, propriety, the question of allowances and offerings. His blood was beating hot, the first shimmery fibers of arousal coalescing, tightening, and yet all he could do was hang on to her wrist like it was the rope his life depended on. At his eye level, the hem of her skirt—so blunt and practical—stood in contrast to the curves of her legs.

He felt *lost*. He looked up at her face, where that placid and protected look she sometimes wore was on the brink of cracking, and he wanted to crack it. So, with his free hand, he brushed the backs of his knuckles along her skin, along the unnamed province between the front of her thighs and the insides. Her skin pebbled, her muscles jumped, and he found the back of her knee with his fingers.

"Will . . ."

He looked up to watch her, and he gripped her wrist more tightly. He brushed the skin above her knee, ran the pads of his fingers behind it, felt the expanse of her thigh beneath his palm. She didn't stop him. Beneath her soft skin were rivers of hardened muscle. His fingertips brushed along goose bumps. He gave her plenty of warning, plenty of time to reach out and say *Stop*. But she held still. His hand moved higher, past the thickest part of her thigh, her head fell back, and he found the truth: she wanted him. Now. At least, for this moment, she did.

He moved closer to the edge of the sofa, but would not let her sit. Not even when her muscles began to tremble. Not even when her legs began to shake and she gripped his shoulders to stay on her heels. She steadied herself on his shoulder. He held her hip with one hand, fascinated by the quickening of her breath, the whimpers in the back of her throat, the heat that meant there was nothing in the world for her, no sensation but those he gave. Moments passed that might have been hours—until she cried out, nails digging into his neck, and her body jerked forward. He stood fast, held her up just as she went slack against him. Her breath was ragged in his ear.

He didn't know how long they were standing there while she waited to recover. He closed his eyes and leaned into her—the pain of his own desire burning, the minutes taut.

Later, he would wonder about the order of events—if he'd opened his eyes before Arlen had come through the door and said, *Oh,* or if he'd opened them after. He would wonder if Lauren had pulled down her skirt to cover herself, if she'd even needed to, or if she hadn't thought that fast. But in the moment, there was only Arlen's face, the confusion, then embarrassment, then disgust, then anger—frames of emotions on a reel. And Lauren was turning around in his arms calling, *"Wait!"* but Arlen was leaving, the moment clipped short. And then the two of them were alone again.

"Don't worry," Will said. "I don't think he realized."

When she spoke, she was breathless. "He realized," she said.

**Lesson Twelve:** Body language isn't just an unconscious outward reflection of our internal thoughts. It's language, just like words are language. By communicating with our bodies—the nodding of our heads, a hand placed jauntily on the hip—we can speak volumes to others without saying a word.

Nowhere is the language of the body more important, and perhaps more innate, than during sex. Sometimes, nearly all communication during sex is nonverbal. We tell our lovers: *Yes, like that. No, like this. Here. There. Wait. Please. Now.* And yet the whole conversation often moves forward without a spoken word. The language of love is a language of the body; when we connect with someone deeply, chemically, spiritually, the body just knows.

# CHAPTER 12

Not everyone who heard that Arlen Fieldstone was innocent believed that justice had gone wrong. After the retrial, Lauren had sought out her ex-colleagues who still worked in the prosecutor's office. The head prosecutor was an acquaintance with whom she was sometimes friendly: she'd gone to his house for a New Year's party, and she knew all his children's names. She'd asked, *Shouldn't the state make a formal apology?* To her surprise, her friend—who had been sitting behind his desk and drinking a fast-food milk shake at the time—laughed.

"Apologize?" he'd said. "For what?"

As far as he and his compatriots were concerned, Arlen's original trial had gone off without a hitch and Lauren was beyond reproach for her part in it. Sure, the jury had put the wrong guy behind bars. But as far as the prosecution was concerned, Arlen's conviction was proof not of the system's failure, but of its success. During the first trial, the jury had found Arlen guilty based on what evidence they had—evidence that had been compelling enough to make them conclude he was guilty beyond reasonable doubt. If they'd found him *not* guilty based on such airtight evidence, the jury would have been either stupid or bribed.

"But Arlen wasn't guilty," Lauren had said.

And he'd shrugged. Actually shrugged. "I know he wasn't guilty. And now he's being let out of prison and he'll be compensated. As far as I can tell, that means the system's working. You're making this into too big a deal."

Though she'd suspected him of trying to make her feel better, Lauren had decided that day that *someone* needed to apologize to Arlen Fieldstone. And that it probably needed to be her.

But now, with the feel of Will's hand still burned on her skin, she wondered if she was doing more harm in Arlen's life than good.

She stepped out into bright sun that made her squint, not yet fully trusting her muscles to carry her weight. She walked fast toward her car—it was parked down the street—and she fumbled for her sunglasses only to realize they were perched on her head. At one point, she paused, leaned against a wall. She wanted the afternoon to freeze, to stop, because it was going by so unexpectedly that she couldn't get a firm grip on it. She felt as if she'd just been lifted high out of her body, out of normal life, and then dropped like a thousand gallons of water to splash back down into it. And yet, here was the day—doing its usual thing. Going on.

She dug her cell phone out of her bag and saw that she had a new voice mail. Her boss. She didn't listen to it; she called him back.

"Burt."

"There you are," Burt said. "Haven't you been getting my e-mails?"

"I didn't check them yet today . . ."

She heard him say something to his assistant, then—the sound of a closing door. "I'm worried about you, Lauren."

"About my heart?"

"Yes. But other things too."

"My heart's going to be fine. I just have to get some things under control. I'm really close," she said. And yet, she'd seen Arlen's face—the disbelief, then the anger. She wondered how much he'd seen. Anything at all was too much.

"What exactly are you doing down there in Richmond?" Burt asked. "I thought I was giving you time off for your health, but you're down south on some pleasure trip?"

Lauren hesitated.

"Come on, Lauren. We know I'm your boss. But I'm your friend too. I wouldn't be calling you if I wasn't. Believe me."

"Honestly?" Lauren leaned her shoulder against the brick of an ice cream shop. "I thought I came down here just to apologize to Arlen Fieldstone. But now I think there's something more."

"So . . . what? This is some soul-searching mission?" Burt asked, his voice tight with frustration. "You're going to throw everything away?"

"Of course no—"

"You're going to quit doing real work and pick up cases for one of those ramshackle 501(c)3s that try to break criminals out of jail."

Lauren paused. "That hadn't even occurred to me."

"Bunch of hippies," Burt scoffed. She bristled, but bit her tongue. "They undermine the system. And anyway, Lauren, you're *already* doing good in the world. You help defend defendants. If you weren't looking out for the underdog, who would? Isn't that giving back?"

Lauren drummed her fingers on the wall behind her. Burt

seemed to be ahead of her in some way, so that she was racing to catch up with him. He seemed to know a thing about her that, until this moment, she herself hadn't known. She worried that she wasn't doing enough good in the world.

But she was . . . wasn't she?

She heard Burt's sigh. "How long have we known each other now—professionally? Over ten years? Since before you took our breath away with your work on the Fieldstone trial. And in all that time, you've worked so hard to get where you are. The only thing you've ever wanted was to be a partner here. And now that you're finally a few steps away . . . you're panicking."

"I'm not panicking. I earned this promotion. I *deserve* it."

"You deserve it if you can handle the pressure."

"I can," she said, annoyed now that she needed to assure him— as if her track record gave him room to doubt. She shouldn't need to justify her work ethic with lip service; apart from Arlen, her success spoke for itself.

"I *thought* you could handle the pressure," Burt said. "But now I'm not so sure. I've seen this before. The stress . . . it can wear you down. And that can lead to self-sabotage. I don't want to see you self-sabotaging, Lauren. I want to see you succeed."

"That makes two of us."

"Then come back. You have to."

"I will."

"No—I'm saying, *you have to*. Now. Bryce convinced the board to move the vote to Tuesday."

"What? That's two days away. They can't do that."

"Well, they did. Lauren, you know you're a shoo-in. But if you're not here, there's a good chance you'll lose your support and the votes will swing the other way. I can only do so much."

Lauren shut her eyes and, for a moment, blocked out all of Richmond. She thought of her office, with its silver desk lamp, bright windows, and shelves of books—her office that sometimes felt more lived in than her own living room. She thought of her clients at the pharmaceutical company—they'd been depending on her firm to help defend them against unreasonable claims. She thought of how good it would feel to walk through the hallways of her office—like she *owned* it.

When she was a partner, she would be the sole owner of her time. She wouldn't have any boss to answer to. She wouldn't need to defend her life's work because she'd taken a week off. She wouldn't have to justify herself to her father. She would be the captain of her fate—finally—when she was a partner. Her mind was focused and clear.

"I'll be back before the vote," she said. "I promise. Can you and Rizzi watch my back until then?"

"You know you've got my support."

"Thanks," she said. "By the way, my father didn't put you up to this, did he?"

"He doesn't know I'm calling."

Lauren knew a nonanswer when she heard one. But she said, "Okay. I'll see you soon."

By the time she hung up the phone, her blood was beating normally, aftershocks of pleasure now merely the faintest echoes of thunder long after a storm. Her heart in her chest had settled into its old spot, fixed firmly as an anchor. She pushed back her hair, started forward, and rejoined the foot traffic on the sidewalk as she headed to her car.

An hour passed, then two. Will stayed at the antiques shop, sorting, dusting, taking pictures of things to post and auction on the Web. He heard Arlen upstairs, his feet making the boards creak. Will was torn between staying out of Arlen's way and going to speak with him. He didn't debate with himself, vacillating this way and that, but instead he was squarely wedged between both the notion of going and the notion of leaving Arlen alone. He owed Arlen an explanation. And yet, there wasn't much to explain.

As he worked, his fingers fumbled. His brain had drifted a million miles away from his body. Lauren—her eyelids heavy, her lips parted, her head lolling so her hair fell across her cheek—was burned on his retinas. And instead of feeling satisfied or triumphant over what he'd just achieved, or what he'd just made *her* achieve, he was instead feeling strangely let down. He got what he wanted and found it wasn't what he'd wanted at all. He needed something else. Something more.

He was on the telephone with a friend, trying to get a quote on an old gumball machine, when he realized that Arlen was in the store. He appeared like a ghost might appear, in silence and with a vacant stare. He must have walked with purposeful soundlessness down from his apartment.

Will got off the phone quickly. "Arlen."

Arlen nodded.

Will wasn't quite sure what to say. And when he opened his mouth to speak, Arlen held up his hand.

"I'm gonna stop you right there," Arlen said. "I didn't see anything. And I don't want to know."

Will pressed his lips together, uncertain of everything except that it was Arlen who needed to lead the conversation.

When his friend spoke again, his voice was quiet. "What if we get out of here for a while? Go do something."

"Yeah," Will said. "Let's."

Though it was the middle of the afternoon, and so hot that even the glint of sun off the roof of a car was offensive, Will drove them to Byrd Park. They went in relative silence, talking here and there only when necessary. Will went out of his way to park in a shady spot, and then they got out to walk for a while. Arlen looked around with passive interest at horseback riders, joggers, and picnicking families—all trying to make the most of the afternoon despite the heat. Will felt sweat trickling down his back.

"Wanna sit?" he asked. He gestured to a bench under the browning leaves of an old tree.

"Yeah."

They sat together on opposite sides of the bench. Amid gentle, rolling hills, a gray lake sprawled and steamed under the summer sun. Houses dotted the periphery, just visible through the trees. A few Canada geese glided lazily on the water.

Arlen cleared his throat to speak. "So, all I'm asking here . . . is why *her*?"

Will started to say, *I don't know*. But he did know. He knew exactly. He'd known since way back when, since he'd first seen her on television when Arlen was tried. He put his hands in the loose pockets of his cargo shorts. "I feel like this is the part where I promise to stay away from her."

"And . . . ?"

"And I don't know if I can."

Arlen gave a low laugh. On the lake, a few ducks began a noisy argument, splashing water with their wings, then settling down.

"Are you going to ask me to steer clear?" Will asked.

"Naw."

"Why not?"

Arlen put his arm over the back of the bench, sprawling out in the heat. "Not my business. And besides, not for nothing, but she'll be outta here soon. She's only gonna stick around for so long. That's what the note said."

Will looked down. A goose was wandering toward them cautiously, probably looking for food. It stopped about ten feet away and settled in to watch them.

"An eavesdropper," Will said.

Arlen didn't reply—and Will hadn't expected him to. But he wished it were easier to talk to his old friend. Arlen's stint in prison had erected a wall of bricks between him and the rest of the world, and Will wished that he knew a way to break through it.

"Hey, remember that time we got that old moose head and scared your mom?" Will asked.

"What made you think of that?"

"The goose, I guess. Taxidermy."

Arlen chuckled, shaking his head. "The moose head. Yeah. We could hardly carry it—the two of us."

"But we did," Will said. Arlen's mother had been having dinner with a couple of ladies from her church, and Will and Arlen had found the stuffed head left out on the curb with somebody's garbage. They'd walked it to and fro past the window until they heard one of the women shriek. "It was worth the grounding."

"Yeah. Getting in trouble was fun back then." Arlen glanced at him across the bench, then looked back to the low and thirsty lake. "I should tell you I lost my job."

"At the coliseum?"

"Yep."

"What happened?"

Arlen shrugged. "I did something stupid."

Will didn't ask for details; he didn't need them. "Did they fire you?"

"No. I just left. And I didn't tell the church people yet. But I'm sure they already know."

"Will they cut off the money they're giving you?"

"Doubt it. They're real salt-of-the-earth types. Anyway, I just wanted you to know."

"Well, you're welcome to keep working for me."

"I appreciate it. I do."

"Why do I get the feeling there's a *but* in there somewhere?"

Arlen sighed heavily. He picked up the white front of his shirt and fanned it up and down. "All these handouts. All the help. I'm grateful; I really am. But I keep on wondering, when's it gonna be that I give the handout? That I can help? You know? When am I gonna be in a position to do some good for somebody, instead of the other way around?"

Will could have said, *You do good*. But he wanted Arlen to know he was heard, and so he kept quiet.

When Arlen spoke again his voice was tight. "Look. About that woman. Whatever you do or don't do, I don't care. I'm the last person to stand in the way of anybody being happy."

"You should be happy too," Will said.

"I'm learning," he said. They watched as a young woman on an old bicycle rode past. She wore the tiniest shorts on the longest, tannest legs Will had ever seen.

"Yeah, I'm definitely learning," Arlen said.

Will chuckled.

"You remember the time we found that dog out back behind your house—what'd we call it?" Arlen asked.

"Twitch."

"I thought for sure your ma was gonna kill you when she found out you were feeding it your dinner every night."

"She thought I had a tapeworm," Will said.

Arlen laughed, a high and soft hooting, and he slapped his leg. When his face relaxed there was a new light in his eyes that Will was glad to see. "Good times," he said.

Will smiled. Arlen was talking—not just answering questions or being polite. But talking. Though the sun beat down hot on the paved paths, the warm lake, the parchment-dry trees, neither of them made a move to go.

"Yeah," Will said. "Good times."

\* \* \*

Eula had never meant to live alone in the house that she and Arlen had bought, and in the beginning, her mind played tricks on her. She saw things out of her peripheral vision—movements that, when she turned her head, were not movements at all. She caught herself talking on more than one occasion to people who weren't there, and she wasn't sure if that was more or *less* crazy than talking to herself. She sometimes cooked dinner only to realize that she'd cooked too much, and when she grew tired of leftovers, she walked them across the street to a neighbor who also lived alone.

Gradually, the notion that her house was too big for a single woman began to fade. She took lovers occasionally. She got a dog. She got engaged to a new man, who moved in with her for six months before he began to feel underfoot, and then they went their separate ways. Though she had no husband or family, the house took on her life, her stories. At times, she liked being single: no one's mess to clean up but her own, no one to fight with over the bathroom in the morning. She'd had to struggle and make sacrifices in order to hang on to the house, to pay the mortgage by herself. Some days, she didn't know why she stayed. But other days, she liked the feeling of mastery she had over her own space, decorating it with her mother's cookie jars, framed posters of nature scenes that caught her eye, and oversized pottery.

Lately, her house had begun to feel strange to her. And the feeling of not being alone was nagging her once again. In the morning after her last date, after she'd sent the good doctor home with a virtuous kiss good night, she'd gotten up and made herself pancakes for breakfast. She poured herself a tall glass of orange juice and breezed through a kitchen utensils catalog. Life was not bad. There was nothing to complain about.

Out of the corner of her eye, she caught a flicker of movement. But when she turned her head, nothing was there.

Because Lauren knew she didn't have many hours left in Richmond, she decided to take aggressive action. She had no more patience for waiting around to see if Arlen would hear her out. She wanted to do something good for him before she left town, and she had only one card to play.

At Maisie's house, her leg twitched involuntarily against the side of the bed while her laptop seemed to take forever to boot up. With fingers shaking from coffee and the sense of time bearing down, she looked for Eula's address. It was simply a matter of doing an Internet search. But where Eula's name came up, hers did too. The words about her, though she'd read them before, still glared:

> Stand-in prosecutor Lauren Matthews, a fresh-faced young woman who might be playing Frisbee at SUNY-Albany instead of trying the most hyped-up case of the decade, misses nothing. She scans the jury with eyes that bore in; one wonders if she has X-ray vision, the ability to see lungs, ribs, hearts. At times it seems she can look at a bench of jurors and can watch their brain waves lighting up in quadrants that signal a vote of guilty or not.

She shut down the Web page. Nine years ago, Arlen had been the monster and Lauren the hero. Now they'd switched. At times, Lauren wished she could shout to the world: *I meant well!* But then she wondered: Did she? Or had she cared more about her career than justice? She knew there was no single answer. Instead, all the minor elements of Arlen's case—the judge, the jury, the evidence, her own ambition, the natural human urge for settling scores—all of it had cemented together and created a singular and monolithic mistake.

She scanned the search results. There was a new page, one that she hadn't seen before, that mentioned her name and Eula's—a blog post by some anonymous, antigovernment anarchist. She couldn't help herself; she took a moment to read:

*The problems with the SO-CALLED justice system is that nobody gives a crap about anything except HOW MUCH MONEY THEY MAKE and whether or not they get envied when they go out to steak dinners at the Four Seasons or wherever. THIS IS NOT PARANOIA! THIS IS FACT! EGO TRUMPS TRUTH AND MONEY TALKKS!*

*If we were all our own SOVEREIGNS like God himself put us on this earth to be, then innocent men woudlnt' go to jail because each man would have his own justice. If you ask me, justice would be Arlen Fieldstone going after Lauren Matthews by mailng her a improvised explosive device IED of the explosively formed penetrator variety. THAT'S JUSTICE. THE BROTHERHOOD HAS SISTER'S IN IT, AND WECAN'T DESCRIMINATE.*

Lauren shivered. Typos and spelling errors aside, she'd never gotten used to the idea of perfect strangers wishing harm on her—though she could tell from the writer's out-of-control style that he was just blowing off steam. She'd run across militia guys before in her travels. They were volatile and angry, their rage fueled by an infinite and natural resource: helplessness. Sometimes she wished she could talk back to them, say, *You do realize that Arlen had a defense counsel, right?* But in the eyes of her critics, *she'd* been the all-powerful and tyrannical aggressor, and Arlen's defense was a puppy dog. If any one individual person deserved censure, it was her.

She had no time for getting fearful and wobbly now; she had things to do before she left Richmond, and no time to do them in.

She drove with her hands tight on the wheel, drove until she found the house that her GPS system said belonged to Eula. At the front door, she knocked and waited. Her heart felt fizzy and pressurized, and at the very edges of her peripheral vision, the light was going blurry. She blinked the dizziness away.

A woman opened the door. The youthfulness of her face, her smooth skin, her high cheekbones, was startling. Lauren hadn't expected her to be so young-looking. "May I help you?"

"Eula?"

"If you're another reporter, I'm calling the cops."

Lauren gripped the cast-iron railing at her side. "So they've been getting to you too."

"Who are you?"

"I'm Lauren. I was part of Arlen Fieldstone's trial. I . . . I stepped in as the prosecutor when he—"

"Uh-huh. I know who you are now," she said. "You okay? You're looking a little green."

Lauren nodded. "May I come in?"

"Come sit down," Eula said, frowning. Lauren followed her inside.

Eula was a petite woman, but she was not small or frail. She held her shoulders pulled back under a deep V-necked shirt that showed significant cleavage. She was shoeless, but she wore black tights with a run on her foot that had been painted with purple nail polish. Her skirt was small and black.

"Here you go." Eula gestured to an armchair. "You need water or something?"

"I'm fine," Lauren said, and she found that once she was sitting down, inside Eula's home, she *was* fine. Her heartbeat went back to normal, a tentative peace.

"What is it that brings you here, Lauren?" Eula asked. She did not sit, but stood in the center of the room, her arms crossed, her stance wide. Lauren read the signs: she wasn't up for a long conversation.

"I've been in Richmond. Hoping to apologize to your ex-husband for my part in his conviction."

"Is that so?"

"I feel some personal responsibility for what happened. I'm doing my best to make things right."

"But let me guess: Arlen won't see you."

"No."

Eula chuckled and shook her head. "I'm not surprised. The man always did know how to hold a grudge. Better than anyone I ever met."

"He's got reason to," Lauren said.

Eula's face darkened. "You asking me to apologize too?"

"No—"

"Because as far as I'm concerned, I did the best thing I could do at the time. Not much more a person can ask of herself than that."

"I know," Lauren said. "I'm not here to make you feel bad."

"Could have fooled me."

"I'm here because I want to know if you would consider going to see him."

Lauren watched her, the twitch of her upper lip, the brightness that flashed in her eyes before she managed to smother it. When she spoke, she'd regained her poise. "Did Arlen ask for me?"

"Honestly? No. But that doesn't mean you shouldn't go anyway."

Eula walked to the mantel over the little fireplace in her room. The living room was quaint—more comfortable than stylish, with soft pinks and soft greens and ruffled beige flounces on the windows. In some ways, it was a room for a woman much older than Eula. A woman still living a decade ago.

Eula stood beside the shadowed, glassed-in fireplace, drumming her fingers on the mantel. "You see that?"

Lauren followed Eula's gaze to a small silver box that was sitting not a few feet from her. It was tin, etched with motifs of elephants and baobab trees. Eula touched it; Lauren wondered if she knew how tender the gesture appeared.

"It's empty," Eula said. "Arlen gave it to me as a wedding present. Said that he was gonna fill it up with gold and diamonds, a little something for every year of our marriage, until it overflowed."

Lauren did not have to know human behavior to understand. There was something universal about the countenance of heartbreak—and of a woman still in love.

"But don't feel too bad for me," Eula said. "I made a choice, and now I have to stick with it. I thought Arlen did it. Just like everybody. I thought he was guilty. I can't believe he would want to see me now."

"You don't know that," Lauren said, leaning forward on the cushion beneath her. "He's hurting too. At least give him the opportunity to *not* see you, if he doesn't want to." She stood and went to Eula, whose eyes were clear and tearless. She pulled a bit of paper from her pocket; she'd written down Arlen's contact information before leaving her car. "Here," she said, and she pressed it into Eula's hand. "I hope you'll think about it."

Eula nodded, her face resolute.

Lauren squeezed her arm gently; then—because she thought Eula could understand her, could know more than anyone else what it felt like to have messed up—she hugged her.

For a long moment, Eula hugged her back. "I'll think about it," she said.

*    *    *

Will's attic—what was left of it—was so crammed with stuff and junk and things that to make his way through it was to do a kind of spelunking. He'd had to wedge open the door with his body to get inside, because the swing of it was blocked, and now he climbed carefully through the dark and dusty space with a flashlight. At midday, the attic was as dark as something out of a nightmare—ragged-edged shadows, dolls with missing hair and eyes, stacks of books like brick chimneys, clothes and shoes he hadn't been able to throw away. All of the unique things that he'd collected over the years had, at some point, stopped being unique at all and become instead one large mass. He made his way as best he could to the far end of the attic, half thinking that he should be wearing a hard hat, half thinking that he could get stuck here if the great walls of clutter ever tumbled. He could picture the headline: *MAN TRAPPED IN OWN ATTIC FOR DAYS.*

As far as he knew, Lauren had no idea of his problem, despite her ability to see things that others could not. He'd been nervous to bring her to his house last week, when she'd hurt her hand. He'd worried that she might have discovered him. His ex-girlfriends—if he could call them that—became restless when he wouldn't show them the upper floors of his home. They had asked him, playfully, where he was keeping the bodies. They hinted about crazy wives locked in the attic. They told him: *I want the Grand Tour.*

But not Lauren. She'd seemed content to stay with him on the first floor only. When he was feeling paranoid, he thought the reason that she hadn't asked to look around was because she *knew.* And then he thought of how liberating it would be if she did find out by accident. He fantasized for a moment about the way she would look at him and the relief he would feel. He supposed the line between paranoia and fantasy could be thin, deceptively thin.

With the flashlight beam going before him, he moved through the bulk of the attic, picking his way over half-remembered finds. He righted a toy boat with a moth-eaten sail, leaning it against a crate. Despite the damage, he guessed it would be worth a lot some day. The monkey with the cymbals; that too, someone would love to collect. The longer he could hold on to these things, the more money they would be worth. And the more they ate him alive.

Finally, he climbed to the farthest end of the attic away from the stairs. Under the pointed roof, a single square window let in a trickle of choked light, so that the space felt like some perverse monastic's refuge. He cleared a spot to sit down on the dusty floor. He could trace his years in this house, almost six years now, on a timeline of junk. The newest accumulations were in one of the second-floor bedrooms. But here in the back corner of the attic, *this* was where it all began. He'd put a box here, a plastic container there. At the time he'd thought: *Just until I clean out the barn.*

It seemed almost funny now.

He sat feeling small and swallowed up by the piles of things: a beat-up Monopoly board, a box of fishing lures, a basket, a single geode bookend, a lamp, a couple of two-by-fours. These things that kept him grounded also weighed him down. He thought perhaps if he had a *reason* to dig himself out, to find the superhuman courage that it would take to begin dismantling his compulsion to hoard, he might be able to get free. Maybe if he had a chance at a normal life, he could drum up the focus and drive to not only tread water, but to swim.

Lauren might have been that temptation. That lure. He might have used the possibility of a future with her as a target; if he could change, maybe they would have a chance. But since she was going back to her life in Albany whether he fixed himself or not, there was no goal line to run toward. Not now, anyway.

He picked up a bag of marbles; they caught the light of his

flashlight and glowed in swirls of blue, red, and green. He sometimes felt like he was a prisoner with mortar and trowel, building,
brick by brick, his own jail. He tested the weight of the bag in his
hand. Then tested himself. Could he do it? Could he throw this
thing away? This, and all the others?

The desire was there, but the will was missing.

He sat among his things, listening for what they had to tell him,
waiting for them to speak.

Lauren had meant to wait until dark. She could picture herself
showing up at Will's house, standing under the porch light, the
Virginia hills falling into shadow behind her, the cows in the fields
having wandered in for the night.

But now that she'd made the decision to leave Richmond, the
hours were so thin and stretched that she did not have the luxury
of waiting to make a dramatic entrance under the curtain of dark.
She reached Will's house by eight o'clock in the evening, when the
sun still was shining bright and golden. Not the time for a romantic liaison at all. But it was what she had.

Her heart was beating hard when Will opened the door. Her
skin felt hot.

"Lauren?"

"Hi, Will. Um . . . *surprise?*" she said, though the word
sounded like a question.

A smile tugged the corners of his lips, and Lauren knew he
wasn't shocked to see her. She'd texted him earlier to ask where he
was. She supposed she was predictable—of course she would show
up after what had happened in his office today. And yet, even if
he'd expected her, he didn't welcome her in.

She pulled herself up straighter. She'd only half prepared herself for the possibility that he might reject her. She should have thought about it more, to lessen the potential sting.

"I have to tell you something," she said.

He leaned against the doorjamb and smiled, friendly enough. But he didn't move aside. "Shoot."

"I'm leaving."

"Now?"

"Tomorrow."

He regarded her long and hard, his arms crossed over his chest. He was wearing a cotton T-shirt and black workout shorts. His feet were bare. "Come in," he said, less welcoming than resigned.

He turned sideways and she walked past him. The scent of juniper was in his cologne. His chest, turned in the doorway, seemed wide as a gate, and already she was second-guessing. He was cagey and suspicious. She wondered if there was a chance that he didn't want her after all, that she'd read their interlude in the antiques shop all wrong. Maybe what he'd done to her had been nothing more than a minor and temporary kink. As she made her way into the kitchen, she resisted the urge to flee right back out the door she'd just walked through. She thought: *I shouldn't be here.*

In the kitchen, Will leaned the small of his back against the center island; she stayed a few feet away.

"I thought you weren't leaving until you talked to Arlen," he said.

"That was the plan. But I think, at this point, it's probably safe to say he won't see me. I mean, it's been a week. And if I don't get back to Albany, I'm going to lose an important opportunity," she said, and she heard in her own voice the inflections of her father and her boss.

"Sure. I understand. You wanna get back to work."

"I have to," she said.

"You don't *have* to do anything."

"No," she said. "I do."

He was quiet. He made no move to come toward her. And while she hadn't ripped her clothes from her body or thrown herself at his feet, they both knew why she was there. She was certain they'd been on the same page—and yet, Will was making this difficult for her. All this *talking*. She'd always been good about saying what she wanted, but now she found herself in an uncertain and unusual place—one in which speaking her intentions did not mean she would get what she wanted. She was bargaining from a position of weakness—and she was sure her body language said as much.

"I think I should go," she said. She adjusted her purse a little high on her shoulder, but didn't move to leave.

Now Will pushed off the counter so he no longer leaned, his hips directly over his feet. "You came all the way out here to tell me that you're leaving? That's it?"

"It seems so."

"You could have called," he said.

She clenched her teeth. She had the sense he was stringing her along, dragging things out unnecessarily—but she didn't know why. "I thought I needed to say good-bye in person."

"That's all you want?" he asked. "That's all you came here for? To say good-bye?"

She lifted her head with as much pride as she could summon, but it was all bluster. Her legs were shaky and her head felt light. "No. That's not all."

He walked toward her. "Lauren . . ."

She lifted a hand, felt the flatness of his chest, the pumping of his heart. She closed her eyes, awash with need and unexpected gladness to feel his heartbeat so steady and strong. Some ancient cultures believed that emotions, thoughts, decisions . . . all of them resided not behind the eyes, but behind the breastbone. Today, she could almost understand.

When she opened her eyes again, Will was looking down at her with desire so fierce it was both thrilling and frightening. "I'm leaving tomorrow," she said.

"Yes." He took her hand from his chest, kissed the back of it so firmly it felt less like a kiss than a pact. "You want to stay the night."

"Yes."

"Then you just . . . go?"

"Do you see any other way?"

His eyes were focused hard on her, a smokier gray green than before. She held her breath, saw that he was weighing his options. She trembled to be kept waiting. She hated that he made her wait.

The moment he decided, his eyes darkened. His breath filled up his lungs. "One thing at a time," he said. And he kissed her.

The evening was long and drawn out, as summer evenings in Richmond could be long and drawn out, so that when the sunset finally came it was like the colors of the sky were being sucked down the horizon like water down a drain. Heat lightning flashed silently in the distance, though no one noticed, and all of Richmond turned lazy under the summer sky. Even the birds seemed to fly more slowly, less like darts than smears.

In Carytown, the owner of a sub shop watched the evening fall, longing for his wife's curry and thinking of why the fellow who'd just ordered a sandwich from him was so familiar. He and Arlen, whose name he did not know, shot the breeze like they'd been talking their whole lives. And when Arlen said, *So long*, the man thought he seemed nice enough and asked him to flip the sign on the door to CLOSED.

His belly full, Arlen made his way down the street, where the buildings were blunt silhouettes. He counted blessings: shoes, food, health, sky. He made his way to the church for a meeting, where bright lights glowed behind stained glass, and a group of ex-cons and former junkies had gathered with metal folding chairs. He was going to tell everyone about losing his job, but he would keep his near run-in with Eula to himself. He cleared his throat and sat down.

Towns away, Eula had no notion of who was thinking about her or who was not. She was on her couch, watching a movie. A bowl of cool popcorn was just out of arm's reach. Her feet were on Mitch's lap, and he was rubbing them, and she was not thinking about the movie on the screen at all, but instead was thinking, *I should ask Mitch what to do about Arlen.* But she knew that would be wrong.

Day merged into night, light flowing into darkness with fluid grace. Maisie got a text message from Lauren. She picked up her phone from the coffee table. *I won't be home tonight*, the text read. And Maisie thought, *Good for you.*

Mostly, Richmond was quiet. The last of the sunlight slipped away with no more fanfare than a lullaby. Traffic on side streets waned and the moon showed through the haze of dusk. Students laughed in doorways or walked to bars, mothers coaxed their babies to sleep, and, one by one, the people of the city gave themselves over to the shadows, expecting that tomorrow they could finish what they hadn't finished today.

In the darkness of Will's bedroom, Lauren learned things she did not know. She learned that Will had a taste for expensive sheets, sheets that tangled around her ankles like the ocean's foam. She learned the scars of his arms, the heat and power of his body's secret places. She learned the play of shadows along his back as he reached away from her toward the drawer in his nightstand. She learned of his generosity, and also of his greed. And somewhere around midnight, she learned that he would not let her discreetly put on her clothes and head home, that he would make love to her a dozen more times, if it meant she was too worn-out to leave before dawn.

At times, the night was a rush of minutes, a loosened dam, gusty and strong. But it was also the soft fall of moonlight, the glaze of silver on bare skin, an oasis where Lauren could drink her fill, fearlessly, though the night was wild. She learned that Will was exactly what she thought he'd be, that her head fit perfectly in the crook of his shoulder, that the way he looked her in the eye as his hips rocked against hers was an intimacy—startling in its demand and naked insistence—she'd never known before. And what she learned about herself was that she had not learned enough about him to satisfy her, not at all.

Sometime in the night Will woke. Lauren lay beside him, her hair falling onto his pillow in soft knots. He pulled her closer, and in her sleep she moaned slightly, reached for him. He kissed her head, thought: *Whatever tomorrow brings will have been worth it.* Then, because he loved the night so much and did not want it to end, he lay down closer to her and slept again.

**Lesson Thirteen:** Few would argue that modern life isn't harried, wired, intense. If you notice a change in a person's appearance, consider whether or not stress might be a factor.

The symptoms of stress are well-known, though it expresses itself in people in unique ways. Stress may appear as dark shadows under the eyes from sleepless nights. It may show as weight loss or gain. Stress could make itself known as a skin condition, such as blemishes or zits. Although none of these markers is an infallible symptom of stress, it may be helpful to watch for them—in others or yourself.

# CHAPTER 13

It had always seemed to Lauren the important decisions in life stored themselves up until the last possible moment: a woman is offered a new job the day after her boss gives her a big bonus and a promise for a raise; a couple spends years looking for their first home, then discovers they have to make an offer within a few hours or they'll lose their chance; a man about to purchase an engagement ring discovers that his old girlfriend is back in town, looking for him.

The hours passed; she and Will dozed more than slept. She couldn't quite believe how easy it was to fall asleep beside him, how safe she felt there. She would remember this—the smooth weight of his knee between hers—on some future night when a nor'easter was blowing up the coast and her apartment was dark and cold. She got up and put her feet on the floor softly, not to wake him. She padded down the hall. Her body was sore and chafed.

She caught a glimpse of herself in a dark mirror, her own reflection superimposed on the peeling white paint of the barn behind the house. And she saw what a mess she was, swollen lips, beard-burned face, mussed hair. With Will, she'd been sloppy and needy and entirely unhinged. She could never have been that way with Edward, who was never fully out of control in anything he did. She ran a hand down over her breast and found how much more she wanted— from Will, from Richmond, from everything. How much she reveled in possibility. Her return trip to Albany should have been thrilling, since she was up for a promotion and since returning home was essentially all she needed to do to achieve her dreams. But instead, the journey hung over her head like a heavy cloud.

Since her phone call with Burt, her life's work had been weighing on her mind. He'd told her in certain terms that he considered her above the charities that gathered evidence and arguments to free convicted men. Exonerating criminals wasn't glamorous or well paying; many of the lawyers who worked such cases were volunteers or students, and those who did have a salary often needed to supplement it with something else, such as teaching or writing. And yet the notion that she might join a group of people who understood wrongful conviction left her feeling energized, ready, challenged—and full of self-doubt. It was only hours ago she'd been firmly committed to returning to her life in Albany. Now, fresh from Will's bed, she wanted something else.

She went to the kitchen sink, filled a glass with water from the faucet. It was cool, and she drank thirstily. She couldn't sleep. She put her glass of water on the counter, then decided that, rather than toss and turn for the remainder of the night and keep Will awake, she would do a little research about exoneration projects— if only to rule them out and reassure herself that her future was fixed firmly in the halls of her Albany office.

She went looking for Will's computer. He had to have an office somewhere. She knew he wouldn't mind. She could be quicker if she wasn't limited to the small screen of her cell phone. She peeked into his living room, where his key collection hung in shadows, a dozen little mysteries pegged to a board. She found his dining room—it could have been in a living history museum—and she even opened a random door only to find herself staring at a closet, before she headed upstairs. By the time she realized what she'd done wrong, it was already too late.

She flipped on the light switch, and then she knew.

She stopped, shaken.

The second floor of Will's house may have had a bathroom. Bedrooms. Maybe even an office. But what showed of the floor was just a narrow trail between precarious piles of things, like a deer path through brambles. She peered into the room across the hall. The windows had no curtains. There was no furniture to be seen in any of the rooms, though here and there Lauren thought she could discern the choked shape of a dresser or bed. There was only junk that looked like garbage—piles and piles like the kind she had seen in so many outbuildings, accretion that strangled itself. The smell of dust hung in the air.

She was afraid.

She hurried downstairs as silently as she could, cursing the steps that creaked under her toes. A moment after she returned to the kitchen, to stare at her glass of water blankly while her mind worked, Will appeared, sleepy and with a lopsided smile. He wore boxers, nothing more. She was glad for the dark. He came to her, kissed her softly on the lips, wrapped his arms around her waist so that his T-shirt rode higher on her hips and she felt the night air on her bottom.

"Nice shirt," he said when he pulled away.

She smiled. "I've always had good taste."

"Clearly."

She laughed, lifted her water to drink. All the time she'd spent trying to puzzle Will out—and now she had more information about him than she knew what to do with.

"What are you doing up?" he asked.

The answer came with embarrassing quickness. "I don't know. I guess I should probably get going."

"At"—he glanced at green numerals on the microwave clock—"three a.m.?"

She was quiet. She didn't really want to leave. But the tides of wood, and plastic, and metal, and dust upstairs—with all the startling wildness and chaos of a junkyard—had lodged in her mind. She needed perspective, distance. She didn't know what to make of his secret—or whether she had any right to make anything of it at all.

He squeezed her and clasped his hands at the small of her back. "You don't have to go."

"No?" she asked, wanting him to convince her.

He kissed her lightly—a kiss that felt like he'd tugged her toward him, though in fact his touch had been light. "I think you can stay."

She looked into his eyes, which were so unguarded, so pleased to be looking back at her, and her heart warmed. She smiled when he smiled.

Surprise receded. The urge to retreat collapsed.

Will had taken pains to hide his story from her, from the world. And yet now that the mystery had been solved, she felt even more intrigued by him. She wanted him to know that he could unburden himself with her, and that she could be strong enough to hear anything he might have to say. She wanted to understand and—maybe—help. But they had only this one night. Such a short time for pleasure. And she loved so much seeing the light in his eyes.

She touched his cheek, the dry stubble. "You know what? You're right. The day will be here soon enough."

"The day can wait."

She was barefoot, and as she reached up to kiss him, her weight rolled to the edge of her toes and she suddenly found herself coming off the ground. Will had sat her on the counter. She pushed her fingers through his hair; he pulled her shirt—his shirt—over her head. Instead of kissing him again, she drew him to her, wrapped her arms around him. His cheek pressed her chest. She held him hard, her heart full of a thousand wishes for him, full to bursting.

"Don't go in the morning either," he said.

"Mmm."

"It's your last day in Richmond. Spend it with me."

She didn't answer; he bent his head, found her breast. The heart-bursting feeling of protectiveness was infused with waves of deep pleasure, and she thought, *My God, this is why people fall in love.* She grasped at sanity. "It's not fair to ask me to think rationally when you're doing that."

"I don't want you to think rationally," he said. He tugged her forward by the backs of her knees. "I don't want you to think at all."

She closed her eyes as he kissed her neck. *One day.* Her groggy and sex-drugged brain could hardly process it. *One day with Will.* One day that would belong to her, fully. Not her work. Not her boss. Not her father. Just her. And just Will.

She thought again of all the years of clutter upstairs. She thought of how difficult it must have been for him to shoulder all those things—emotionally, physically—on his own. And she wanted to tell him everything would be okay.

"Say yes," he said, easing her back.

She smiled at him, bowed with desire and exhaustion both. "Yes," she said.

*     *     *

Sometimes, in prison, it was easy for Arlen to imagine that he was not alone. His imagination was vivid. He could smell in his dreams. Taste. He could see colors in detail: pine green, mint green, pea green, the green of spring grass. So intense were his dreams that on certain nights he opened his eyes to the white, white walls of his cell, and yet the dream continued, going on in the semidarkness, his brain making improbable and nonsensical connections between the world his eyes saw and the fantasy that still lingered in his mind. The result was that his dreams sometimes seemed superimposed, briefly, on his cell, the way that cartoonists would pencil the muted colors of a background and then draw their characters overlaid. He saw his mother standing in the cell, looking down at him. He saw his old dog, sitting on the floor and wagging his tail, waiting to be taken out. He saw Eula, leaning her hands on the little sink and staring at herself in a mirror that wasn't there.

At one point, the dreams had come so often that he was compelled at times to question his own sanity. But Arlen knew that he was fully awake on Monday morning when Eula came through the door of the antiques shop—although it seemed to him that she was apart from the background that framed her, that she stood out from it and apart from it as if she were a dream. Her hair was neatly turned under at her chin—a fine, warm brown shot through with almond. She wore high black heels and a white satin shirt with no sleeves.

"Hi, Arlen," she said.

He felt the hard, swift jolt of panic, a collar tugging his throat, and for a moment he couldn't speak. Eula waited, looking at him, perched on those high heels and with those breasts that were larger than he remembered. He had lost weight in the time that had passed, and she had gained it. The curviness suited her; she was more beautiful than he remembered.

"I heard you were here," she said.

"Yep," he said. "I am."

His heart pounded. He wanted to ask her: *Why'd you come to see me? What do you want?* But such questions were too big to ask right up front. And yet, some smaller comment, like, *Did you hit traffic on the way over?* also seemed wrong.

She began to look nervous, her lips pursed and her gaze darting. "Arlen . . . ?" She was shifting from foot to foot. "I . . . Are you mad that I'm here?"

"No," he said. "I went to see you. You waved to me."

"That was you standing across the street?"

He nodded.

"I'm sorry. It's been such a long time. You look so different now. You look good. Not that you didn't look good before. But—yeah—you look good."

His fingernails were pressing into the skin of his palm. He wanted to be angry, and yet, there was no reason for anger. Whether she'd divorced him or not, they wouldn't have been together. The divorce decree hadn't changed things: it simply had reflected what was.

Arlen tried to sound as normal as possible. "How are you doing?"

"Oh, fine. Just fine. I'm manager at the bank now."

"The same bank?" Arlen drew his lips into the shape of a smile. "Good. Good." He wanted to ask if she was with anyone. If she was married. But of course he could not. "And your family?"

"My sister's married. Got two kids. Mom's doing okay. She's in a home now—doesn't always know what's going on. She's got her good days and bad."

"Don't we all," Arlen said.

Eula was quiet, her heels close together as if she was trying to take up as little space as possible. "Are you . . . are you having better days? Now that it's over?"

He looked at her for a long while before he answered. He wanted to go to her. To feel the warmth and plush softness of her against him. He wanted her to wrap her arms around him and squeeze him as hard as she could. But this was more than tender fondness: this was desire. For her. Everything about him that had felt old, felt young again. He took in a deep breath. He told her: "Things are looking better every day."

"Arlen . . ." She had tears in her eyes. She walked toward him, her hands clasped before her. He remained still. "Oh, Arlen."

He took a risk, said, "Come here."

And then she opened her arms and wrapped them around his middle, until all of her was pressed up against him. She smelled of jasmine, not like he remembered, but beneath her perfume there remained the smell that was so familiar, so *her*, that it broke his heart. She pressed her face to his chest and he knew she was crying. His strong, strong Eula, who never cried. He held her as she shook.

"I'm so sorry . . ." she started.

But he cut her off. "None of that now. None of that."

He closed his eyes, giving himself over to the feel of her, of the two of them alone, and the deep familiarity of a moment that he'd never known before. In prison he'd imagined their reunion a thousand times. A million. And though he knew there was no promise of anything more, that this was as close to her as he might be ever again, for now it was everything he'd dreamed—only better, because it was real.

Lauren passed the morning hours in Will's bed. They slept and not, at the whim of the sunshine and shadow moving along the floor. Lauren marveled at the way hours flew as quickly when there was nothing to do as when there was much to be done. They lay naked

under the sheets, hands always seeking and finding, no lines to
mark beginnings or endings, to distinguish when they were making love and when they had stopped. At ten a.m., Lauren looked at
the clock with the feeling that the whole night had been a dream.
It occurred to her, while she was in the shower and Will traced
soaped hands along her waist, she hadn't thought of Edward once.

They went to a local diner for breakfast, bright light bearing
down on blue Formica. They ordered plates heaped with eggs and
sausage, grits swimming in butter and cream. They talked about
nothing important—and yet, Lauren hung on every word. Will's
favorite color was the burnt red of brick faded by weather and sun.
He loved Doritos and any type of meat that ended in *wurst*—
though not at the same time. He confessed that *Gone With the
Wind* had made him cry.

Lauren was transfixed by him, by the way he'd opened up since
she'd arrived at his house last night. He told her more now: about
being poor as a child—the dizzying contrast of so much scarcity in
a house that was full of so much love. He'd mentioned to her in
passing that he'd hoped to have a family someday, and then, to her
amazement, he'd blushed slightly and changed the subject, as if
he'd just confessed the most intimate desire of his life.

As they talked, her mind occasionally wandered back to the
second story of his house, where she'd seen the forgotten printers
and schoolroom desks, handkerchiefs and bowling trophies. He
was letting her into his life as much as he dared—and she admired
him for that. She too had felt that it was easier to open up than it
had been a day ago. After all, she was leaving. She could share her
deepest secrets with him, if she wanted to, with no more repercussions than tossing a handful of petals into a strong wind.

They ate slowly, and when the food was gone, they ordered
second cups of coffee and laughed about needing to stay awake.
Over the rim of her coffee cup, she watched him.

She'd once met an analyst who worked as a marriage counselor. He'd conducted an informal study of as many couples as he could find—a scientific parlor trick mostly for colleagues and friends. He put the couples in a room, recorded their behavior. For two minutes he asked them to talk about each other: *Tell me the story of how you met. Tell me what you like about your fiancé. Tell me what drives you crazy.* Within two minutes of watching—reading the micro expressions that flashed fast as lightning bolts through otherwise placid smiles—he could predict with an accuracy of 80 percent if the couple would separate within the next few years. The talent was frightening. She wondered: If that man were here now, watching, what would he say?

In their booth at the diner, Lauren thought she and Will might have looked like lovers of months, weeks, or years. They might have been husband and wife, or just friends. To outsiders, they were no more noticeable or memorable than the pictures of movie stars framed on the walls. And yet, Lauren could feel that this was important—this moment—branded on her memory.

"What are you thinking?" Will asked.

She smiled, the edge of a straw between her teeth. "What are you?"

"I'm wondering what I can do to talk you into staying another night."

"Is that an invitation?"

"A standing invitation," he said.

She thrilled to think of it—that she could stay, and more, that she might always be welcome in his bed. In the back of her mind, she was captive to the fantasy of a different kind of future: one where they had breakfast together like this often, one where she wore jeans to work instead of panty hose, one where she and Will lived together and fussed about what color to paint the upstairs bedroom, one where they had children who played in the sprinkler in the front yard.

She put down her mug, rubbed her eyes for a moment. How ridiculous she was being. She'd known Edward for months before she'd let herself begin to trust him—with terrible results. And yet here she sat at a diner, like some college kid after a night of gluttonous indulgence, mooning over the future and everything that could be—with a man she'd known for a mere handful of days.

Will noticed her hesitation. His eyes were fathomless, honest and open, all the way down. "You don't need to make a reservation."

She smiled. "No reservations, then," she said. For this one morning, she could let herself imagine what it would be like to spend the night with him again, to spend many nights with him. What would it hurt—really—to momentarily pretend?

The waitress brought Will's change. He reached for Lauren's hand as they walked to his car, like any two people who had been together so long that holding hands was second nature. Somewhere beyond the noise of the roadway, sirens blared.


Eula and Arlen talked of old times. Arlen wanted to know: What ever happened with the new washing machine that the family had bought her sister for her birthday? Had she liked it? And what about the neighbor who played his music so loud all night? Had Eula ever called the cops?

They went out for an early lunch—a big meal of pasta and sweet white cheese. They'd forgotten to bring wine, but the sodas were effervescent and for all Arlen knew they might have been champagne. Sconces on the walls cast a soft glow over the hand-painted stucco, scenes of gondolas and bell towers and small ships out to sea. Eula's rings caught the light and sparkled gold as she picked up her glass.

*Eula.* Sitting across from him, right there. Sometimes, he couldn't quite make out what she was saying because his brain was too filled up by her to take it all in at once. He felt as if he'd just picked up a book that he'd stopped reading in the middle; he could remember the basic premises, and the details came back with prompting. Eula was patient in answering his questions: Yes, her sister had liked the washing machine. No, she'd never called the cops on their noisy neighbor. Shortly after Arlen had "left," the man moved away. Eula couldn't remember his name.

He was glad she was so willing to talk—she'd always been generous with her thoughts. She'd never shied away from telling people the intimate details of her life—and Arlen relished everything: whether she was talking about paying off the mortgage or how loud one of her coworkers blew his nose.

But for all the questions that he'd asked about her life, she'd asked him none. He knew what she was wondering. If she were a different woman, she might have said, *What was prison like?* with the same look of wonder in her eyes as if she were asking what it had been like living on the moon. She, like everyone, probably wanted to know: What kind of violence had he seen, had he faced? What kinds of killers, robbers, and rapists?

But she asked none of those questions. She just talked. And talked. And Arlen's heart was filled up by her talking, as if she poured herself right into him and he thought he might overflow. It wasn't until the waiter brought dessert—a tiramisu that looked like God Himself had come down and beaten the eggs—that her look changed and her voice grew soft.

"The coffee isn't very good," she said.

"Compared to what?" He laughed. "One thing about prison—you learn to appreciate things more. In some ways."

She looked down. The tiramisu was between them, powdered sugar on the plate. "I have to tell you something."

Arlen braced himself. He was desperate to know: *Was she seeing someone? Did they still have a chance? Could she love a man who'd been in prison?*

She cleared her throat. "I went to your mother's funeral."

Arlen held the coffee cup in his hand; the handle was too tiny for his fingers. He didn't know what to say. He supposed that whether she had or had not gone to the funeral service, neither decision would have been wrong. "Was it . . . nice?"

"They had it at her church. Everybody who knew her came. She wore her blue dress with the yellow flowers."

"Yeah. She loved that dress."

Eula arranged her fork in a line even with her plate. "I tried to help her, when she was sick. But she wouldn't let me."

"No, probably not. She might not've let me help her either, if I was there. You know she was proud."

When Eula looked up at him, her eyes were slightly wet. "Arlen, do you think she would have been mad that I went—to the funeral, I mean?"

"She would've wanted you there."

"I went partly because I needed to say good-bye. Because I owed her that respect. But also, I went because I felt like, in some little way, I went for you too."

Arlen scratched the side of his nose. "You went for me, meaning, in my place?"

"No. I mean, I went to say good-bye." She dabbed at her eyes with her napkin. "You were only supposed to have been gone for three days. *Three days.* I would have done things different if I knew I wasn't gonna see you again."

"They wouldn't let me out," he said.

She laughed through her tears. "Prisons are like that."

"For the funeral, I'm saying. The superintendent had a thing against me because nobody could make me admit that I was innocent. See—a lotta guys say they're innocent when they first come in. They'll look you square in the face and say, 'I didn't do it,' and you can tell they believe every word. But eventually, they fess up to being guilty."

"But not you," Eula said.

"No, not me."

"So the superintendent wouldn't let you out for the funeral."

Arlen bit the inside of his lip before he spoke. He hated to talk about prison; he'd said very little about it since they let him out, because he thought if he could keep from talking about it, it would disappear. But now, he wanted Eula to understand at least one small thing of what he'd gone through. His mind flashed an odd image, one in which he was breaking himself out of his own mind like a prisoner digging with a spoon.

"They might've let me out," he said. "If things had been different. But I was in the isolation unit. I knocked out a guy who tried to . . . well . . . Let's just say I didn't take any nonsense."

"I'm glad to hear that."

He looked at her, her soft hair, her pert nose that was wide at the nostrils and dipped between her eyes, her mouth that was plush and red. He wanted to put his hand on hers, but he didn't.

"I'm glad you went to the funeral," he said. "It makes me feel better. Knowing you were there."

"Even though I went to say good-bye?"

"You can say good-bye to me now, if you want to. It's up to you."

She sat still for a moment, then reached out her hand for his. He took it—an awkward, suspended handshake. "I'd rather say hello again."

Arlen felt tears come to his eyes—damn and blasted tears. He hated to cry in front of Eula. But he couldn't help it. The tears came. "I'm gonna be a better man," he said. "Believe me. I promise I am."

Her smile was like the sun on a winter's day. "Arlen. You couldn't be a better man if you tried."

In the afternoon, Will made love to Lauren again, though she was half-asleep and turned on her side. He simply couldn't get as much as he wanted from her. Afterward, he dropped beside her into a deep and exhausted sleep, only dimly aware of her hips nestled against his thighs, the heat of her under his arm.

When he woke again, the light in the room had changed, the square of afternoon sun on the hardwood having stretched into a rectangle. He got up sleepily. The first floor of his house had central air, and the hair on his arms stood on end as he crossed the bedroom, stepping over discarded shirts and shoes. Lauren was not in the bathroom; no light shone under the door. He walked down the long hallway that led to the kitchen and when he did not see her at the table or the sink, he began to worry that she'd left.

Only afterward did he realize that should have been his *second* worry, not his first.

He walked up the stairs slowly, running his hand along the banister. And though the hair at the back of his neck stood on end, he felt oddly empty. The fact of the moment confronted him; the meaning of it did not.

He found her sitting in the middle of one of his more recently filled-up rooms. She'd cleared a space for herself on the floor in the center of the heaps. She was cross-legged, wearing an old pair of his shorts and one of his tees. It fell from her shoulders like a slack sail.

"What are you doing?" he asked, his voice flat.

"Looking." She picked up a child's toolbox—a plastic hammer

and screwdriver were on the floor. "I used to have one of these when I was a kid."

"I still do," he said.

She smiled; to his surprise, he didn't see any traces of judgment or disappointment there. He didn't even see repulsion. He leaned his shoulder against the doorframe. He didn't want her to know he was trembling. "So now you know."

"Am I the only one?"

"Other people have their suspicions, but I've never acknowledged it to anyone. Obviously, you're the exception."

"Then we're even," she said. He must have looked confused, because she put a hand over her heart to remind him. Last week, she'd told him about her palpitations, when he'd been the only one to know.

"Even Steven," he said, flat.

She got to her feet; her toenail polish was chipped now. He could picture her talking into her cell phone to schedule a pedicure when she returned to Albany. "How long has it been like this?"

"Probably since forever. But it only got bad since I bought the house."

She stood before him, looking up. He realized she wasn't going to ask him the hard question: *Why?* She'd come to know him over the last week—know him and understand him. He should have been angry by her intrusion; instead, he felt relief.

"Does it disgust you?" he asked.

"It's dirty. There's a lot of dust."

He nodded. She stepped away, bent to look at an old diploma frame. He'd thought, at one point, he might need it. He still could.

"Can we go downstairs?" he asked.

She took his hand, and they walked to his kitchen. She sat on a high stool, tucking her feet beneath her on a silver bar.

"Cold?" he asked.

She shook her head.

"You should have napped; you've got a long drive tonight."

"I couldn't sleep."

"Why not?"

She pushed her hair back with two hands; it curled neatly around her ears, a comma at her earlobe. "Just . . . thinking."

"About?"

"Whether I'm making the right decisions."

He leaned against the kitchen table, pleased that she was willing to direct the conversation away from his illness for a time. "Do you mean decisions about your job?"

"I've been working toward getting this promotion since I was first out of college."

"Why do you want it so bad?"

She hesitated. "So many reasons. I want it because I *can* want it. I hate the feeling of my time belonging to someone else."

"Like a boss."

"If I get this promotion, I make my own decisions from now on. I'll be the only person in charge of me."

"And you'll be in charge of all the people who will work for you."

"That too," she said. "Plus, my family will be absolutely thrilled. My dad's planning a run for the Senate one of these days. Maybe."

He paused, thinking. Over the last twenty-four hours, she'd told him more about her family: her ambitious father, her retreating mother, her brother whom she loved like a best friend. He wondered if she felt any need to compensate in her family for Jonah—who probably wasn't considered presentable in public among the Hudson Valley elite. But he wasn't going to make that guess aloud.

"Those aren't *reasons* for wanting the promotion," he said.

"They're excuses. The only reason for wanting one is that you enjoy the work and love what you do."

"Sometimes it's hard to know," she said.

He went to her, put his hands on either side of her neck. He looked into her face. When she'd first come into his shop, he'd thought she was hard and calculating. Now there was not even the slightest shadow of that hardness there anymore. The last vestige of it had melted away in the night. "Stay here a little while longer. You shouldn't make snap decisions. You should think things through."

"They're voting tomorrow, and I have to be there. Besides, the reason I came to Richmond was to see Arlen. And he doesn't want me here."

"I want you here."

"Will . . ."

"I do. I want you here. You know it—even if I don't say it aloud."

"My life's in Albany."

"Your *job* is in Albany."

"And my family."

"They can visit," he said.

"This is crazy."

"It's not crazy." He took her wrists, gathering her hands between them. "Don't go back. If you go back, what's there waiting for you? A life where you have to walk around pretending to be perfect all the time? That's not a life at all."

"It's my life," she said, and he saw a flash of anger in her eyes.

"It's a fake life."

"And you know that from personal experience."

He dropped her hands. The barb had struck.

"I'm sorry," she said.

"No. You're right. It is a fake life. The first floor of it, anyway."

She reached for him, then let her hand fall, empty. "I don't want to spend my last hour here fighting with you."

"Why were you upstairs? What were you doing up there?"

He thought he saw her blush. "I guess I wanted to get to know you a little better. Some part of you that no one else sees. While I can."

"This doesn't have to be over. Albany isn't that far."

"You told me it was Oz," she said.

He winced, remembering his own words. How hard he'd tried to make her seem so much different from him during those first days. He knew that it couldn't work between them; they would struggle. They would be separated not only by miles, but by the strata of society, and by the bulwarks of *things* that were useless except that Will clung to them for dear life. Perhaps they might try for a while to be with each other, but inevitably, as with all the women Will had ever thought he might connect with, it would come to an end. Her sense of duty was a double-edged sword: it had brought her to him, and soon it would take her away.

"You have to promise me something," she said. "You have to get help. You can't keep living like this."

"What's the difference to you?"

"I care," she said.

"You won't have to see it. You're leaving."

"So let me leave knowing that you're going to take good care of yourself. I know how this must feel . . ."

"No, you don't. You have no idea how it feels. You have *no* idea."

"What I mean is, I think I understand."

"Why? Because you have your own baggage? Because you're hoarding all these invisible things like I'm hoarding bread boxes and skateboards?"

She straightened. "I'm not hoarding anything."

"Everybody's got a safety blanket. It's just that mine collects dust."

She filled her lungs; he saw the rise of her breasts under his shirt, and even now—while he was furious—he wanted her. He'd come on too strong. Maybe if he'd played it more nonchalantly. Let her go as if it was no big deal, then called to say, *I happen to be in Albany this weekend and I wondered what you were doing . . .* But he'd never been cool or sly.

"I should go," she said.

"Wait." He moved quick, touched her. He was glad when she didn't tug away. "You don't want to go."

"No?"

He bent down, kissed her. "One more hour." He pushed his fingers into the short hair at the nape of her neck. He saw her eyes go hazy with want—the same that he felt. He looked into them as deeply as he could, as deeply as she would let him. "Read me, Lauren. What am I not saying out loud?"

"Will?"

He held her shoulders. "Read me."

"No."

"Do you want me to say it, then? Do I have to tell you?"

"Don't do this. Please? Let's not—"

"If you won't just read it, then I'll say it: I'm falling in love with you. And you're falling for me too."

She closed her eyes, and he kissed her. She lifted his shirt over his head; he hooked the elastic of her shorts with his thumb. They were both sore and exhausted, but Will went as slowly as he could. He thought if he could draw the minutes out, if he could make her crazy with wanting and keep her in that place, he might make her see— might make her at least want to *try*. He brought her to his bedroom, to kiss every part of her body, to smother her with patience, stoking the flames until she came apart under his hands.

Afterward, Lauren stood up from the bed, bent down, and kissed him. She stooped to gather her clothes, then looked at him for a long moment, standing naked in the doorway. "I'm going to take a shower."

"All right," he said.

He was still in bed, staring at the ceiling, when he heard the front door close.

**Lesson Fourteen:** Many people come to the study of body language because they want to be able to tell when a person is lying. And certainly, body language can tell us when we've been fed a falsehood. However, when a liar *believes* what he or she is saying, it can be more difficult to discern truth from lies.

# CHAPTER 14

Lauren had done a lot of leaving, mostly because she'd done a lot of traveling. She'd left Houston. She'd left Chicago. She'd left Martha's Vineyard. Denver. Fairbanks, Alaska. She'd left Phoenix, and she'd left Edward there.

But when she left Will's house, she'd felt as if she were fighting against a current. She'd left enough places to know that drawing out a departure and wishing things were different could extend the moment's sweetness, but it could draw out bitterness too. If she'd lingered, Will would have tried to convince her. Deep down, she wanted to be convinced.

But because she wouldn't make promises that she perhaps couldn't keep, she'd slipped out, saying good-bye only in the quiet of her heart. She'd gone to his living room, to stand before his display of antique keys. Before, the keys had spoken to her as tools that opened doors, that exposed secrets. But in the moments before she walked out the door, they struck her not for the mysteries of what they might open, but for the dead ends of the things they locked away.

Now, as she turned into Maisie's neighborhood, one additional key hung from her key ring; it opened nothing anymore. She touched it where it hung beside the steering wheel of her car. Years down the line, when she thought of Will, she would not permit herself to think, *What if I'd gone another way?* But at least she would have something to remember him by.

She wiggled her car into a parking spot a few blocks away from the house. The sun beat down brutally hot in the early evening, the air so heavy and burning that it was difficult to breathe it into her lungs. The tasks before her helped to focus her mind: she would pack, shower, maybe take a quick power nap, load up her car, and then she would head out to celebrate Maisie's birthday—though she wouldn't stay long. If she left Richmond at eight, she could make it back to Albany with enough time to grab a little sleep before tomorrow's vote.

Walking down the street with her purse on her shoulder and her underwear tucked in a pocket, she marveled to think that she'd meant to spend only two days in the city. That had been a lifetime ago.

She was nearly on Maisie's block when her phone rang in her purse. Her first thought was that Will was calling her. Her second was that, if he was planning to yell at her for leaving the way she did, he probably would have done it by now. She dug out her phone, and when she held it up to glance at the number, what she saw made her stop. She heard someone behind her swear—a young couple had to split apart to go around her. The stoplight changed. She took a breath, moved out of the center of the sidewalk, and answered. "Edward."

"I'm glad I got you. Sorry if it's early. Or late. I have no idea what time it is where you are."

"It's late afternoon."

"Where are you?"

She bristled at the notion that he thought he had any right to know where she was. But she told him: "Richmond."

"What are you doing there? I heard you were up for some big promotion . . ."

"I'm on vacation," she said. Then she was quiet. She walked forward slowly, listening, waiting for him to lead.

"You? Vacation?"

"Yes."

"Alone?"

"I'm staying with a friend from college."

"A woman?"

"Wouldn't you like to know," she said.

There was silence. Only a week ago, she'd been in the habit of glancing at her phone, waiting for his call. Now she hated to hear from him at all.

"So how are you?" he asked.

"Fine."

"No, I mean . . . how are you *really*?"

She thought over the last week. "*Really*, I'm fine."

"I miss you," he said, and the softness of his voice was pitch-perfect, just the right amounts of gentleness and longing.

Lauren bit the inside of her lip. Edward had always been a fantastic orator; being a trial lawyer required a certain amount of showmanship and flair. And yet, Lauren believed him—just like she always did. Probably, he did miss her in his way.

"What are you calling about?" she asked. "Is there something you want?"

"I'm leaving my wife."

Now she did scoff. "Uh-huh."

"No. I really am. Margaret is just so . . . I love her. But I just don't feel that—you know—that thing anymore. I'm not *in love* with her. And I'm leaving her."

"Do you still live with her?"

"I told her that I'm leaving."

"But you're still living there."

"I'm sleeping on the couch."

Lauren was nearly at Maisie's house, with its front door set back a short way from the sidewalk and its green awnings to shield the sun. Her body was sore. The night had passed and she hadn't closed her eyes except to squeeze them shut when the pleasure was too much to stand. And though she wondered if she might never see Will again, the whole afternoon suddenly seemed to fill her up with a sense of freedom and optimism and promise. She switched her phone to the other ear and got out her key.

"Edward, I wish you good things. I really do. But please don't call me again."

"But I'm leaving her *for you*."

"No, you're not," she said. "You're only telling yourself that you're leaving her because you're bored. Say good-bye to me now."

"I won't stand for this. I'm not giving up this easily."

"I am," she said. And then, because she knew there would be no polite way to get off the phone with him, because he was tenacious and pushy and didn't like to lose, she hung up. Not her most graceful moment, but effective. She stopped before Maisie's door, and she'd just taken in a deep, triumphant breath when her phone rang again.

She laughed—Edward was so predictable—and looked down at her phone. But it wasn't Edward. It was her office.

The phone buzzed and buzzed—a loud sound that seemed to be buzzing through the whole neighborhood, all the way to the center of her skull. Before she could talk herself out of it, she hit *ignore*. And, just like that, the street was quiet again.

After she dropped by Maisie's birthday dinner, she would leave Richmond, and tomorrow, she would throw off the covers and go back to the hard grind of daily life. Whatever someone at work was calling her about, it could wait. Whatever *anyone* was calling about could wait. She flipped her phone open and then, for the first time in more years than she could remember, she turned it off.

She pushed open Maisie's door—thinking about packing, showering, dressing, napping, a thousand things at once—and the sound of paper scraping across the floorboards made her look to keep from tripping.

At her feet, she saw an envelope with her name on it. Slowly, and with a feeling of dread, she bent down.

Eula led Arlen through her house in the late afternoon. She wanted to say, *And here's the living room, and down there's the bath, and the bedrooms are down the hall.* But he already knew the layout, though it had been a long, long time.

She took him into the small dining room, and she was surprised when he recognized the oak table as the one that had been in her mother's house before they sold it. In the kitchen, she watched him run a hand along the Formica countertop as fondly as if he were a musician touching a baby grand. She walked him down the hall to the bedrooms that were meant for children, but which had instead become a craft room, a guest room, and a relatively unused gym.

"Hey." She stopped him at the bottom of the stairs that led to the second floor. Under her hand, his shoulder was firm and warm. "You doing okay?"

"Great," he said. "I'm great." They walked slowly up the carpeted stairs, Arlen following behind her. "You did a lot with the place."

"But not too much."

"Nope. Not too much."

At the top of the stairs she pointed out the space where she'd had a wall adjusted to make a bigger closet in the master bedroom. And Arlen stood with his hands on his hips, looking over the wall and nodding his head, considering the handiwork. He asked polite questions about builders and permits. He wanted to know how long the work took and how much it cost.

His voice was low and thoughtful. "Shame I wasn't here. I would have done this for you. Piece of cake."

"Oh, well," she said, pleased. "There's plenty of things to repair. Believe me."

They peeked into the upstairs bathroom with its seashell motif. And then they were standing in Eula's room, which had once been Arlen's room too, for a short period of time. The dressers were decorated with lace runners made by a great-aunt; the windows let in light through sheer yellow curtains. The bed sat like a life raft, square in the middle of the room, a soft pink bedspread tucked neatly beneath white pillows.

"Looks like you got some water damage," Arlen said, looking up.

"Just a little. From a snowstorm last spring. It hasn't leaked since."

"I can take a look at the roof. See if I can't figure out what's going on."

She smiled. Arlen was wearing his serious face; though his features seemed longer now and thinner, his expressions hadn't changed. "You ever think of doing handyman work? I bet you could be real good at it. You always were good at working with your hands."

"Maybe," Arlen said.

"Arlen . . ." He turned to her. She didn't quite know what it was that she wanted to say. A feeling of deep tenderness had welled

up inside her—but it was more than tenderness too. It was gratitude for the fact that he was here with her. It was the fierce urge to
promise him that things would be okay. That she would make
them okay if he let her. She hadn't spent too much time with him
last night; he was in many ways still a stranger. But her heart was
telling her in no uncertain terms: here was the man she'd married.
Generous, forgiving, strong, and, most of all, not gone.

She looked at him, and—*bless him*—he could not hold her eye.
But she wanted him to. Oh, how she wanted him to. *Look at me*,
she thought. And when he did not, she stepped closer, stood up on
her tiptoes, and kissed him. His lips were soft under hers—a kiss
not quite returned.

She didn't need to ask him. She knew it had been a long time
since he'd been with anyone. And she didn't need him to lead. She
took him by the hand to the edge of her bed, sat him down among
the pink ruffles. Then she stepped back, and, button by button,
with her head high, offered herself, as if with her skin she might
somehow smooth over even the smallest part of his hurt. He
watched with his hands on his knees, flexing and curling, until she
was in only her panties and bra.

She walked toward him, feeling slightly outside herself. She ran
her hands along his hair. Where it hadn't thinned, it was still thick
and rich brown.

"Eula." Her name seemed to break on his lips. He still did not
touch her. "I haven't . . . See, it's been a while, and . . ."

She shushed him, then bent to kiss his lips. They were soft and
sweet—until his arms came around her, pulling her hard to the
bed, and then his weight was on her and his mouth was so demanding that for a moment she worried about what she'd done. But her
confidence returned—this was *Arlen*, after all—and she met him
with a need that had been dormant until now. She'd meant to give

to him, to *only* give. And yet, for the first time in years, she actually *wanted*. She felt a loosening like a cramped muscle, part pain, part relief, and then there was only Arlen, his hands, his mouth, his breath on her skin.

Will did not get out of bed for a long time after Lauren left. He lay and watched the late-afternoon light skate across the floor. He got up only to open the window when a little roving thunderstorm came through because he wanted to smell the rain. When the sun began to set, he dragged himself to the kitchen, his rumbling belly leading the way. He made himself a peanut butter sandwich and ate it standing at the counter. Then, because he didn't quite know what to do with himself and he was feeling lost, he called his sister.

"What's going on today?" she asked brightly.

"Nothing much," he said. He washed a bit of peanut butter from his hands. "How's the baby?"

"Loud. I'm calling him my little fire engine. Because when he's hungry he wails and turns beet red. I wouldn't be surprised if his head spun around." For a moment, Annabelle slipped away from the conversation to coddle the baby. "Am I talking about you?" she sang. "Yes? Are you the little fire engine? Yes, you are!"

Will climbed the stairs to the second floor very slowly. He could picture the baby looking up at his sister with bright but utterly uncomprehending blue eyes. A great heaviness made his feet hard to lift, one over the other, until he reached the top of the stairs. Lauren was gone, but his stuff—all his stuff—was still right where he'd left it. It wasn't going anywhere.

"So what's going on with you?" Annabelle asked. "What's Lauren up to today?"

"Leaving," he said through clamped teeth. "Back to Albany."

"Will you see her again?"

"Not likely. She was here for Arlen."

"That might be why she came in the beginning, but it wasn't Arlen who she was looking at like he hung the moon."

Will sighed. Around him, in the hallway that stretched along the second story of the house, his collection had taken on a dull, gray-brown sheen. Normally, when he saw his stockpile, it seemed to him to be vitally alive, full of promise and verve. But now it was just a collection of crap that the life had gone out of. It was garbage—other people's garbage that he'd made into *his* garbage. He had no love for it at all.

Lauren had not been the first woman in his life to see that he had an illness. One woman, with whom he'd been serious for six months, simply hadn't been able to understand that his problem was more than mere laziness. She'd told him he was a slob and he'd been glad to let her go. Another woman who'd discovered his problem early on had simply turned tail and run. Men who hoarded like he did were not suitable husband material. It wouldn't be possible to raise kids in a house that looked like a junkyard.

Already, Will missed Lauren. He would miss going picking with her, would miss listening to her "interpret" the people they met, would miss the way she always tucked her hair behind her ear when she was thinking. Although her leaving corresponded almost immediately with her discovering his illness, he didn't get the sense that she'd been scared off. More than any woman he'd met before, she seemed strong enough to actually handle what he was. She was tough enough to be with him. If she wanted to. *If.*

"So what are you going to do to get her back?" Annabelle asked. "You're not just going to let her go like that. Are you?"

"She wants to go."

"Oh, come on. Will—it's a teeny tiny little world these days. Just because she lives up north and you're here doesn't mean you can't see each other."

"We can't," Will said. He kicked an old claw-foot end table with his toe, and the whole pile of junk that sat on top of it threatened to collapse. He put out his hand to steady it, but still, a few pieces of paper fell. He felt himself to be on a dangerous precipice, and he was shuffling inch by inch closer to the edge. "I've got no future with her. There are things besides geography standing in the way."

"What things?" Annabelle asked slowly.

He took a deep breath. His legs felt weak. His mouth suddenly felt overly full of teeth. "I . . ." The years flashed in frames, the rooms filling box by box, bag by bag, thing by useless thing. "I have a problem," he said.

Already he felt a little better.

"Oh, Will," Annabelle said. And it wasn't pity he heard in her voice, but relief. She'd known. She'd always known. Probably, the whole family did. "As soon as you say the word, we're all here to help. You know that."

Will rubbed his eyes. "I'm saying the word," he said.


The envelope in Lauren's hand had her name on it—handwritten letters in the thick black script of a felt pen. She stepped into Maisie's house, into the rush of air-conditioning, and locked the door behind her. *Arlen*, she thought. *He'd written to her.* She set down her bag, then dropped herself onto Maisie's butter-cream couch. Her heart was pounding now. She had a sense of time stopped—as if whatever she was about to read was going to change things, and until she read the letter, time would not go on.

She wedged her thumb into the envelope and tugged until it was open with a ragged edge. The note inside was written on an unlined index card. The words gave her pause.

*What you did is unforgivable.*

She stared blindly at the letters of the sentence. The words were blunt, so without mystery or the slightest bit of room for interpretation. Arlen was done with her. Will must have told him that she was leaving—and this was Arlen's response. In some ways her errand to Richmond had been over before it had started. She let the note fall to her lap. A great wave of exhaustion came over her, mental and physical.

She'd once heard of a man, a detective in Arizona, who was known for his brutal, endless interrogations of suspects. If a colleague needed a confession, this man was sent in. He could get any suspect to break down. At his hand, three men were sentenced for murder based on their confessions. They spent years in jail.

Later—when it became clear that the men's alibis checked out, that their DNA didn't match what was found at the crime, that there was no possible way in the natural world that the four men could have committed the murder—the detective was questioned about his brutal tactics. Lauren had caught an interview with him replayed on a news program. The man was defensive and antagonistic, sitting in his gray suit behind his desk. Despite the clear indication that his life's work had hinged on his talent for browbeating and coercion, that his ability to wring false confessions out of scared men would have made the Spanish Inquisition proud, he insisted he was without blame. *I still believe they're guilty,* he said, again and again, with all the conviction of a man looking up at the sky and swearing it was night instead of day.

Now there was this note: *What you did is unforgivable.*

She wished she could assure Arlen. She wouldn't forget. She wasn't going to just go on with a life of denial, pretending his conviction had never happened, pretending that she was blameless. She wished she could tell him that—how her life, too, had forever been changed.

She did not get up from the chair in Maisie's living room. She called her father.

"Dad?"

"What's wrong, darling?"

She meant to say that she would be driving home late tonight. That she'd see him tomorrow after work. She meant to tell him to pass the word along to Jonah that she would see him soon. But when she spoke, other words were on her lips. "He won't forgive me."

She heard her father sigh. "I'm so sorry."

She rarely allowed herself the luxury of sniveling, but now, she didn't deny herself a few silent tears. They felt good and overdue.

"Come home now," her father said. "Your mother and I miss you. Jonah misses you."

"I miss you too. I just . . ." She felt the words on the brink of slipping from her lips. And though she hated to appear pathetic before her father, she didn't stop herself. "I wanted to make things right."

"I know."

"I hate that I disappointed everyone. That I disappointed myself."

"Lauren, no one expects you to be perfect."

She was quiet.

"You gave it your best shot, but Arlen *wants* to hold a grudge. And that's his right. Maybe it's time you just . . . let him."

"Think so?"

"I do." His voice was tender. "Come home now, sweetheart. There are amazing things waiting for you here."

"Yes," she said.

"It's time to start fresh."

"Start fresh?"

"Turn over a new leaf. Be there when the board votes tomorrow. You can only go forward; you can't go back."

"I guess you're right." She looked down at Arlen's note—his neat handwriting. Her watch was ticking off the seconds. It was nearly six. "Tell Mom and Jonah I'll see them soon."

She said good-bye and hung up the phone. The early-evening light was coming in full and bright through the windows, the heat of a relentless day. She thought of the coming darkness, of leaving Richmond, and she waited to feel a release of tension. But still, the anxiety remained.

**Lesson Fifteen:** You can read love in a person's body language. You can read respect. You can read disgust. And you can also read violence.

A person about to do something violent will often show the white lower halves of his eyes—head lowered, chin tipped down, the thickest part of the skull presented (think of a football player lining up against an opponent—a natural starting point for aggressive movement). If a person is considering doing something violent, nervous energy will be released, maybe with fidgeting, opening and closing the fists, shallow breathing, or shifting foot to foot. As the body is pumped full of chemicals to prepare for a fight, fine motor skills can become deficient, causing a person to fumble to close a button or even lift a drink. Knowing how to read the signs of aggression might be your best chance at getting away.

# CHAPTER 15

Afterward, after Eula had called out his name and after he too had gone slack with exhaustion, Arlen wept with happiness, quietly and to himself. He buried his face in one of Eula's pillows, into the smell of her detergent and sleep. If she noticed, she said nothing. She lay beside him, her hand stroking along his bare back, her breathing soft.

"You know when I missed you?" she said, not unhappily. "Other than the holidays? And when the drain in the bathroom clogged?"

He chuckled. "When?"

"Monday nights. Monday is always such a rough day—you have to drag yourself out of bed, go back to work, get in it with your coworkers. Monday nights I wished I could have come home and had somebody to talk to. To complain to. That's when I missed you a lot."

He turned over to face her. They'd pulled back the sheets, which were such a pale blue they were nearly white, and against the color,

Eula's skin was beautiful, dark and luminous. Arlen ran a hand along her arm and she inched closer. "Sorry."

"Not your fault," she said. "You're here now."

He smiled. At certain points in prison, when he was feeling his lowest, he thought: *I'm never getting out. This is it. Every experience that could ever matter is a thing of the past.* But then he would think of Eula, with hope in his heart, and he knew he couldn't let himself go crazy or be broken. If he ever did get out, he wanted to keep some little pieces of himself still in their right order. For her.

"I'm glad you came to find me," he said. "How'd you know where I was?"

Eula kissed his forehead before she answered. "A woman came to see me. That woman from the trial. Lauren *something*. She gave me your address."

Anger flared briefly when Arlen heard Lauren's name uttered in the intimate peace of Eula's bedroom. But the emotions quickly died out, with one last pathetic puff of heat like a black and curling match. Lauren had found Eula for him. She'd convinced his ex-wife to see him. He thought: *Oh, shit.* In the warm light of evening, with the sun setting outside the window, and Eula looking more beautiful by the moment, it was difficult to stay mad.

He ran his gaze over Eula's bare shoulders, her breasts. She had that look in her eye that said she was biting her tongue. And he knew what she wanted to say: that it was time for him to forgive, to put the past behind him. He felt her disapproval, but something else too. She wanted him to recover, to be *well*, even more than he wanted it. Hope like that . . . it could make a man see things in a different way.

"She's not a bad person," Eula said.

"I know."

"She wanted to do what was right."

"Don't we all," he said. He sat up sleepily and rubbed his face. "You think you'll ever talk to her?"

He shrugged. He'd treated Lauren in a way he couldn't be proud of. He'd driven her off, when it was so clear to him that Will had wanted her to stick around. Arlen supposed he'd wanted to keep her right where she was—because it had felt good to keep staying angry at her. To keep staying angry at something. But maybe it was time to release her—and himself, and Will, and Eula too.

"Well, I think you should see her," Eula said.

Arlen turned to look at her, and he couldn't help himself. He started laughing.

"What?" She sat up, holding the sheet to her chest. "What's so funny?"

"Not two hours I've been in this house and already you're nagging me."

"And you think that's funny?"

He kissed her. "Yes. Don't stop." He stood up. His pants were still hooked around one ankle and he wrestled them off. Eula watched him from the bed. "I'm gonna take a shower."

"You know where it is," she said.

He showed himself to the bathroom. He turned on the shower and stood for a long time under the hot water. When he got out, his skin was reddened and smelled of flowery soap. For the first time in a very long time, he felt clean.

Eula was wearing her bathrobe when he came out. She was sitting on the bed with her hands clasped in her lap. She stood as he walked toward her.

"Are you leaving?" she asked.

He clasped his belt buckle. "I got something I got to do."

"Can I give you a lift?"

"No. I need to do some thinking. A bus ride will do me good."

Arlen picked up his shirt from the floor, pulled it over his head. When it was buttoned, she slipped his hand into hers.

"Arlen . . . will you come back?"

He smiled. "Wild dogs couldn't keep me from seeing you again."

"I mean, will you come back *tonight*? I've been sleeping alone for so long. It would be nice to have you next to me."

"I promi—"

She put a hand to his lips. "Don't promise. Don't promise anything. Just come."

He drew her toward him. They stood like that for long moments as the room turned faintly orange in the red-hot, setting sun.


To celebrate her birthday, Maisie had gathered her friends to go out for dinner at a steakhouse in Shockoe Bottom. The pub was old—leaded glass, dark wood floors, a high bar, low lighting. They ordered fat pints of brown beer, with steaks that faintly sighed in pleasure when cut with a knife. Lauren had bought her friend a little stone penguin for her collection. As the windows darkened to black and the restaurant began to feel like a bar, she smiled, limited herself to one beer before switching to coffee, and tried not to think too much about the time. And yet, she was anxious. Her trip home was sitting heavily on her chest. And her heart was acting up again. She would need to go back to the doctor when she got home.

Maisie sat beside her, sparkling with happiness. And though Lauren had arrived at the bar in a sullen mood, her spirits were lifted by her friend's good cheer.

"Thanks for staying for this," Maisie said. "I know you'll have to drive home in the middle of the night."

"It's better that way. Less traffic." Lauren took a sip of the hot coffee that she'd ordered to keep herself awake. "And besides, it's not every year I get to be around on your birthday."

"I understand if you have to leave soon. It's a long drive back."

Lauren picked up her friend's hand, squeezed it. "You know, this week wasn't what I thought it would be. I mean, I thought I'd be down here for less than twenty-four hours. But . . . it's been nice. Staying with you."

"Don't make me get teary-eyed on my birthday," Maisie said. She glanced around the table at her friends, who didn't seem to notice that they were talking privately. Then she leaned a little closer to Lauren. "I still think you should reconsider going back. I mean, screw the promotion. Do you really want it anyway? Usually people get those kinds of promotions after they've already got married, sent their kids off to college, and settled down. You're too young to have so much responsibility."

"I admit the timing of it doesn't feel right," Lauren said. She pushed her hair behind her ears. "But . . . for my whole life I've been working for this. And for my whole life it felt right. I can't throw away that much dedication for one week's worth of doubt."

"Can't you?" Maisie asked. "What's the worst that can happen if you decide you want something else?"

Lauren glanced at her watch. She wasn't eager to get on the road, but the looming pressure was becoming too much to stand. "I should get going."

Maisie nodded. Now she was teary-eyed, and Lauren felt her own eyes moisten as she hugged her friend. She and Maisie had always been close, but in recent years, as Lauren's work had consumed more and more of her time, focus, and energy, it was nearly impossible to maintain such closeness. Lauren's heart cried out now, wishing that she could take Maisie with her back to Albany, and knowing that her friend's life was solidly and squarely *here*.

Lauren said good-bye to Maisie's friends, then walked herself to the door. Outside, the street was busy. The sky was dimmer than normal thanks to a thick layer of low clouds. The streetlights' were on and the shadows seemed darker and harder than they should have been at eight p.m. Lauren got her keys and headed to her car, trying to work through the motions, to follow blindly the path that she herself had created, the path that would take her directly back to the life she was supposed to lead.

Will sat in his kitchen, drinking alone at the table. It was an old table, sturdy as a tank but scratched here and there from use. He liked it that way because it had character. He leaned his elbows on it, hard, and peeled the label from the green bottle of his beer. He didn't look up when he heard Scoot thumping down the stairs or when his brother came into the room.

"Well?" Will asked.

Scoot sat down across from him. He slouched in his chair and stretched one thick arm on the tabletop. "It's bad. It's pretty bad."

Will snorted a little under his breath.

Scoot pointed. "Got one of those for me?"

"Help yourself," Will said.

His brother stood and went to the fridge. When he returned he seemed a bit more relaxed. "Well, the good news is that you've got yourself a family of rednecks."

"Not following."

"Trucks," he said. "We all got trucks. We can move stuff around in no time."

Will smiled. He forced himself to sit up a little straighter. "Like pulling the Band-Aid off fast."

Scoot took a drag of beer; he pulled back his lips in a grimace before he swallowed. "We don't have to rush. You can go through some things. Figure out what you want to save."

"If I do that, I'll want to save all of it."

"All right, then. Band-Aid-style, it is."

Will spun his beer in a circle. "Thanks for coming over."

"Naw." Scoot looked out the window. "So what brought this on?"

"A lot of things."

"A certain woman?"

"That too." Will smiled.

"Sucks," Scoot said. "Sorry it didn't work out. You know I keep telling you I want you to meet this girl who works in the office . . ."

"That's okay," Will said.

He knew he was being ridiculous. Overreacting. He'd known Lauren for only a handful of days—in person, anyway. And he'd spent most of his adult life hating her and making her into his archenemy for what she'd done to Arlen. There was no logical or mature reason for him to feel as low-down and saddened as he did by her leaving. But he felt what he felt. He missed her already. He missed what might have been.

"Anyway," Scoot said, "you must feel a *little* better. Knowing you'll get your house back. Knowing it's all out in the open. I mean, the worst is behind you now, right?"

Will drank the last swig of beer in the bottom of his bottle. He knew it was going to get harder before it got easier. But he also knew now that to hold on to all the things he'd amassed would hurt him more than letting them go. He could collect everything that came across his path, he could build up piles the size of Richmond's flood walls, but it wouldn't guarantee him anything. The thought wasn't depressing; it was liberating. It meant he was free.

He stood up, tossed his bottle into the recycling bin. "Yeah. The worst is over," he said.


As usual, Lauren couldn't find parking. So she left her car in front of a fire hydrant with the hazard lights flashing, a few blocks away from Maisie's house. She'd been halfway out of Richmond before she remembered: she'd left a file in Maisie's spare bedroom. It was incredibly unlike her to be so forgetful, especially about work. In the back of her mind she was suspicious of herself: she'd forgotten the folder so she could not leave.

She walked down the dark sidewalk toward Maisie's and, as usual when she walked alone at night, her senses were heightened, including her awareness of herself. Her heels clicked as she walked hard and fast down the cement walk; her heartbeat was a little high. The street was unusually dark and quiet, quiet enough that Maisie's question posed earlier in the evening was echoing in her head: *What's the worst that can happen if you decide you want something else?*

She walked faster. The worst that could happen, she thought, was that she would make the wrong choice—and then where would she be? How could a person spend her entire life knowing exactly what she wanted, only to second-guess herself because of a single, atypical week? She could go slowly and as planned into a future that was pretty much guaranteed—one in which she would get her promotion, her raise, and then perhaps everything else would fall in line. Or she could rush headlong into a future that had nothing guaranteed at all but might give her a shot at love, at a different kind of work, and a thousand other tempting but elusive things.

She shook her head to clear it. She simply needed to push forward as planned—to get herself up to Maisie's spare room, grab the wayward folder, and head home. She was nearly to Maisie's house when she noticed the man. He was standing on the sidewalk, leaning against a street sign. He was bent slightly as if talking on a phone. She didn't know why, but she felt a jolt of warning. She took stock of him: the fact that it was summer in the South, and he was wearing a hoodie. His white sneakers and baggy pants. She reassured herself: She had her pepper spray on her keychain. And the street was relatively bright where he stood leaning against the sign.

Her heart was beating a little harder as she neared him, and she readied herself to look him square in the eye. Firm eye contact could be enough to put someone off because it signaled that she would not be an easy target. She was almost to Maisie's house now and she laughed at herself silently: most likely, there was no reason to be afraid.

The man looked up when she walked past him, though not all the way, and she met his gaze. He seemed startled for a moment. He was very young and baby-faced. His hair was so blond it was nearly white, and buzzed close to his head. His eyes were wide-set and militant blue. She walked past him and saw his profile: he hadn't much chin to speak of, and his triangle nose made the shape of his head look vaguely sharp and triangular like a blade.

"Excuse me, ma'am," the boy said. And then he was walking beside her. He was short for a man—about her height. She was caught between the urge to run and the desire not to be rude. He was just a kid, after all. She gripped her pepper spray. "Can you tell me whereabouts is Jefferson Avenue?"

"No, I can't," she said curtly. She was only a few steps from Maisie's door. She was hurrying. "Sorry."

"Oh," he said.

And then, quicker than she could have imagined it, he'd grabbed a big fistful of her hair and was pulling her toward Maisie's door. It was then that she realized he hadn't been waiting for just any-one: he'd been waiting for *her*.

Her fingers weren't working and she couldn't activate her pepper spray. She reached for her self-defense training, tried to stop his foot, to grab and twist, but it was like he held her everywhere at once.

She called out loudly, "Help!" but the man's hand wrapped tightly around her mouth, crushing her lips against her teeth, her spine against his belly. He'd gotten a knife from somewhere and he held it up before her face. It was a tiny little blade, but it was enough to make her stop yelling.

"Open the door," he said. And when she didn't, he pulled her hair so hard she thought it would come out. Tears filled her eyes. "I said, *open it.*"

She could hardly feel her hands. Some small voice said that she could not let him drag her into the privacy of Maisie's house. She flipped her key chain around in her hand, making to open the door like he'd asked. But instead of turning the lock, she tossed her keys as high as she could over her head and backward. She heard the clink of them behind her, hitting the street.

The man yelled in her ear—at least, it sounded like yelling. It might have been a whisper. He pulled hard now on the hair on the side of her head, not letting up on the pressure for a moment. "You want to do this the hard way? Fine. We do it the hard way."

He walked her, jostling, deep into the alley that separated Maisie's building from the house next door. When he tried to reorient her to face him, she took the advantage: she kneed him hard, began to run. She called for help. But she'd barely gotten a word out before he was on her. Her head connected with the brick wall. His hand was over her nose and mouth. He stomped her foot so hard that she suddenly understood what it was to be blind with pain. Among garbage cans and roaches, he pushed her face down. She thought: *So that was it*. She no longer had anything to decide.

Years before the Arlen Fieldstone trial, before the word *trial* had become a regular part of Lauren's everyday vocabulary, a good friend and professor had called Lauren into her office and began asking questions. *You're different,* her teacher had said. *You can see more than the rest of us. Isn't that true?*

Lauren was not modest about her talents, and so, sitting on the worn-down love seat in her teacher's tiny office, she talked about Jonah, of how he saw even more than she did, and how she had a knack for people-reading, but it was Jonah who'd taught her everything she knew. Her professor had listened carefully, and when the story was over, she suggested that Lauren would make a good jury consultant. Lauren had said she hoped to go into law. But she'd never known a jury consultant and she wasn't yet sure what she wanted to do, exactly. She'd had no plan at the time. She told her professor: *I'll think about it.* She felt a slight shiver—that was all—and then the conversation, and the years, went on.

Arlen had walked the long blocks of Monument Avenue enough times now that he half wondered if the police weren't going to question him for suspicious behavior. He'd tried knocking, and when there was no answer, he'd wondered just for a second if Eula had given him the wrong address. Then, he'd started walking. The night air was cooler and fresher than it had been in some time. He felt lighter in his shoes. He needed to be careful, he knew, about falling in love. About *re*-falling. But something about Eula—she'd always made him reckless, which he supposed was another word for *brave.*

He was near the house where Lauren was staying when he heard voices. A woman. A man. And the erratic and primitive sounds of struggle that he might not have recognized before he'd gone to prison but which now made his ears prick up with alarm. Instinct kicked in. He ran without hesitation.

In the alleyway he found them. He knew the man by the shape. But the woman—he couldn't see her. He could tell she was there only by the sound. He grabbed with two hands for the man's shoulders, picking him up off the ground. He was surprised to find that the guy was small.

"What the—"

The kid didn't have a chance to get out the word. Arlen threw him. The boy was scrambling to his feet, cursing, and the woman was facedown and scrambling to get away. He had only a moment to register these things before the boy's feet were pounding the pavement, his sweatshirt billowing behind him like a cape.

Arlen thought about chasing him. But the woman was still there and he hated to leave her. She was sitting up now, her back against the brick wall. She had her phone next to her ear.

"You okay?"

"I'm calling nine-one-one."

He waited at a distance, to let her know he was with her, that he would protect her, but that from him she had nothing to fear. She argued for a moment with the operator about not needing to stay on the line. When he heard her phone click closed, he moved closer again. He wanted to be sure she wasn't going into shock.

"My foot," she said.

He crouched down. Her high heel had come off and was lying on its side in a damp spot. Her ankle was swelling. Arlen rubbed his face.

"Will you help me get out of this alley?" she asked. "It's too dark back here. I want to wait out there, in the light, for when the ambulance comes."

"If you're sure you can move . . ."

"I'm fine," she said.

He helped her stand. All her weight was balanced on one foot. She brushed herself off and, in the near darkness, lifted her head. He couldn't make out her face, but there was something about her that he recognized. She relied for balance on his hand, then hopped—just an inch, on one high heel, toward the light. She hopped again.

Arlen cleared his throat. "May I?" he asked.

"Yes. Please."

He bent down, picked her up. He felt the cool sweat behind her knees where they folded over his forearm, the slight drape of her arms around his neck. "Did he get anything? Your wallet? Money?"

"He didn't want those things. He just wanted to hurt me. He kept saying it was punishment."

"You knew him?" Arlen asked, making his way around garbage cans and boxes to the front of the alley.

"No. But I think I knew his brother, once. In my line of work, a person makes enemies."

He was nearly to the street now. He could hear sirens in the distance, too far away. "What on earth could a woman like you do for a living that would piss a person off like that?"

"You'd be surpri—" She stopped talking as they reached the sidewalk, the gold wash of the streetlight. Arlen had been eyeing the far end of the neighborhood, looking for the flash of blue and red. But he stopped looking when she stopped talking. And then he saw her face.

"Arlen . . ." she said.

He held her, barely registering her weight. Her head was bleeding, though not much. Her pupils were so big that her eyes seemed nearly to be black.

"You're—"

"Yes," she said. "I think you just saved my life."

He must have smiled, unintentionally, because when his head cleared and he looked down into Lauren's face, he saw that she was smiling timidly back. Something fiercely protective rose up within him. He felt triumphant. He shifted her weight in his arms. That was when he heard the sound. Behind him. Sneakers, beating the pavement. A dog's bark. And then the boy in the sweat-shirt, this brother of someone he didn't know, raised his arm in front of him and squinted. Arlen heard angels. The streetlight wasn't light anymore; it was beaming music. The dark was bright as day. He knew what was going to happen. He turned away.

When the shot rang out he was ready, Lauren protected by the wall of his body. In the distance, he saw the faint wash of red and blue lights, splashed like watercolors up against the brick build-ings. And behind him, he heard the sound of someone running away. He dropped to his knees, careful with his cargo, and he set her on the ground before he fell onto his shoulder.

"Arlen? Arlen!" Lauren leaned over him. "Arlen!"

He tried to tell her. Everything was going to be okay. But he was dreaming with open eyes. He saw his mother; she was touch-ing his shoulder like she used to when she woke him up for school. His dog's tail thumped the ground. He knew he was in his house, the house where he grew up, because wintry drafts were blowing in through the closed window, making his skin pebble with cold. And he knew that today was another day, for school, for friends, for chores, for all those overlooked things that—when he saw them, *really* saw—he loved so much it broke his heart. He finally understood what freedom was and what it meant to be free. His whole body filled with gratitude that was unspeakable, inflating him until he became light as air, light as light, gladness so big that it carried him like a balloon, high over Richmond, over the clusters of lighted neighborhoods, over the silver slick of river, over all the sleeping people who couldn't begin to know what it felt like, sail-ing toward the moon.

**Lesson Sixteen:** Once you have been studying people for a while and learning to read them, you may find yourself becoming increasingly confident in your abilities. You might even get cocky. Overly assured. You might think you know people better than people know themselves—and, on occasion, you might be right.

But I've seen the most tenderhearted mothers turn into snarling demons when their kids are in trouble. I've seen little old ladies with crosses around their necks come into a courtroom and tell me they're advocates for marijuana and free love. And I've seen brutes of men with barbed-wire tattoos and shaved heads stop to pick up a little girl's dropped doll.

If you want to be an expert reader of people, never forget this: People will always surprise you. You'll surprise yourself.

# CHAPTER 16

As Richmond's early risers woke to their radios, as they stood in their kitchens hurrying to chew one last bite of a bagel or take one last gulp of coffee, they were struck down by disbelief at the story on the news. Those who weren't alone called out—*Honey, come here.* Those who were alone stared at their television screens, or they paused where they were listening, trying to explain it to themselves. At office buildings and teachers' lounges, they told one another: *Did you hear?* The baker across from the antiques store went to Will's door, his arms full of hot bread, the least he could do, but no one answered. The local news anchors made the seamless transition from talking about back-to-school shopping to relaying Arlen's selfless act.

*A hero,* they said. *A hero.*

In the hospital, Eula sat at Arlen's bedside, worrying the corner of a sheet. Machines beeped and clicked, their soft sounds louder than any sound Arlen had so far made. She prayed—sometimes pleading for God to have mercy and not make her suffer his loss a second time, sometimes threatening to never say another prayer again. She held Arlen's hand, his fingers dry but warm, and she talked to him.

"Come on," she said. She had a sense that once again he was imprisoned, this time by his body, which was keeping him away from her, locked inside. "I need you to stay. Who's gonna fix my roof if you don't stay?" she asked him.

The nurses brought her cups of coffee and the doctors spoke soft and low. If there was a clock in the room, she didn't notice it. She rubbed her left hand, the finger where her wedding ring used to gleam. "Come on," she said.

All over the city, people stole moments of quiet, at delis and libraries, at parks and playgrounds. There was the staid infrastructure of everyday life: copy paper, pencils, telephone wires, buses, the work desk, the stepladder—but none of it was the same. Husbands and wives, sisters and brothers, touched one another's backs, arms, hands. Blessings had to be not only counted, but attended to.

At the police station, a young man sat in a holding cell after a long night of not sleeping. Until now, he'd thought panic was a thing that happened in a split second, then was over—like when someone snaps a picture unexpectedly, and everyone jumps to see the flash. But this panic was the slow, steady withering of a candle burning down—a voice playing on an endless loop: *Oh, no. Oh, no. Oh, no.*

He couldn't hear the detectives, who were talking about him in a cramped cubicle, complaining as they filled out papers upon

papers. The kid fit the profile: Antiestablishment. Antigovernment.
Anti-everything. He had a blog that said he didn't believe in courts.
That the justice system needed to be brought to justice—Lauren
Matthews especially.

He'd refused an attorney. He told the cops everything they
wanted to know. Prior to the Fieldstone trial, Lauren played a part
in his brother's conviction for cooking and selling crank. When she
became very visible during the Fieldstone case, his anger at her
spiked. Arlen's release from prison had finally pushed him over the
edge. He'd found her easy enough, just by making a few sly calls.
He was good and drunk when they arrested him. But he was
sober now.

Morning brought to the police station the sound of tired good-
byes, the smell of coffee, the ringing of phones. The words *press
conference* were uttered, sometimes placating, sometimes annoyed,
sometimes feeble and apologetic. Cops and dispatchers made their
way to peek into the cell of the man who had done such a terrible
thing, the *boy* who had done it. They shook their heads and com-
miserated with one another. *How unfair.*

In the night Lauren sat with Will on a blanket on the second floor
of his house, among all of his things. Arlen was in a hospital in
Richmond, fighting for life for the second night in a row—they
could do nothing but wait. They'd filled their bellies with Chinese
food and soda. They'd made love on the hard floor, fast and desperate. The need to keep moving drove them, and so they worked.
Though neither said it, they were both waiting for a call.

"This?" Lauren asked. She held up a box; in it was a pair of
never-worn jogging shoes. "Do you want it to stay or go?"

"Those can go to charity," Will said.

She put the box aside, held up a broken basket. She made no

assumptions. She asked him about everything, even the most broken, worn, and obviously useless things. The basket was coming apart in her hands. "Stay or go?"

He laughed. "Go."

He looked at her. She knelt beside him in a clearing, towers of rubble on either side. His heart filled up and he reached for her hand. "What about you?"

She tipped her head, puzzled.

"Stay or go?"

"Will . . ." She lifted herself, closed the space between them. She put her head on his shoulder and kissed his neck. "You tell me."

"Stay." He held her close. "You're worth keeping."

He kissed her, his hands catching in her hair. And they moved, finally, only when the phone rang.


By November, the weather had cooled. Sunbaked side streets were filled with children holding their backpacks by the straps. Pumpkin and squash filled the storefront windows. And the memory of what had happened during the summer began to fade with the falling of the leaves.

In the auditorium of a community college, Lauren adjusted the microphone, which was old when Will had found it in his attic and which now worked only when it was raining or when it didn't need to be used. She tapped the mesh and a breathy puff reverberated over the rows and rows of empty seats. Will appeared from behind a fortification of boxy black speakers, coming toward her and wiping his palms on his pants.

"Working?" he asked.

"So far," she said, and her voice boomed through the auditorium. She laughed and stepped back.

"Don't turn it off," Will said. "It might not turn on again."

She heard noise on the roof; it was raining harder now—a cold autumn rain. She worried her lip. "Do you think the weather will keep people away?"

"I don't think so. Not from something like this." He stole a moment to wrap his arms around her. She closed her eyes, grateful for the feel and smell of him. Her heart was quiet. His warmth had gotten her through the last few months.

Last night, somewhere around three a.m., while he sat with her at his kitchen table and they sifted through letters upon letters written by incarcerated men, she'd looked up from her work and realized she loved him—and that she had for some time. Who but Will would have so thoroughly and completely supported her when she'd said, *No, thank you*, to more money? When she'd said, *For a while, I'm going to work for charity*? She hadn't told him yet that she loved him, but she would. Until then, she would hold the knowledge inside her, to savor it—but not for very long.

"What? Is there something in my teeth?" he asked when he pulled back.

She knew she was looking at him funny. And she realized she didn't need to tell him she loved him for him to know. "They're fine."

"Then what are you staring at?"

"Ask me later," she said.

Eula opened the doors of the auditorium, both at once, and walked inside. She walked alone down the long, long aisle. She wore a fire-red suit, and Will and Lauren both stood up a little straighter. Lauren thought that in another life, Eula must have been royalty.

"Everything set?" Eula asked.

"We're ready for them," Will said.

Eula stood close and leaned in. When she spoke, her voice was a whisper. "I've got a promise from the fund-raising council that they'll match any donations that the kids come up with, until the end of the year."

"That's amazing," Lauren said, pleased. Outside the gym doors, she could hear a loud group of students gathering with parents, teachers, and friends. Some camerapeople from the local news station had come in through a side door and were setting up their tripods.

Eula glanced around the auditorium. "Where's the main act?"

"Right here," Arlen called. He'd come in through the handicapped access door on the side of the building, wheeling himself with two strong arms. The bullet had made it difficult for him to walk, but it had not paralyzed him. When he reached Eula, she leaned down to take his arms and help him stand.

"Want to hear my good news? The school is going to match donations that the kids come up with. Isn't that great?" Eula said.

"That's fantastic." Arlen shuffled a few steps to sit on the stool near the mike. "What've you got lined up next?"

"Next month, a senior center in Florida. Then a high school in Missouri. And after that, another gig here in Richmond," Lauren said.

From the back of the auditorium, one of the men was signaling to them, waving his hands. People began to file noisily into the room, their voices loud. Will put his arm around Lauren's waist and gave her a squeeze. "Got your introduction ready?"

"All set," she said.

One by one, the children dropped into their seats, some looking to the front of the room, their eyes flashing speculation of what was to come.

"Let's tell people what happened," Arlen said.

# ACKNOWLEDGMENTS

Thanks once again to everyone who made this book possible: especially Cindy, Kim, Leis, Erin, Rita, and Lee. Thanks to Cathy and Michael for a great tour of Richmond—complete with personalized tour book and visit to the Richmond vampire. Thanks to Betty (a one-woman publicity machine and the best mother-in-law a girl could ask for). Thanks to my family and friends for letting me disappear for months at a time while writing.

Books on body language that helped with this story are *What Every Body Is Saying* by Joe Navarro and *Reading People* by Jo-Ellan Dimitrius and Wendy Patrick Mazzarella. I've taken liberties with some minor logistical elements, including the hierarchy of the DA's office in Albany and their accident procedures. To learn more about joining the fight against wrongful incarceration, visit www .innocenceproject.org.

# READERS GUIDE FOR
# A PROMISE OF SAFEKEEPING

Dear Reader:

I hope you liked *A Promise of Safekeeping*. There's certainly a lot to talk about in this story! I would love to host your next book club meeting by joining your conversation and by sending you my *A Promise of Safekeeping* book club care package, which includes goodies and adorable antique-looking key charms. If you would like to read *A Promise of Safekeeping* with your friends (and with me!), please see my website for details. Otherwise, enjoy the group discussion questions that follow!

Best,
Lisa Dale

# DISCUSSION QUESTIONS

1. All of the characters in *A Promise of Safekeeping* hold on to various objects (or they reject objects) for various reasons. Eula stays in the house she bought with Arlen. Will keeps trinkets from his boyhood (which Arlen can't bring himself to touch). Lauren says she doesn't hold on to anything (though she takes overly long to delete Edward's number from her phone). What objects have special meaning in your life? (HINT: For a little extra book club fun, have each reader bring in her object of choice and tell about it!)

2. If you could see into people the way Lauren sometimes does, how do you think that ability would affect you? Will can read Lauren as well as she can read him. Discuss the irony in that and also her confusion at being attracted to him physically, despite her thoughts that she only wanted to be friends.

3. Early in the novel, Will describes Lauren as "morally deformed." What does he mean by this, and how will it come to shape his burgeoning feelings for her? Do you think he's actually reflecting

on his own issues, or is he confused by his own feelings of having hated her for so many years and now finding her attractive?

4. Arlen is anxious and agoraphobic at the beginning of the novel. Discuss the parallel with Lauren and her palpitations.

5. Although Lauren and Arlen are two very different characters, they're connected by a similarity in the sounds of their names. What do you think this means?

6. At one point, Lauren talks to a colleague who indicates that "as far as the prosecution was concerned, Arlen's conviction was proof not of the system's failure, but of its success." He believes the jury made the best decision possible given the evidence, and therefore justice was not obstructed. Do you agree?

7. Why does Lauren deem it her personal fault that Arlen was convicted and not believe that it was the system at work, as so many people have told her?

8. Discuss some of Lauren's reasons for righting Arlen's wrongful conviction as you came to read in the book. Do you agree with her need to apologize to Arlen? Would you do the same?

9. It's sometimes said that a person's greatest talent is also his or her greatest weakness. How does this idea pertain to the characters in this story?

10. Throughout the novel, the author explores themes of keeping, holding, hoarding, and locking away. And yet, it is not always secrets that are being hidden and kept, but rather something

more fundamental. What is each character holding on to? How do they learn to let go?

11. When Lauren finally goes to Will's home, she admires his key collection and understands why he likes them. Do you agree or disagree with her assessment and why?

12. Lauren and Will both know secrets about each other that no one else knows. Discuss what this says about their individual character and their pride.

13. Discuss how the lessons at the beginning of each chapter relate to the story. What are your favorites and why?

14. Maisie, talking about Richmond as a city with a difficult past, tells Lauren: "When there are no answers, a person learns to live with the questions." What does this mean? Do Lauren's actions indicate that she agrees with this idea? What do you think of it?

15. At one point, Will accuses Lauren of hoarding behavior. He says, "Everybody's got a safety blanket. It's just that mine collects dust." Is he right? What are the parallels of their self-preservation strategies?

16. Discuss the idea that Will is emotionally attached to Lauren like he is to one of his antiques. Does he prefer the polished Lauren that he'd sell in his shop, or the real gem that he would keep on his second floor, only for him?

17. Lauren and Will's first serious sexual encounter is surprising to both of them. Why? When Lauren goes to Will's house the night

before she leaves Richmond, what changes that closes their emotional distance?

18. Chapter 13 begins with: "It had always seemed to Lauren the important decisions in life stored themselves up until the last possible moment . . ." Has this ever happened to you?

19. Early on in the story, when Arlen steps out of the antiques shop for the first time, he toys with the idea that freedom is about not caring. Later, when Arlen saves Lauren's life, he finally understands what freedom means to him. What does it mean? What enables him to reach that realization?

20. Will describes himself as "fundamentally alone," which he means as who he really is, the hoarder. Why do you think Will aligns himself with this thinking? And why does it take Lauren to make him want to change?

21. When in the story did you realize that Will has a hoarding problem? Is Will's hoarding endemic of something missing in his life? Why doesn't he think he can lead a normal life? Discuss why Will is relieved when Lauren finally knows his secret.

22. Did you see the ending coming—that Lauren was in danger?

23. After Lauren's time in Richmond, where she actually ceased her workaholic mentality, why does she still feel the need to follow a path that is no longer right for her? Is she doing it for herself or to make other people happy? Discuss.

24. An early draft of *A Promise of Safekeeping* had a much different, darker ending. In that version, Arlen doesn't recover from his

wound. How do you feel about the final version of the ending? Was it the right ending for the book?

25. Truth is a major theme of the book—both real and perceived. Discuss how each character took a perceived truth and made it real to him or herself.

# NOTES